JAILBREAK

R.M. OLSON

To Frances, who knows all the best prison tropes

JAILBREAK:

The unauthorized act of removing restrictions on a device or system placed there by the manufacturer or operator.

Also, an escape from jail.

1

Jez grinned at the man sitting across the table from her. He smelled of sour sweat and too much sump, and his pilot coat was thick with grease and dirt.

He didn't grin back. "Well, you scrawny plaguer? You going to call, or fold?"

She leaned back on the rickety metal stool, still grinning. "Neither. I'm raising."

The small kabak was noisy, crowded with hard-drinking, grim-faced men and women in tattered pilot's coats or grubby peasant smocks, but a handful of the man's crewmates had gathered around the gambling table. At least, she assumed they were his crewmates. Couldn't imagine anyone else would stand that close to him on purpose.

"Raise with what?" he grunted, clearly skeptical.

She grinned wider. She didn't look like much right now, sure. But she plaguing well smelled better than he did. That should count for something, right?

Casually, she reached into her coat and pulled out a small chip. She kept her fist closed around it for effect as she touched it to the betting chip in the centre.

The six pairs of eyes widened as the numbers clicked higher, and the man's heavy eyebrows dropped into a scowl.

"What?" she asked innocently. "Can't meet it?" She shrugged. "You could always fold."

"You damn—" he half stood, leaning forward.

Her heart was pounding, every muscle in her body tingling with anticipation.

This was what she lived for.

"Or," she said casually, "I suppose you could put in that information chip my friend was asking you about earlier. I'd take that as a call."

He would probably just kill her. Or try, of course. But what the hell. If you weren't about to be killed at least a couple times a week, were you even really alive?

"Why do you want it so badly?" he grumbled. She shrugged.

"That's fine, you can fold. I don't care. Got plenty of credits in there, I could buy myself enough sump to last me five standard years. Or maybe one really, really good night."

"How did some scum-sucking lowlife pilot like you come up with that kind of credits?"

She raised her eyebrows. "You calling, or folding? Don't got all day."

He looked down at the symbols on the smooth tokens in his hand and scowled.

He had a good hand.

She'd checked.

Slowly, he pulled a small chip out of his inner pocket. "I lose this, my job's not worth spit."

She shrugged and made as if to scoop the betting chip towards herself. He slapped his meaty hand down on her wrist.

"Damn you." He dropped the small chip into the centre of the table. "Now, I say we're dropping tokens."

With a dramatic flourish he spread his tokens out on the table and broke into a slow, mean smile, the expression ugly on his stubbly face.

It really was a good hand.

She would have let her grin drop if she could. But she couldn't help it. Never been that good at modesty, really.

So she was grinning so wide her face felt stretched as she tossed her tokens casually onto the table.

There was that one delightful moment, as he saw the symbols and made the calculations in his head. Then his eyes bugged out, his face darkening with rage.

She scooped up the betting chip and the information chip and shoved them in the inside pocket of her jacket. Time to leave.

His fist caught her in the ribs as she stood, and she grunted and stumbled sideways. He shoved the table out of the way and grabbed her by the shoulder, hoisting her bodily into the air.

"You cheated! You plaguing scum-sucker."

She turned her head and bit down as hard as she could into the fleshy part of his hand. He howled in pain, and she dropped to the ground. She grabbed the stool she'd been sitting on and swung it into position just as he lunged down at her. The stool legs caught him under the ribcage, and for a split second he stood, face frozen in agony, gasping for breath. She rolled out from under the stool, spun around, and flung it into the face of the man next to her, who, in fairness, looked like he had been about to recover his wits and grab for her. He grunted and stumbled back, cursing, and she turned and brought her forehead down on the bridge of her erstwhile gambling partner's nose. He fell against the broken table, clutching his bloody face, just as another one of his friends grabbed her from behind. She threw her head back, connecting squarely with his jaw, and then took advantage of the momentary slackening of his grasp to drive her elbow hard into his sternum. She dropped to the floor as another man and a woman grabbed for her and rolled between their legs. Then she jumped to her feet, checked her coat pocket, and sprinted for the exit, still grinning, the man and all of his friends hot on her tail.

She burst out of the kabak, glanced quickly in both directions, then took off down the dirt street towards the edge of the shabby town. She slapped the com on her wrist as she ran.

"Hey kids, time to go!" she called. A moment later, Lev's long-suffering sigh came through her earpiece.

"Where are you, Jez?"

"Be there in a jiff."

"And someone's after you."

A heat blast scorched the dirt beside her, sending up a thick scent of ozone and burnt earth. She yelped and dodged as another blast sizzled past her and left a charred mark across the colourful shutters on the dingy prefab house across from her.

"Yep. Don't call you genius boy for nothing!"

She ducked down an alley, dodged into another street, and took a sharp right.

There, ahead of her, was the wall marking the end of town, the intricate carvings and once-brilliant colours now faded and shabby. And after that …

The crew behind her were gaining. She half turned, and squeezed off a shot from the modded heat pistol she'd borrowed from Ysbel.

The street in front of her pursuers disappeared in a ball of smoke and flame, and from behind it she heard strangled cursing.

"Ysbel! You're beautiful," she called over the com.

"Piss off."

"Pees oaf yourself," she called back, imitating the woman's heavy outer-rim accent.

She sprinted through the gates of the town—no city force field on this dump of a planet—and slowed, grinning.

Three figures stood in front of the loading ramp to the most stunning ship she'd ever seen in her life—a sleek long-haul, with beautiful old-fashioned rivets and smooth metal panels, its body the dull, glossy sheen of something old that had been restored and polished to perfection.

Yes, she'd been flying this little beauty for the last two weeks, but honestly, every time she saw it again her heart skipped a beat.

Tae was glowering at her—nothing new there—Ysbel was giving her the usual flat stare, and Lev was shaking his head slightly, his expression resigned.

All three of them had drawn heat-guns, and they were holding them in a no-nonsense way.

"What did you do, Jez?" Lev asked as she jogged up to them.

"Nothing," she said. "Just making new friends. Hey! You figured out how to hold a gun!"

Lev gave her a look that was almost as flat as Ysbel's. Granted, he didn't look nearly as intimidating as the stocky, muscular woman, with her shaved head and obvious familiarity with weapons, but Jez had to admit that being on the run had been good for him. He still looked more like a scholar than anything else, with his messy cropped hair and the thoughtful, calculating expression on his face, but at least he'd figured out which end of the gun to point at the bad guys. Or the good guys. Whoever was chasing them at the moment.

Two weeks of Ysbel's tutelage would do that to a person, even a soft boy like genius over there.

She reached them and turned around, drawing her own pistol. "Ysbel, don't take this the wrong way, but I think I might love you mostly for your weapons."

"That's good. I might kill you with them one of these days."

Tae shoved his dark hair out of his eyes and glared at her. "Can we spend one day getting supplies without you getting into a fight Jez? One day?"

"Nope." She grinned at him.

The gambler's crew had come through the gates and slowed on seeing their company. They'd all drawn weapons, and now they were approaching cautiously.

"Your pilot stole something from me," the man in the dirty pilot's coat called out. Jez was gratified to see that his nose was swollen to twice its previous size.

"Hey now, can't handle the pressure, stay out of the game," Jez called back. "Not my fault you can't pay what you play."

"You cheated!" he growled.

She shrugged, still grinning. "How do you cheat at fool's tokens?"

Lev sighed and slapped his com.

"Masha, you were right. Jez found someone who wants to kill her. We've got to go." He glanced at the scowling young man beside him. "Tae, can you throw the last few boxes in? Ysbel and I will hold them off."

"And me," said Jez. Lev glared at her.

"Hand the pilot over and we'll call it even," the man called. "There's more of us. You don't want a fight, and neither do we."

Ysbel turned her flat stare on the approaching group, and they slowed further.

"It's tempting," she said. "But I have dibs on killing this idiot, so

I'm afraid I can't."

The man shifted his grip on his pistol.

Ysbel raised one eyebrow. "I don't think you want to do that."

"Tell your pilot to give me back what's mine."

"Was yours. Until I won it," Jez shot back. She glanced quickly over her shoulder. Tae was carrying the last of the boxes up the ramp, and she could feel in her bones the slight vibration that told her that the ship was running.

Damn.

She slapped her com. "Masha, stay out of my cockpit!"

The man in the dirty pilot's coat whipped his pistol up and cracked off a blast. Jez dove for the ground, knocking Lev out of the way as Ysbel fired.

The force of the blast from Ysbel's modded gun threw Jez against the ramp, practically on top of Lev. He shoved her off him, and she rolled to her feet, yanked him up, and pushed him up the ramp.

"Get in, genius."

Ysbel had holstered her weapon and was running in after them. Jez took one last look around, grinning, paused long enough to make a rude gesture at the stunned gamblers, and swung herself up the ramp.

Tae was already closing it behind them.

She shoved her way past him into the cockpit, where a pleasant, competent-looking woman in a long pilot's coat sat in the pilot's seat, her black hair pulled back into a simple rat tail and her expression one of bland helpfulness. You'd hardly see the calculation beneath it unless you were looking.

"You've already blown up one of my ships, Masha," Jez growled. "Move over."

Masha stood, giving Jez a cold look. "If you had fewer people trying to kill you, I suspect it would be easier to keep your ships from getting blown up," she said, words tinged with ice.

"Shut up," Jez grumbled, sliding into the pilot's seat. She rested her hands on the controls for half a moment, letting the perfect, perfect feeling of the ship wash over her. Then she touched the stick, ever so slightly, and the ship lifted delicately off the ground.

"Strap in, kids," she called over the ship's com.

On the holoscreen in front of her, the right shield glowed as a heat-blast bounced off it.

She gave a beatific smile, settled herself into her seat, and pulled back smoothly on the control stick.

The ship pointed its nose to the sky and streaked towards the blue line of atmosphere, leaving Jez's stomach far behind. The speed of it shoved her back into her seat, and she half-closed her eyes in pure bliss.

This was life.

This was what she was born for.

The shields glowed a dull orange as they shot through the atmosphere, and the controls trembled against her hands, and then they were through.

She let out a long breath as the rich black of shallow space enveloped them, tension draining from her body.

Finally.

They'd been planet-side for less than a day, but she already hurt from missing this.

She leaned back in her seat, staring out at the vast expanse, the tiny pricks of fire that were the stars, the brown-blue glow of the planet through the rear window.

Every time. It almost made her cry, every single time. She'd spent three plaguing weeks on a prison ship back when she'd been picked up for smuggling, and every moment of every day in that tiny, miserable cell she'd longed for this. She'd needed it like she needed the blood in her veins and the air in her lungs, and every day she couldn't have it she'd died just a little bit more.

And now that she was back in the sky, it took her breath away every single time.

Freedom.

Home.

The only thing she'd ever wanted.

She let her hand rest on the control stick and closed her eyes, feeling the ship in her bones, the rightness of it.

She was jolted from her reverie by the sound, from somewhere behind her, of someone swearing loudly.

That would be Tae. Probably hadn't strapped down in time.

She opened her eyes and turned back to the cockpit window, staring at the endless expanse surrounding them. Then, reluctantly, she glanced at the com screen, set a few calculations into the controls, and stood.

Even after two weeks, leaving this perfect, beautiful cockpit was almost a physical pain.

She patted her coat pocket and grinned.

This time, though—

She couldn't wait to see the expression on Ysbel's face.

2

Lev took a deep breath and released his harness.

It wasn't that he didn't like flying. But what Jez did wasn't flying so much as it was some sort of aerial acrobatic routine.

At least he hadn't thrown up this time.

He shook his head, ran a shaky hand over his face, and stood cautiously. As long as they weren't being chased, Jez would probably have set a course. Which meant he was probably safe. And from the look of those gamblers, he doubted very much they had a ship that could come close to the *Ungovernable*.

To be fair, he'd spent the last two weeks pouring over every piece of information on board the ship they'd stolen so spectacularly out from under the nose of the system's most dangerous weapons dealer. He was increasingly coming to the conclusion that no one had a ship that could come close to the *Ungovernable*.

The others had gathered on the main deck by the time he arrived. Masha's arms were crossed, and there was a dangerous glint in her dark eyes.

She didn't look happy.

Lev sighed.

A few moments later, the lanky pilot sauntered into the room. Her black hair was tousled, and there was a broad grin across her tawny face, and despite everything, he couldn't stop his heart from skipping slightly, like it seemed to every time he saw her these days.

Which, of course, was utterly ridiculous.

"Well Jez," said Masha, her tone cold. "Would you like to explain what just happened?"

Jez grinned. "Sure. I went to the town kabak, took all the credits you gave me, and used them to gamble on a game of fool's tokens against someone who turned out to be a sore loser."

Lev winced. Masha closed her eyes and took a deep breath.

"I didn't get drunk," Jez added helpfully. "I thought about it. But the sump there was absolute crap."

Lev sighed and stepped forward before Jez could actually get herself murdered. "Jez—"

"No." Masha's voice was solid ice now. "I appreciate your efforts, Lev. But I'd like Jez to explain to me why she told me she needed supplies for the ship, and then went to buy sump and a stake in a game of fools's tokens."

"I did need supplies," said Jez. "Tech-head over there got them for me." She gestured to Tae.

Tae exchanged an exasperated glance with Lev, then turned to scowl at Jez.

"For heaven's sake, Jez, you didn't tell me—"

Jez shrugged. "You didn't ask. Anyways, I waited until you were all basically done getting what we needed. I thought you'd appreciate that." She reached into her coat. "And, I got your credits back with interest. You should be proud of me." She pulled out a gambling chip and tossed it to Masha. The woman caught it neatly without removing her gaze from Jez's face, her eyes narrowed.

For someone who appeared so remarkably average, Masha could

be surprisingly intimidating.

Jez, of course, was surprisingly difficult to intimidate.

"Besides," the pilot said, reaching into her coat pocket again. "I saw Ysbel trying to buy this. I thought I'd give her a hand."

She pulled out a small chip, dyed a bright orange, and held it up.

Lev stared at it, frowning. That was a transport log chip.

His heart beat faster, and he swallowed down the tightness in his throat, excitement or fear or guilt, he wasn't sure which. He glanced quickly over at Ysbel. She was looking between Jez and the chip as if she couldn't quite believe her eyes.

"How did you get that?" Ysbel asked at last, her voice slightly awestruck. "I offered that transport captain more credits than he knew what to do with for a five-minute look at it. He said it was more than his job was worth."

Jez grinned. "Fool's tokens. He had a good hand, but—" she shrugged. "I cheated."

Lev shot her a faintly disapproving look. She winked at him, and he blew out a long breath.

Ysbel shook her head as she took the chip, her face still slightly awed. "You know, you crazy idiot, most days I can't decide if I think you're brilliant, or I want to blow you up."

Jez grinned. "Couldn't blow me up. You'd miss me."

Ysbel looked at her with a flat expression. "And this is exactly what I mean. Most people wouldn't talk like that to a mass murderer."

"Yeah? Well I'm not most people."

Ysbel muttered something that sounded like, "thank goodness."

"Anyways," Jez said, leaning up against the wall, "you threatening to kill me all the time is kinda hot."

Ysbel shook her head in exasperation. "You remember how I'm

married? And how right now, at this moment, as we speak, we're going to find my wife? And how that was the whole point of getting this chip, to help me find my wife, who I'm married to?"

"Bet your wife would be jealous."

"I bet my wife would think you have a death wish. *I* think you have a death wish."

Masha opened her mouth, but Lev held up a hand. "Alright. Alright. We have our supplies, Masha, and no one died. And she did get Ysbel's chip. Let's call it a day."

Masha turned and looked at him calculatingly. "Very well, Lev," she said at last. "You're right. There has been no permanent damage done, through, I can only assume, some minor miracle. But," and here she turned back to Jez, "I am not impressed. I'm beginning to think I will not be able to leave you unsupervised."

Jez was still grinning, but there was something sharp in her expression now. "Well Masha," she drawled, "but here's the thing. I'm a pilot. I'm flying this ship. And you are not my damn boss. So you can take your supervision, and you can shove it up your—"

"Jez!" Lev snapped.

She smirked at him, turned on her heel, and sauntered back to the cockpit. Masha stared after her for a moment, her expression cold. Then she turned and left out the other door, boots clicking sharply off the deck floor.

Tae, Ysbel, and Lev looked at each other.

"I don't know how she's still alive," said Tae at last.

"I don't know how none of us have killed her yet," said Ysbel. She looked down at the chip in her hand. "I suppose I can't kill her now, anyways. I can't believe she got this." Even through her usually-stoic expression, Lev could read the strain in her face, the faint hint of excitement or fear in her voice. "I'll look through it, Lev, and I'll let you know if there's anything on it." She turned, then paused, shaking her head. "I honestly don't know how that crazy pilot does it."

"She cheated," said Lev. "At fool's tokens. How do you cheat at fool's tokens?"

"This is why I would never play fool's tokens with her. Or anything else, for that matter." Ysbel pocketed the chip. Even with the tightness behind her expression, she managed to shoot an amused glance at Lev. "Millions of people in the system, and that's the one you go soft for," she said, low enough that only he could hear. He glared at her, but she only gave him a slightly smug grin before she turned and left.

"What'd she say?" asked Tae. Lev took a deep breath and shook his head ruefully.

She was right. Millions of people in the plaguing system. Billions. And somehow he'd gone half-way soft for the idiot trigger-happy pilot who'd been responsible for landing him in jail. And who clearly had no time for romance at the moment, and at any rate, was likely the closest thing to his polar opposite he'd ever find.

So much for 'genius boy.'

"Nothing. Come on. Let's get back at it. Ysbel isn't going to be happy until we come up with a plan to get her wife and kids out of jail."

Tae nodded silently, and followed him back to their makeshift workroom.

Masha was waiting for them when they stepped through the door to the cluttered cabin-turned-office, sitting at the small ship's table Tae had set up in the centre of the room. It was crowded with scraps of paper, chips, clipped wires, and assorted information tech, but she'd cleared off a space in front of her, and somehow looked much more comfortable there than by rights anyone should. Lev sighed, shoved a bundle of charts he'd found stored in the hull of the ship off another chair, and sat down. Tae hesitated, then followed suit.

"Lev, Tae," said Masha, in her usual pleasant voice. Lev could hear, though, a trace of her earlier coldness. "What do you have for me?"

Lev paused. "I'm—still looking. I'm sorry. Not much. Tae?"

Tae shook his head, a frown creasing his forehead. "Not much from me either. Lev was able to find the prison sector, but even so I just barely figured out what planet she's on. I'm having no luck hacking into the sector system. I'll figure it out eventually, but it's a system-type I've never worked on before. Most of what they use on Prasvishoni are linear systems with mods. This is—" he shook his head. "It's a web-type system, I think. Every time I hit a fork I have to re-work the whole thing. It's taken me two weeks just to get this far." He let out a short breath, frustration clear on his face. Lev studied him unobtrusively.

Even before he'd met Tae, Lev had heard rumours about him. A street kid who was possibly the best hacker and techie in the system. And after working with him, Lev wholeheartedly agreed. The street-boy-turned-escaped-convict was a prodigy. If he was having trouble hacking in, it meant the system was next to impossible. But what he hadn't said—what he hadn't had to say—was the reason he was struggling so hard was that he'd been working blind. Lev hadn't managed to get him specs on anything.

It wasn't for lack of trying.

Lev had taken to splashing cold water on his face in the mornings after a sleepless night, to disguise the dark circles under his eyes.

Masha was watching them as well, her eyes sharp and calculating. "Are you certain this is what you want to do?" she asked softly. "I understand wanting to help Ysbel's family. But unfortunately, I don't have the information to help you, as I did with the last job we pulled."

Lev gritted his teeth against the irrational surge of irritation and took a deep breath. "Masha. We've discussed this. We're getting Ysbel's family out, and I quite honestly don't give a damn how long it takes, or how you feel about it. I hope I've made myself clear."

She was still watching him, and for a panicked half-moment, he wondered if she knew, if she could tell what lay behind his reasons. Then he shook his head wryly.

She didn't. She'd have mentioned it by now, if she had. Ysbel, Tae, Jez, even Masha—they all thought he was doing this out of the goodness of his heart. Because he was concerned for Ysbel's wife and children.

None of them knew about the guilt that ate at him every time he laid down on his bed and tried to close his eyes.

None of them knew that he was the one responsible for this.

He'd planned the extraction, five and a half years ago, where Ysbel was kidnapped and dragged away from her home planet to work for the Svodrani system government. Where she'd watched her wife and babies burn to death in their cottage, collateral damage of the operation. Or she'd thought they'd burned to death, until two weeks ago when Lev had turned up a record of them alive, somewhere on a prison planet.

Still—

Two children, she'd said. Eighteen months and three years old.

Two children who'd watched their mother dragged away, who'd somehow survived a fire that should have killed them. Who'd spent the last five and a half years on a prison planet.

He knew enough about prison planets to know they were no place for children.

And the thirty-five people Ysbel had killed when she'd blown up the shuttle station she'd been hauled in to work on—he'd been indirectly responsible for their deaths as well. And for the five years Ysbel had spent in prison for it.

He hadn't known, of course. He hadn't known who the operation he was designing had been for.

He hadn't even asked.

"Lev?" Tae sounded concerned. He looked up and tried to smile.

"I'm sorry. But Masha, that's my final word on the matter."

Masha was still watching him, and he couldn't read her expression. "Very well," she said at last. "We'll do this. I'll help you as much as I am able. It will not be as much as I'd wish—I worked in the government, but the prison sector was a world unto itself. But Lev, Tae. This—" she gestured around them at the long-haul ship they'd called home for the last two weeks. "This is an opportunity not many have had. We're completely wiped from every database in the system. Two weeks ago, a hundred people saw our ship explode. As far as anyone in this system is concerned, we're dead, or we never existed in the first place, as long as our pilot manages not to compromise all of that every time we stop in for supplies. And you know as well as I do, Lev, what this team is capable of. We can't afford to squander that on unjustified risks."

The thing was, a month ago he would probably have agreed with her. Back when he could still think rationally about the people on this team. Back when he hadn't realized he was as good as murderer himself.

"This risk is justified," said Tae quietly, and looking at him, Lev could tell he meant it.

He'd have to figure out a solution. Tae was working too hard on this. The circles under his eyes didn't show on his dark skin quite as much as they did on Lev's, but they were there. He was taking Lev's lead on this. Treating it like he was the one responsible.

For someone who couldn't be much older than twenty, Tae seemed to think he was responsible for a lot of things.

Masha nodded and stood. "Keep me appraised on your progress," she said. "We'll want to attract as little notice as possible before we get onto the prison planet, despite what our idiot pilot seems to think, and I hope we'll attract little while we're there—get in, get the woman and the children, and get off with no one the wiser. Once I have a timeline, I can calculate what we need so we make the least possible supply stops."

Lev nodded. "I will, Masha. But I suspect this will be measured in months, not weeks. If we're going to do this right, we'll need time for Tae to get into the systems, and for me to get the information."

Masha gave a small smile. "On that, at least, we agree. I'll help the rest of you pull this off, but I expect there to be no surprises, and no unknowns. I know enough about the prison system to know that one mistake there would likely be the last mistake any of us would ever make."

She turned and left the small cabin. When she was gone, Lev ran a hand over his face.

"Tae. You got me the name of the planet. Jez can find it on her charts. That's a start. But you need to take a break. Get some rest. This will all go faster if you have specs, so let me find the specs."

Tae shook his head, his dark eyes intense under his scowl. "No. You've seen Ysbel. She's going crazy. We need to figure this out, and —" he half-shrugged. "I'm the only one here who does tech. No offence."

"None taken," said Lev with a small smile. "But I'm going to tell you the same thing I told Ysbel. Wherever they keep this information, it's somewhere I never had access to when I worked with the government, and I had access to almost everything. And even if I do find the specs—" he spread his hands. "It's going to take at least three months to plan and prepare for. We don't have anything on this, so we have to move slowly."

Tae's scowl deepened. "Ysbel's not going to be happy to hear that."

Lev raised an eyebrow. "Trust me. She wasn't. But three months planning for a job that works is still more efficient than three weeks planning for one that fails."

Tae gave a heavy sigh and stood reluctantly. "I suppose." He paused. "Do you think Jez and Masha will survive three months?"

It was a fair question.

"Get some rest," Lev said at last. "It's been a long day."

For the first time, Tae gave a reluctant smile. "You could say that, I suppose."

Lev tipped his head in the direction of the cockpit. "Never a dull moment."

Tae yawned and chuckled ruefully. "I could use a dull moment once in a while. You're right. We'll try again in the morning. Maybe we'll see something we missed."

Lev nodded, and Tae turned and made his way out of the room.

When he'd gone, Lev tipped his head back and stared sightlessly at the ceiling. He smoothed his fingers absently across the worn tabletop and breathed through the tight fist of guilt constricting his chest.

Eighteen months and three years.

They'd grown up in jail. They'd grown up on a prison planet.

He sighed and pulled up his holoscreen.

He wouldn't be getting much sleep tonight.

3

Jez hummed tunelessly to herself as she ran her fingers across the control panel, feeling every dip and divot, every smooth surface, every tiny imperfection.

She still could hardly believe this ship was hers. Well, everyone's, technically. But it was her ship. It talked to her. It listened to her. It *believed* in her. And it would go to hell and back for her if she asked it to, she was certain of it.

And she'd barely scratched the surface. She could spend her whole lifetime trying to figure out what this ship could do, and she would love every single second of it.

There was a light tap at the cockpit door behind her.

"Come in," she called, not bothering to look up. Whoever it was couldn't be nearly as interesting as her perfect, beautiful, angel ship.

"Jez."

She turned as Lev slipped into the cockpit, and smiled despite herself. Something about this soft-boy seemed to do that to her.

"What are you doing still up?" he asked. "I thought you'd set it on autopilot."

She shrugged. "I did. What time is it?"

He tapped his com and peered at it. "It's 0400 standard time."

"What are you doing waking me up at 0400?" she countered.

He gave her a look of sorely-tried patience. "I didn't wake you up. You weren't sleeping."

"Well, I could have been."

"Not unless you hum off-key in your sleep."

"Maybe I do," she said with a smirk. "Bet you wish you knew." She took her hand off the control panel reluctantly. "Sorry, beautiful," she whispered. "Got visitors."

He raised one eyebrow at her, but she could see a tiny smile twitching at the corner of his mouth. She rolled her eyes, and he chuckled softly, sliding into the copilot's seat.

"Glad the ship suits you."

It was a little like saying, "glad breathing suits you," or "glad eating food suits you."

She glanced over at him. He looked tired, but then he always looked tired these days. "What about you? Why are you up?"

He shrugged one shoulder. "Couldn't sleep, I guess."

She looked at him a little more closely. There were dark shadows under his eyes, and his face was paler than it usually was.

Not like she made a habit of looking at him. Obviously.

They sat in silence for a few minutes. It was something she'd found herself liking about Lev. Sure, he was an eggheaded scholar-boy softy, but he seemed to understand that she wasn't much of a people person. And he seemed to not mind. Most of the time. He had looked a little irritated when she'd cheated that idiot out of the information chip, but honestly, that had been absolutely spectacular. If he didn't appreciate something like that, his loss.

"How do you do it?" Lev asked at last, gesturing at the black expanse surrounding them. "I mean, you … seemed upset when Masha told us all to stay in the hangar bay, back on Prasvishoni."

She grinned. "You mean when I smuggled in sump and got completely smashed? And Masha absolutely lost her crap? Is that what you're talking about?"

He sighed. "Yes, Jez. Among other things." He paused. "And now here we are in a ship in deep space. Nowhere to go. We've been here for two weeks, and yesterday was our first time off-ship. Why aren't you going crazy?"

She studied him for a moment. Then she turned back to the cockpit window.

How did you explain something like this? How did you explain how it felt to breathe after weeks of no oxygen?

"It's different," she said at last. "Just … different."

He turned to look at her. "I was talking with Tae last night. We're thinking it will take a solid three months to plan Ysbel's prison break. Maybe more. And we can't spend much time planet-side between now and then. We're off-radar, and I'd like to stay that way. You're used to smuggling, which, if I'm any judge, is lots of action. This is … waiting. That's all. Are you going to be alright for that long?"

She shook her head. "I haven't even begun to figure out this sweet, sweet angel's capabilities. I've barely played with the hyperdrive. If I'm in the pilot's seat, three months with her is nothing. Besides, deep space isn't nearly as boring as you're making it out to be."

She glanced over at the holoscreen. The blurred shape she'd been watching for the last hour was growing closer.

Much closer.

Her grin widened. "For example—"

She settled herself in her seat and touched the tips of her fingers lightly on the controls, breathing in deeply.

"Jez!" Lev hollered as a meteoroid shot past the cockpit window.

"Strap in," she murmured. She barely had time to notice the

blood drain from his face before they were in the middle of the narrow asteroid belt.

She half-closed her eyes and leaned her head back, flying by instinct. The ship danced between the hurtling balls of space-rock, responding to her lightest touch. She barely had to think a command and the ship read her thoughts through her fingers.

Beside her, Lev's knuckles were white on the arms of his seat, jaw clenched, cords standing out on his neck.

"Loosen up, genius boy," she said over her shoulder.

"Just fly, Jez," he said through his teeth. She shrugged.

"I am."

Another meteoroid skimmed the cockpit so closely that she could have reached out her hand and touched it. Adrenalin pumped through her body, and the world slowed, and everything was perfect.

And then, far too soon, it was over.

She pulled back on the controls regretfully, and the ship slowed and steadied on course.

Lev let out a shaky breath. "For heaven and the Lady and the Consort's bloody sake Jez, what the hell was that?"

She sighed patiently. "I told you. I need to figure out what she can do. I can't very well pilot her if I don't know how she responds."

"You—I'm fairly certain that sailing her out through Vitali's vaults would be considered piloting her," said Lev, still sounding shaky. She rolled her eyes.

"No, that was just flying. I need to get to know her. That's why I don't care about being in deep space. It'll be fine. As long as I can do that every so often—" she trailed off, tipping her head back against the seat. "It's all I need, Lev. Freedom, and a ship, and deep space."

Lev shook his head, but he was watching her with the smallest hint of a smile on his face—not amusement, something else.

She frowned slightly. Whatever it was, she wasn't sure she wanted to deal with it.

The sharp crack of knuckles against the cockpit doorway made her jerk her head up. She didn't even have time to call 'come in' before Masha strode into the cockpit.

Jez narrowed her eyes and got to her feet.

"Jez." Masha's voice snapped out like a whip. "What do you think you're doing?"

Jez gave her a lazy grin, her heart beating faster and her muscles tightening with anticipation. "I was taking her through her paces, Masha."

"You took us through an asteroid belt. What were you thinking?"

"I was flying my ship."

Masha narrowed her eyes. "Your ship? If I remember correctly, Jez, I found you on that prison ship because you'd crashed *your* ship into an astroid."

Lev jumped to his feet and grabbed her arm before she could smash Masha's smug face in. "Jez," he said in a warning voice.

She jerked her arm out of his grip, not taking her eyes off Masha. "That wasn't my damn fault," she hissed.

"Perhaps not. But you've shown me clearly in the past two weeks that you are incapable of making responsible decisions. I'm sorry, but I can't have you putting my entire crew in danger any time the urge strikes you. Someone could have been killed yesterday. The *Ungovernable* could have been damaged if the steering hadn't reacted the way you assumed it would. This has gone more than far enough. You will not put this crew or this ship in danger again."

"I didn't realize you were the boss of me," drawled Jez.

Damn this woman. Damn her to every hell that ever existed.

"Perhaps you'd better learn how to have a boss, Jez," Masha said sharply. "You will set a course for deep space, and you will leave the ship on autopilot until Lev and Tae are ready to take us onto the prison planet. Do you understand me?"

Three months.

For a moment Jez couldn't breathe.

Three damn months on autopilot. Three months sitting in deep space with a ship that spoke to her, that sang to her, and Masha expected her not to answer.

It would be almost as bad as being stuck in that damn hangar bay.

Worse. It would be like starving to death right in front of a plaguing feast.

She'd die. She'd walk out the airlock herself before she'd make herself do that.

"Jez," said Lev again, stepping up beside her. "Listen to me."

She took a deep breath. "Sure Masha," she said through her teeth. "I'll do exactly what you say. Over my dead frozen body, you bastard."

Lev tapped his com. "Tae, Ysbel, I need you in the cockpit, please. Now."

Masha's eyes had narrowed further.

The woman was a stinking scum-sucker as far as Jez was concerned, but she'd always proved remarkably competent every time it came to a fight. Jez wasn't entirely certain, if it came to it, which one of them would win.

One way to find out.

She grinned at Lev over her shoulder.

Tae appeared in the doorway, took one look at the scene, and stepped quickly beside Lev, placing himself between her and Masha.

Plaguing idiot.

"What's going on?" he asked.

"Masha and Jez are having a discussion," said Lev through his teeth, "and I think it should take place another time. Where's Ysbel?"

"I don't know." Tae looked like he'd just woken up, long black hair tousled, eyes swollen with sleep. "What in the system happened back there?"

"Jez decided to take us through an asteroid belt," said Masha in a cold voice.

Tae shook his head and rubbed his eyes. "What?"

"I was testing the controls," she said, rolling her eyes at him. "Like a responsible pilot."

"I don't think the word 'responsible' could be applied to anything to do with you," Masha snapped. "This discussion is at an end."

"This is my damn ship, Masha."

"It's not your ship."

"Jez, Masha." Lev stepped forward beside Tae, holding up his hands. "Let's—"

"No!" she snapped. "I'm sick of this. Masha decides what we do. Masha decides where we go. We get Masha's permission before we plaguing sneeze. And I'm finished. I don't know what she wants, but I know damn well what I want. I want a ship, I want deep space, and hell, I'll help Ysbel get her family back. But not like this."

Masha had gone very quiet, and there was a look on her face that might have made Jez nervous, if she hadn't been so angry.

"Well, Lev?" Masha asked, her voice sharp as a razor blade. "Tae? I won't command a crew who doesn't agree with me."

"Command? All you've done is almost get us killed," Jez growled. Masha gave her that piercing look of hers.

"No, Jez. That was you. I got you out of jail. I brought you together so you could pull off the heist. I wiped you from every database in the system, I made it appear that you'd all died in an explosion."

"By blowing up my ship," Jez growled.

"And you, Jez?" Masha continued, voice hard. "I brought you in because you are a very good pilot. But you seem intent on making sure all my work was for nothing, by putting everyone's lives in danger. You may not believe it, but the five of us on this ship are not the only people in the system, and getting into deep space is not the only thing that matters. That's not why I did this."

Jez wrenched her arm free from Lev's grip and grabbed Masha by the collar. She didn't even see Masha move, but she felt the unmistakable shape of a heat-pistol muzzle pressed into her stomach.

"Stand down, Jez," said Masha, her voice dangerously quiet.

Jez's whole body was buzzing with adrenalin, every sense sharp and clear. To her side, Lev and Tae stood helpless and horrified.

"Sorry, Masha," she said through gritted teeth. "You'll have to shoot me, then. Because I'll be damned before I take one more order from you."

Masha narrowed her eyes, and Jez's heart rate sped up. She'd seen heat-gun wounds. It wasn't a nice way to die.

The door to the cockpit burst open, and Ysbel stumbled through. All four of them whirled around, Jez's hand loosening from Masha's collar and Masha's pistol slackening from Jez's stomach.

Ysbel hardly seemed to notice the scene in front of her. Her face was set and expressionless, but there was something haunted behind her eyes.

"Ysbel?" asked Lev at last, his voice strained.

"Lev," she said hoarsely. "That chip our crazy pilot got—it has some information. I think you should see this."

4

Tae rubbed his eyes again, blinked hard against the sleep he'd been rudely jerked out of a scant few minutes earlier, and shook his head in a sort of awed exasperation as Jez let go of Masha's collar, an expression of disgust on her face. Masha holstered her pistol, expression cold, and turned to follow Lev and Ysbel out of the room.

What a way to wake up.

Bloody idiots. It was probably inevitable at some point. It just would have been nice if it could have happened while he was awake.

Jez hesitated a moment, then followed the others, and, with the two main combatants out of the room, Tae went after them.

Back on Prasvishoni, before he'd been arrested, he'd been the oldest surviving street kid in their sector, which made him their motley gang's de-facto leader. He'd broken up plenty of fights between starving, angry kids who'd been pushed past the breaking point.

He watched Masha's stiff posture, Jez's slouch and the anger steaming off her like heat, and sighed.

Maybe this was almost the same thing.

Ysbel, Lev and the others had already gathered around the makeshift table in the cramped cabin by the time he stepped in behind them. He squeezed in through the doorway, and pushed between Masha and Jez to the table.

He could almost feel the loathing between them. Although Jez, typically, seemed already distracted.

He wished, for just a moment, that he could forget about everything that was stressing him that quickly. His jaw ached from where he'd been clenching it, even in his sleep, for the past two weeks.

He'd thought after they'd pulled off the job on Vitali and made their escape he'd be able to relax. He hadn't counted on waking up every night to the faces of the starving kids he'd left behind on Prasvishoni.

Masha was right—there wasn't anything he could have done to help them. If he'd gone back there, he would have been back on the streets in days, and back in jail in weeks, government pardon or no. Street kids were considered an infestation, and the government's views on how to deal with an infestation were depressingly brutal. Even if he'd gotten them out of the city and off the planet, they'd have simply starved or frozen on one of the outer-rim settlements, trying to eke a living from the thin, terraformed dirt or begging or stealing in the dirt-eater settlement towns from others who'd been forced, or had chosen, to do the same. It was no life. No matter how much he'd dreamed about it, it was no life.

But he was all they had. And he'd left, and they probably thought he was dead. Would Caz be their next leader? The kid was only seventeen, but he'd already grown up way too quickly. Like Tae had. Like they'd all had to.

He shook his head and pulled out a chair beside Lev.

At least he could help Ysbel get her family back. That was one thing he could do. And maybe, if he was busy enough, he could stop thinking about the people he'd failed.

Ysbel's grim face, the haunted look in her eyes—that, at least, he could relate to.

"Alright, Ysbel," said Lev. "Show me what you found."

"This chip has some information on the prison itself, but probably not much more than you already know," she said, her voice not quite steady. "It's a political prison, and it's as isolated as the government can make it. There are settlements for the workers families on the other side of the planet, and workers only go in and out weekly. No visitors. A situation I'm sure you, Lev, are familiar with."

From the corner of his eye, Tae saw Lev's rueful nod. "Yes, Ysbel. I am. And this is all useful information. But I'm not certain—"

"I haven't finished." She tapped her com and expanded the glowing holoscreen that appeared above her wrist, then pulled it around in front of her so they could all see. "The chip Jez stole—"

"Won," cut in Jez.

"He was a transport driver. They go in to bring supplies to the prison planets. Once a week they stop in, but sometimes their schedule is interrupted. Like, for example, if the prison is moving prisoners. And then they might help with the transport."

She tapped a point on the screen, and expanded it. "See, here. There will be prisoners transported in three weeks' time. They don't say their names, only their prison numbers. And their gender. And their age."

It took Tae a moment to see what she'd seen. Then he sucked in a quick breath.

9877 - F - 37

9878 - F - 8

9879 - M - 6

The only children on the list.

Likely, the only children in the prison.

Ysbel's children.

"Where are they taking them?" Lev's voice was calm, as always, but Tae could hear the strain under it. Ysbel didn't answer, just flicked the screen with an impatient gesture. Another page of data appeared. Lev peered at it, then swore softly and leaned back.

"They're taking them to the Vault."

Something icy dug itself into Tae's chest, and he stared at the screen in front of him.

He'd heard stories about the Vault, back in his days on the streets. He'd never heard of someone making it out, though.

Ysbel nodded grimly.

"Why would they do that, Masha?" Lev asked, not taking his eyes off the screen.

"Ysbel's dead, as far as the government is concerned," said Masha in her no-nonsense tone, but there was still cold anger under it. "I know very little about Tanya. I looked up her records before I came to talk to Ysbel, obviously, but there's very little on her—grew up on a farm, went away to Prasvishoni for university, came back home, got married, started a family. I can understand them putting her and the children in a political prison, if they survived Ysbel's extraction. The government would certainly go to great lengths, including locking up two children, to prevent word of how it had dealt with Ysbel from getting out—her father and mother were cultural heroes during the war twenty years back. But transferring them to the Vault? I don't know." She shook her head slightly, her face grim. "It's possible it has something to do with Ysbel's disappearance. But, Lev, you know as well as I do what this means."

Lev nodded. His face, Tae noticed, was as grim as Masha's.

Jez shoved her seat back so it was balancing on two legs and put her hands behind her head. "So I guess this Vault thing is bad?"

Tae rolled his eyes in exasperation. Ysbel glared. Lev sighed. "Yes, Jez. It's bad."

"It means the only way we would get my wife out would be if I sent you in the front door with a handful of explosives and then set them off."

Jez raised her eyebrows, looking suddenly interested. "That would work?"

"No. It wouldn't work. But it would make me feel better."

"Jez," said Lev. "That's the highest-security prison in the system. What we did with Vitali is child's play next to that. It means in three week's time, we lose Tanya and the kids, permanently."

Jez lowered her chair to the ground, looking, for once in her life, serious. "Oh. So. What do we do?"

Lev caught Tae's eye, and Tae could see his question.

The thing was, what he was asking wasn't possible. What Ysbel was asking wasn't possible. He'd been trying for two weeks to break into the system, and the best he'd gotten was a hairline crack. Three weeks from now? There was no way.

There was almost certainly no way.

Just like every other damn thing he'd done with this damn crew.

There was something heavy and sick in the pit of his stomach.

He was clenching his jaw again, and he consciously tried to relax it. He'd been awake for ten minutes and he already had a tension headache.

Lev glanced around at the others quickly, but no matter where he looked he could see Ysbel's face.

This was a terrible idea. Even if he and Tae had three months to find information and plan it, it would be a delicate thing to break three people out of a high-security political prison. And this?

If he agreed to it, he may well be sending this entire crew to their deaths. And there was almost no chance they'd be able to extract Ysbel's family. Tae knew it too, he'd seen it in his expression.

But—

Eighteen months and three years when they'd watched their mother grabbed from in front of them and dragged off on a ship. When they'd almost burned to death in their own home. When they'd been taken to a prison planet.

They'd grown up in hell. A hell he'd sent them to. And if they were taken to the Vault?

He shuddered.

So he'd risk the crew of the *Ungovernable*. His friends. People who'd been willing to put their own lives at risk for him, more than once. Or he'd sentence Ysbel's wife and children to something that would probably be even worse than death.

But at the end of the day, if he was being honest, those weren't the things he was taking into consideration right now. The simple fact of the matter was, he couldn't keep doing this. He couldn't live for the next however-many years with the thought of Ysbel's children haunting him. He couldn't.

And so, for that, to assuage his own guilt, he'd gamble his friends.

Of course he would.

He gave a small, bitter smile. And they'd go, willingly, because they trusted that he'd somehow have a plan to make it work.

"Well. I guess our timeline has moved up," he said at last.

The tension in Ysbel's posture relaxed, her shoulders dropping, the relief obvious in her face.

"So," she said. "What do we do next?"

Lev sighed and pulled up the holoscreen on his own com. "Honestly, Ysbel, I have no idea. I'm willing to go in. But I won't try to talk anyone else into it. You make your own decisions on this. Ysbel?"

She looked at him as if he were slightly mad. "If you want me to not go in," she said in a reasonable tone, "you'd have to kill me or put me in a coma. And considering that I do not think anyone in this crew is capable of either of those things, I'm coming."

To be fair, it had been a stupid question.

"Tae?" He already knew the answer. But he had to give him the chance to back out. On the off-chance he'd take it. Of course, there was no way they'd succeed without him, but on the other hand, there wasn't much of a chance they'd succeed with him, either.

"I'm in," said Tae dully. He sounded as tired as he looked.

"Masha?"

She was still standing by the door, lips pressed tightly together.

"Lev," she said at last. "You know my position. This isn't just foolhardy. This is walking all five of us into a death trap. You and Tae both have explained to me that it's not possible to do this on short notice. Believe me, I want Ysbel to have her family back. I hate the idea of children locked up in a prison planet as much as any of you. But someone here needs to be realistic. This is an impossible mission, and there is no way we can pull it off. All we'd be doing is throwing our own lives away, and getting nothing in return."

"We've done impossible things before. We could save them, maybe," said Ysbel in a low voice. She sounded lost, and her tone cut him like a knife.

Masha sighed and shook her head. "Ysbel. I understand. And I know you believe the risk is worth it for yourself. But do you believe the same for the rest of this crew?"

Ysbel was silent.

Lev glanced around again.

But it didn't matter. When push came to shove, he'd discovered, he was a selfish bastard after all.

"I'm afraid that's not up to Ysbel," he said, forcing his voice to remain calm. "Ultimately, it's not her decision. Masha, I understand your concerns. In other circumstances, I'd agree. But I intend to do this, with or without your help. I've made a promise to Ysbel, and I intend to keep it."

There was a moment of silence, and he steadfastly refused to look in Ysbel's direction. He wouldn't be able to handle the look of gratitude on her face.

"If you're set on doing this, I'll come," Masha said, reluctance clear in her voice. "I spent an inordinate amount of time and effort to bring you together, and I have a vested interest in your remaining alive. But I can only hope that at some point you will come to your senses. If we're caught, they won't lock us up. They'll kill us."

"Well, I'm in," said Jez loudly, dropping her chair back on four legs with a loud thud. "If Masha's against it, it's probably right up my alley." She flashed Masha a wide, dangerous grin.

Masha gave a tight shake of her head, her face cold.

Lev sighed. "Well Masha, it looks like you're out-voted."

"So it would appear," she said thinly. She turned to Jez, and Lev sat forward in his seat, waiting for the inevitable explosion. "Jez." Masha's voice was cold. "For now, it appears, we will have to work together. But I expect to revisit our conversation once we're out."

"Yeah? I'll be looking forward to it, you bastard." Jez smirked and stretched luxuriously. "Well then, now that's out of the way, let's go break someone into jail."

5

The crate had been used to store cattle of some sort, Ysbel assumed from the smell of it. Tae had grumbled when she'd asked him and Jez to help load it onto the ship when they were gathering supplies on the zestava, but she'd ignored him.

Things like this always came in handy.

"This good?" asked Jez. Ysbel nodded.

"Stand back."

Jez grinned airily and strolled to the other side of the room.

"Farther."

Jez raised one eyebrow, but did as she was told.

For once.

Ysbel watched with a mixture of irritation and affection until she was out of the way. Maybe the idiot had some sense of self-preservation after all. She tapped her ear, and Jez rolled her eyes, but shoved in the ear protection Ysbel had given her. Ysbel waited a moment to make sure she'd actually stay put, then she touched the control in her hand.

For a moment, nothing happened.

Then the world exploded around them.

Ysbel squeezed her eyes shut for a second to block out the jag of light seared across her vision, then coughed and waved the smoke away from her face.

Not bad for a first try. The supplies she'd bought in the zestava weren't as low-quality as she'd expected. An explosion like that would probably take out a force-field, given enough hits.

Across the room, Jez was doubled over coughing, her mouth moving in what were unmistakably swear words.

The crate was gone. Instead, the air around them was filled with a haze of charred prefab dust.

Ysbel pulled one earplug out.

"Thank you, Jez. That was all I needed you for."

Jez had already removed her own ear plugs. She'd recovered from her coughing fit, and, apparently, her swearing fit, and now she was looking around at the hazy room with stunned delight on her face.

"Can you make my ship a gun that does that?"

"I did. I installed it when we were planet-side."

"What? Can I shoot it at something?

"No."

"That was fantastic. I think I love you."

"Piss off, Jez."

She smiled grudgingly despite herself.

She still wasn't sure when this stupid pilot had become something like a friend.

Jez wandered over to where the crate had stood moments before. "What did you do to it?"

"I was just checking my supplies."

"And?"

"And I vaporized it."

"Oh."

This was good. If she could smuggle in her supplies, she could do a lot with minimal equipment.

But …

She shut her eyes for a moment. Tanya was there, behind her eyelids, like she always was. Every dream, every daydream, every other thought was occupied by the willowy woman with long brown hair and limpid blue eyes and wistful smile, a small, determined girl with dirt on her face, and a chubby, solemn toddler. Not a small girl anymore. Not a toddler. But hers. Her life. Her whole heart.

And now they were so close. So close that she could almost touch them. Thanks, in no small part, to the transport chip this ridiculously-irritating pilot had cheated off someone in a kabak.

She'd never not be grateful. And she couldn't afford for anything to go wrong.

"You could make me a gun out of that. That would be amazing. And besides, it would be really useful. What if we have to shoot someone when we're breaking onto the prison planet? Something like this, they'd never know what hit them. No one else would even know anyone had been there. You've got to admit, it would be amazing."

Jez was still talking. Jez was always talking.

"Don't you have work to do?" Ysbel asked, opening her eyes. Jez was looking around her with the sort of wide-eyed wonder she reserved for things that could fly and things that could cause mass destruction.

"Nope," she said, looking back at Ysbel. "My sweet darling is ready. She'll do whatever I tell her to."

"Good," Ysbel grunted. "That had better be true."

"Ysbel. It's my ship."

"And I'm sure it's missing you. Why don't you go back to your cockpit?"

"Ah, she's not jealous."

"I wish you'd do whatever I told you to."

Jez laughed loudly, head tipped back and snorting.

"It wasn't a joke, Jez."

Jez recovered herself, wiping tears of hilarity from her eyes. "I mean it, Ysbel. I really, really need a gun like that. You could mod my heat pistol."

"Jez. Please shut up."

"But—"

"Shut up."

"But—"

"Please stop talking."

Jez let out a long-suffering sigh. "Fine. Use me for my muscles. I don't care. Hey, I think I'll go check on Tae. You think he needs a hand?"

Ysbel was almost tempted to let her go. Still, Tae didn't deserve that.

"Look. You go back to your cockpit. You go through your protocols one more time. And—" she took a deep breath. "And I'll keep Masha busy for a few minutes so you can run some flight tests. OK?"

Jez looked like someone had just handed her a full bottle of sump and a weekend off.

"Now please go away."

Jez gave a mock salute. "You got it, cap'n." She turned and strolled out of the room, calling back over her shoulder, "I need fifteen standard minutes. You promised."

Ysbel sighed. She was probably going to regret this. Still, she would have regretted having the pilot in the room with her for the next fifteen minutes much more, so there was that.

"Masha," she called over her com. "Can you come in here? I'd like to ask you something."

When they convened in the mess hall a standard hour later, Lev still looked pale, and Tae was nursing a bruise on his elbow and scowling darkly at the entire room.

Ysbel felt a slight tinge of guilt.

Still, Jez was probably right that she needed to put the ship through its paces at some point.

Masha glared daggers as the long-limbed tousle-haired pilot dropped into her seat, pulling up one knee and stretching her other leg out in front of her luxuriously.

"You could have warned us, Jez," Tae grumbled.

"Well, but then Masha might have stopped me," she said, without a hint of remorse. "Or tried." She grinned at Lev. "See? Genius-boy's getting used to it. Bet he didn't even throw up this time."

"And that, Jez," said Lev through his teeth, "is a bet you'd lose."

"Ah, come on. You know you like it." Jez tossed him a packet of rations and grabbed one herself, ripping the packaging open with her teeth. He rubbed a hand over his face, and Ysbel bit back a smile. Tae rolled his eyes and grabbed the carton of meal rations from the food stores.

"Here. In case anyone other than Jez wants to eat."

Ysbel smiled at him slightly as she took a rations packet. He was the youngest of them, but somehow he'd become the de facto parent of the group.

"Alright. Once again, what do we have?" Lev asked, ripping open his own rations packet.

They'd been at this for four days now. Every time there was more than one of them in the room it was the same question. But the list on the holoscreen Lev pulled up in front of him was still depressingly short.

Masha crossed to the supplies cupboard, and pulled out a heavy bundle of beige work smocks.

"Here," she said, dropping it on the table. "If we're going to talk while we eat, please get to work on these as well. The prison uniforms are the same colour, thank goodness, but you'll have to cut them to the right shape." She still looked disapproving, but she hadn't said anything to convince them to change their minds. Perhaps she knew it would be futile. Or perhaps, knowing Masha, she knew something the rest of them didn't, and had no intention of sharing.

The thing was, Ysbel couldn't help but agree with her. This mission was an absurd risk.

But she had to go. And despite the guilt that gnawed at her every time she looked at the others—she needed them. If there was even the smallest chance that they could get Tanya and her children back, she needed them.

Tae picked up a smock, still scowling. "Nothing new. I've been trying all day to even crack the system, and I made it down maybe one more line of the web. But I think I may be in deep enough that I can try for the prison records tomorrow. I did get our wrist coms plugged in. They'll read as prisoner ID bracelets."

Lev sighed. "Well, that's better than it was yesterday. Jez?"

"Ship's ready to go," the pilot said, pushing the last bite of rations into her mouth. "Good thing I put her through her paces to test her today, right?"

"That wasn't a test," Tae muttered.

"Yeah it was. I was testing to see how fast you could get into your harness."

For a moment Ysbel thought Tae might try to punch the pilot.

She wouldn't have blamed him, honestly.

Jez grinned, and grabbed a smock from the pile on the table. "Hey, I figured out how to get us on the supply transport to get us in the doors. In case you were wondering." She pulled a ship's knife from the magnetic case under the table and started hacking at the hem of the garment with a noticeable lack of finesse. "I still bet I could fly us in to the transport ship, though, when they fly them out, and we could grab them from there."

Lev sighed. "And, as I'm almost certain I already told you, they will have more than a dozen armed escorts, and even if we could get past them, prison policy is if there's a hint of a security breach, the prisoners in the transport are neutralized, which tends to be another word for killed. They're trying to discourage breakout attempts, apparently. And before you ask, we're also not going to just fly the *Ungovernable* in and blow the prison up, because again, the prison would immediately go into lockdown and, it would likely lead to a similar outcome, at least for the prisoners we're interested in extracting."

Jez looked momentarily sobered.

Lev paused. "Unfortunately, I don't have good news. Masha managed to get me some rudimentary prison specs. I looked up their force-field—there'll be no communicating out from inside the prison. Inside, yes, with Tae's tech. But not past the field. Our plan to have people on the outside with backup isn't going to work."

Ysbel shifted in her seat. Her heart was beat painfully fast.

She couldn't afford to get emotional. Not now. This had to work, and she had to be thinking logically.

"So what does that mean?" she asked, her voice somehow measured.

Lev looked at her, then turned to the others. Whatever it meant, he was clearly reluctant to say.

She half-closed her eyes, trying not to let the strain show on her face.

It didn't matter, in the end, how impossible it was. If the others didn't agree to help, she'd go in by herself.

"It means," he said finally. "We're all on the inside."

Jez sat up abruptly, dropping both the smock and the knife. "Wait. What?"

He spread his hands. "I'm sorry, Jez. I can't think of another option. We're going in blind. We can't make more than a skeleton of a plan out here, because we have no idea what we'll be facing. We have to work from inside the prison."

"You mean I have to go back into a prison?" She looked panicked. Lev shook his head.

"No one's going to make you go anywhere, Jez," he said. "But at this point, anyone who's in on this will be inside. That's all I've got. We need Tae—none of us can get into the systems without him. We'll need me on the inside, because I'm the only one of us who will be able to get us back out. We need Ysbel for more reasons than one —she's our weapons and explosives expert, she's the one Tanya will trust, and also, she'd probably blow me up if I tried to stop her. Masha, you managed to talk all of us into pulling a heist on Vitali. We'll need you in there if we want a chance of getting information from the guards. And Jez—" he paused. "As I said. I won't force you to come. I doubt I could if I tried. But of all of us, you're the only one who's broken out of prison. We'll need what you know, and what you can do."

Jez stood abruptly. "I'm a pilot. I fly things. That's what I do." She was breathing quickly, eyes narrowed, and Ysbel watched her with a sudden pang of sympathy, mingled with guilt.

She never would have believed, a month ago, that the crazy pilot would even have considered it.

She opened her mouth, but Masha spoke first.

"Perhaps it's best if Jez stays behind." Her voice was cold. "My motive is, as it always has been, is to keep this team from being killed. And to be honest, I'm not certain having her there will advance that aim."

"Shut up, Masha," Jez snapped. She took a deep breath, clearly trying to keep herself under control. "Fine. It's just a week. A week at the longest, right?"

"Jez. You don't have to—" Ysbel began. Jez turned on her, glaring. "Ysbel. Piss off."

Ysbel almost cracked a smile, them found herself swallowing a lump in her throat.

"If we don't find Tanya right away, or if things go sideways, our backup plan will be to get out when the supply ship goes out. That gives us a week on the inside." Lev glanced at Ysbel. "I'm sorry Ysbel, but that's the best I can offer."

With or without Tanya.

Well. It didn't matter, really. She'd go in, and she'd come out with Tanya and Olya and Misko, or she wouldn't come out at all.

She nodded slowly, and picked up a smock of her own. "I would not ask any of you to stay longer than that."

He gave her a sharp glance, as if he'd caught the words she hadn't said, but he didn't comment.

"Anyways, it's not like I haven't broken out of prison before," said Jez.

"And?" asked Lev, looking up. "I know the basics, but not the details. Anything could help."

Jez leaned back, appearing to think for a moment. "Well," she said at last, "I don't know anything about the systems. Or the guard schedules. Or weapons or whatever crap Ysbel can do. But," she grinned, "you can make the guards really mad if you make up a song about them and their dog alone in a room with—"

"Thank you, Jez, that's enough detail."

"Or, you can say something about their partner going up to a government building with an official and—"

"Thank you, Jez."

"And sometimes, I'd—"

"Jez! Shut up."

She smirked. Ysbel glanced at Tae's horrified face and bit back a small grin.

"I can't imagine how you got on the guards' nerves," Tae muttered, and this time Ysbel had to bite back a snort of laughter.

"Do you have anything that doesn't involve crude stories about guards?" asked Lev in a resigned tone. Jez thought for a moment, then shook her head, leaning forward.

"I have one more thing."

"Yes?"

"If you're kicking someone in the crotch on the way out, you have to make sure it's the right kind of crotch. If you know what I mean. Because I made that mistake once, and honestly—"

"Jez." Lev was speaking through his teeth. "You can shut up now."

Jez shrugged and leaned back again.

Ysbel shook her head in faint amusement.

Poor boy was in way over his head.

"What's our timeline?" asked Masha.

"The supplies ship comes in at 1500 standard time the day after tomorrow, which is early morning on the prison planet. It docks just outside the prison, and the prison guards come out and inspect it for contraband and for any sort of possible deep-space contamination. That's when we'll have to get in."

Masha glanced around the room. "Then I suggest we finish our uniforms, and pack whatever it is we need to smuggle in."

Ysbel watched the others as they worked, clutching her own smock in her hand so tightly the rough texture of the fabric cut into her palm. Her chest felt as if someone was squeezing it, her muscles tense.

Somehow, this had to work.

It would work. Because to fail—to loose Tanya and Olya and Misko a second time—was unthinkable.

6

Reluctantly, Jez pulled back on the ship's stick, and once again time seemed to stretch and warp around them as the ship came out of hyperdrive, the strange patterns and glowing colours surrounding them giving way to the black of shallow space.

She sighed, the same aching feeling of loss that always came when she pulled out of hyperspace pulling at her stomach.

Still … She glanced at the com.

Perfect. She'd dropped them on the exact coordinates Tae had asked for.

"Not bad," said Lev from the copilot's seat, raising an eyebrow. She gave him a smug smile. He smiled back, then reached down to flip on the cloaking device.

She glanced at the bright glow of the planet in the near distance. She'd brought them in close.

An hour, max.

It would be fine. She'd be fine. Just a week. No sweat.

A week grounded. A week locked up.

Her stomach was tight, her palms sweating on the controls.

"Jez? Are you alright?"

She turned and tried to grin. "I'm fine. We'll get Tanya and the kids and get out, right? Easy peasy."

He was still watching her, his face concerned.

She turned away quickly. He didn't need to see her panic.

She'd been locked up before, on that prison ship, for three weeks. She'd survived.

Barely.

She tried to slow down her breathing and stared out the window, running her fingers up and down the control stick absently.

It would be fine. She'd be fine.

Ysbel's family had been locked up for five years.

"Jez?"

"Be there soon," she said, trying to grin. "Better get ready."

He nodded and stood, but he watched her for a moment before he turned away, and there was concern on his face, and for some reason she had to swallow a lump in her throat.

Which was ridiculous.

She wasn't used to this. She still couldn't believe that, when they could have left her behind back in Vitali's compound, they hadn't. They'd tried to break her out, instead.

And now she couldn't leave them to do this alone either, even though she really, really wanted to.

As soon as Lev was gone, she jumped to her feet and took two quick steps across the floor.

The cockpit had never felt cramped before. Now it was closing in on her like atmosphere, heavy and clinging and poisonous.

She swore loudly, and kicked the pilot's seat.

It didn't help.

Less than an hour.

She wished she'd thought to bring some sump along.

* * *

The planet, when they broke through the atmosphere, was nothing much to look at. The side with the settlement for the prison worker's families, Lev had said, was beside a small ocean, but on this side, by the prison complex, it was more of a desert, with jutting rock cliffs and the hint of brownish-green brush on the sandy flats.

They didn't know the scope of the cloaking tech yet, so she brought them in at an angle from the prison complex coordinates, then flew them in low over the mountainous cliffs. Lev clutched the arms of his seat with white-knuckled hands as she shot through the narrow canyons, and Tae muttered strained curses under his breath, but they'd told her they didn't want anyone to see them, hadn't they? So they couldn't very well complain.

She kept them in low behind the cliffs as they approached the prison coordinates. Tae had marked on the holoscreen the landing pad for the supplies ship, and she brought the *Ungovernable* down maybe a fifteen minute walk away. Desert like this, wasn't like someone would be wandering around looking.

Still, touching down in a sandy valley in the shelter of an outcropping of red-grey rock felt far too much like saying goodbye. She lingered in the cockpit for a few moments.

She'd hardly left it since that day in Vitali's compound.

She would have been happy to never leave it again.

She took a deep breath. "I'll miss you, sweetheart," she whispered, kneeling and pulling the lower panel off reverently. She glanced quickly at the wiring underneath. If she tweaked this one right … here … Yes.

There was a slight change in the air pressure as the newly-modded forcefield ramped up.

That should do it.

Slowly, reluctantly, she got to her feet.

Just a few days. A few days, that was all. Then she'd be back.

She swallowed hard at the lump in her throat, running her fingers gently across the controls one last time.

"Hey, Jez. You coming?"

She jerked around to see Tae at the cockpit door. She blinked hard to hide the tears that were welling up in the corners of her eyes. He didn't need to see that.

But he didn't say anything, just gave her a sympathetic look. "Come on. Transport will be here in a few minutes, and we have to be ready."

She nodded, not trusting herself to speak.

He paused. "Listen, Jez. It'll be OK. I'll get us out, I promise."

"I've broken out of prison once before anyways," she said. "Not a big deal."

He nodded, and didn't say anything about the fact that she'd probably told the biggest lie of her entire life, and he probably knew it as well as she did.

She grabbed a handful of loose bolts and wiring and shoved them into the pocket of her prison uniform. Nothing she really needed, honestly, but it was always nice to have something to fiddle with in your cell, and anyways, she'd feel better if she had something to remind her of the *Ungovernable*.

When they got out, the others were already waiting. Jez stepped through the modded force-field, and the ship seemed to shimmer and disappear.

Despite herself, she was impressed. She stepped in and out a couple times, until Lev snapped at her to cut it out. Then she stuck her finger out of the force-field in a universally-recognized communication, and was rewarded with a snort from Ysbel and a sigh from Lev.

Above them, a prick of light glowed like an expanding star.

The supplies ship coming in through the atmosphere.

Time to go.

They walked across the desert without speaking. The pink glow of the far-off sun rising over the stark horizon was surprisingly beautiful, and the air was cool, but with the dusty scent of a hot day ahead. She glanced around the sandy desert floor uneasily as they walked, trying to slow her racing brain. Probably poisonous snakes or something in a place like this.

At least it wasn't carnivorous vines and centipede snake-monsters like last time. That was something, she supposed.

They stuck to the edges of the cliffs, even after the supplies ship had landed. Lev had calculated it would take about half a standard hour to go through the supplies, and another to scan the ship body. Plenty of time for them to do what they needed to do.

When they came around the corner of one of the rock outcroppings, the prison guards were still inspecting the supplies, figures in masks and hazmat suits scanning the ship's cargo hold with long wands.

She took quick inventory. The corner of the outcropping they were concealed behind was only a few steps from the port side of the ship, and most of the activity was happening on the other side, closest to the prison. The ship itself was a short-haul, with a long, wide body and a deep hold. The hold door, from the looks of it, was built more for ease of use than security. Ship like this wouldn't hold much attraction to a pirate—probably had plenty of external locks and defences. No need to have a hatch that was impossible to open too.

"Ysbel," she whispered. "It's your lucky day. Go blow something up."

Ysbel glanced at her, then reached into her shirt and pulled a diminutive smoke bomb from the padded bag she kept round her neck. She gave it a quick twist, then crouched at the edge of the outcropping. She bounced the sphere experimentally in her hand, then gave it a low underhand toss. It hit the bottom of the ship's hull, in the centre towards the front, with a *ting*, and stuck fast. Ysbel turned and gave her a smirk.

"You're up now, pilot-woman."

Jez grinned and turned to the others. "OK, so here's the plan," she whispered. "I'll go in and get the hatch open, and I'll call you on my com when we're ready. Then you get your lazy butts into the ship. Got it?"

"Thank you, Jez, I think we can handle that level of complexity," Lev whispered back.

She shot him a grin and turned back to the ship.

The guards in hazmat suits were packing up their wands and ducking out of the ship's stern hold. As they stepped outside, stretching and talking in low voices, Ysbel tightened her fingers over the tiny controller.

There was a loud pop, and a black gush of smoke poured out of the front of the ship. The guards looked up, startled, and rushed around the side of the ship to see what had happened.

Jez crouched, then sprinted for the ship, bent low to avoid being seen.

She reached the back corner closest to the cliff, then dropped to the ground, cursing.

A lone guard stood at the back, heat gun at the ready, posture bored.

Damn.

She glanced around quickly, then grabbed a pebble and skimmed it across the sand to clatter off a rock to his right.

He glanced over, in a lazy sort of way, and didn't move.

She gritted her teeth and felt around on the ground for something bigger. Her fingers closed around a larger rock. For half a moment she was tempted to fling it into the back of the idiot's head and see if that would get his attention, but, as satisfying as it would be, it would get them all killed. So she skimmed it past his feet again.

This time he didn't even glance up.

She gave a creative commentary on his birth and parentage under her breath as she groped around again. She bit back a yelp and snatched her hand away as something smooth and dry moved sinuously under her fingertips, and glanced down in time to see a reptilian tail disappear into the scrub beside the ship.

"Jez," came Lev's voice in her earpiece. "What are you doing? They're almost finished inspecting the front of the ship. We don't have much time."

She cut her eyes around quickly. Maybe a rock in the back of the head was the best option after all—

Then she smiled slowly.

"There's a guard back here," she whispered into the com, "but I think he's about to leave. Get ready."

She dropped to her stomach, after quickly checking for anything else moving, and wriggled forward under the ship's hull until the bottom half of the guard's legs were in front of her. She reached into her pocket and sorted through the handful of crap she'd grabbed from the *Ungovernable*.

There. A staple. She fished it out, studying her target. He was wearing tough ankle-high boots, but his legs were unprotected, except for thin trousers. She grinned to herself, and with a quick jerk of her hand, jabbed the two sharp ends into the back of his right leg.

He cursed and jerked his leg up, hopping on one foot and twisting backwards to see what had happened. Then he noticed the two thin trickles of blood running down the back of his leg, and his face went bloodless with sudden panic.

"I've been bitten!" he screamed, limping towards the front of the ship. "Quick! A sand-snake got me!"

"Now!" she hissed into the com, then she rolled out from under the ship, jumped into the back, and yanked up on the cargo hold door.

Tae got there first, and she shoved him in. "Get under some of the supplies, but not too far. We'll have to get out quick," she whispered. Ysbel came next, then Masha, then Lev. She was just in time to roll into the cargo hold herself before the heavy tread of boots signified guards returning.

"I know we have some antivenin," a woman said. "Grab me the first-aid kit."

Someone stepped into the hold above them, and there was the sound of someone rummaging through cupboards.

"No, not that one," came the woman's impatient voice. "The antivenin's in the kit in the cargo hold."

Jez froze as the cargo hold door opened slowly. From behind her came the sounds of four people trying very hard not to breathe.

"Where is it?" came a man's voice from above them.

"Just at the front there. You don't have to go down, it's right there."

A man's hand reached in to the darkness, almost brushing the front of Jez's shirt. She cut her eyes carefully to the side and caught Lev's gaze. He jerked his chin upward.

The first aid kit was wedged in between the two of them.

Carefully, he reached out and pulled it free.

"I can't find it," said the man.

"It should be right there."

Slowly, Lev handed the kit to Jez, and just as carefully, she pushed it towards the man's reaching fingers.

"It's not where it's supposed to be," he said in disgust. "I'm going down."

She held her breath and pushed it the last few centimetres. It touched his retreating fingers, and he paused. "Wait." He felt around the edges of the kit. "Never mind. It's right here." He grabbed it, and the hatch slammed shut, dropping them back into darkness.

She let out a breath of relief.

Now it was only a matter of waiting.

It was probably only a few minutes before the ship started to move again, but in the dark, cramped hold, it could have been hours. She jiggled her foot impatiently, until someone gave her a sharp kick. At last the ship jerked, shuddered, and moved slowly forwards.

Crap ship. Or maybe just a crap pilot.

It came to a stuttering halt a few moments later. She rolled over and shoved the hatch open a crack.

The hold was closed. She pushed the hatch all the way open and beckoned the others up. They crawled stiffly out of the cramped cargo hold, and she gestured them in behind a pile of supplies.

"When they open the hatch, get out," she whispered. Tae glared at her.

"That's your plan?"

She shrugged. "You're smart, right? Just don't get caught."

Before he could respond, the ship's hold lifted, sunlight and hot desert air flooding in. She ducked behind the pile of supplies, and Tae did the same.

Two guards ducked inside and grabbed an armload of supply packages, then ducked back out. She counted the seconds until they came back for a second load.

Thirty seconds. Plenty of time.

She tapped Tae as they stepped out a second time, and jerked her head in the direction of the door. He swallowed, nodded, and slipped out from behind the supplies. He disappeared out the door, and she listened closely.

No shouting. Good. He'd made it. She tapped her com.

"Ysbel. You're next."

When the guards left a third time, Ysbel rose from where she'd been hiding and slipped out after Tae.

Masha went next, then Lev.

Finally, it was her turn. The two guards stepped outside again, their arms full of supply packages, and she stood, straightened her prisoners uniform, and sauntered out after them.

She blinked at the bright sunlight as she stepped outside, the brilliance bringing tears to her eyes.

"Prisoner! What are you doing out here? Step away from the supply ship!" came an angry voice from one side. She squinted in its general direction.

"Now, prisoner! I'll shoot."

"On my way," she called, and took a couple steps to one side.

Now that her eyes had had a few moments to adjust, she could finally see her surroundings.

She was in a dry, barren-looking courtyard, and the bleak walls of the prison rose above her and around her, huge wall cannons mounted every few meters into squat towers. Behind a line of guards to one side, a mass of people in outfits identical to her own were gathered into loose groups or wandering around the open space. Ysbel and the others had slipped in among them. The ground under her feet was a solid concrete, and thick, heavy blocks of prefab made up the wall. They'd probably once been a sterile white, but were now stained a dirty reddish-brown with grime and sand. Even the sight of the blue sky overhead was filtered through the thick prison forcefield.

For a moment the walls were closing in on her, the air too thick to breathe, like it had been back on the prison ship in Prasvishoni. She sucked in a long breath.

It would be fine. Just a week, right? It'd be fine.

Her hands were shaking with adrenalin.

"Prisoner!"

She glanced up. A large guard stood directly in front of her, scowl on his face and shock-stick in his hand.

He didn't look even a little bit happy.

7

Lev, Sector 1, Day 1

Lev swore under his breath, his stomach tightening even more than it already had been.

Across the open courtyard, Jez was face-to-face with one of the prison guards, a huge man with the look of someone you didn't want to mess with. He was scowling, and Lev was all too familiar with the expression on Jez's face.

"You will pay attention when I speak, and you'll do as your told, prisoner!" The threat in the guard's voice was audible even from where Lev was standing.

Lev turned away from the other prisoners and tapped his com frantically. "Jez. Leave it," he hissed. She glanced in his direction, a dangerous expression on her face, and raised an eyebrow. Then she turned and said something he couldn't hear to the guard.

The guard raised his shock-stick, and Lev flinched as he brought it down across Jez's ribs. She grunted and stumbled back, and the guard looked down at her, his face set in cruel satisfaction.

Jez caught her balance and grinned up at him. "Well, I assume she must have been blind, because I figure that's the only way—"

Lev turned away so he wouldn't see the inevitable, but he couldn't escape the sickening sound of the shock-stick slamming into the side of Jez's head. He looked up despite himself as she went down.

"Stay down, you idiot," he whispered into the com. But, of course, she was already struggling to her feet.

He swore again. "Masha, I'm going to keep Jez from being killed," he said through his teeth, then tapped his com off and pushed his way through the prisoners toward her.

A small group of prisoners had gathered at the commotion, but they were staying well back. The looks on their faces told him everything he needed to know about the guard.

He shook his head and stepped around them.

They'd think he was a plaguing idiot. And he wasn't certain they'd be wrong.

Jez pushed herself up on her elbows, her grin sharp, a bruise already rising across her temple, and he bit back a surge of cold anger at the guard. "Here's the thing, though, you bastard," she said. "I'm not used to taking orders from brush-pigs, and honestly, from where I sit, it's hard to tell the difference between—"

The guard bent and shoved the shock-stick under her ribs and held it there. Jez's body jolted back, and Lev had the sudden urge to do something that would certainly be suicidal. Jez somehow she still managed to swear loudly and fluently between her teeth until the guard finally removed the stick. She collapsed in a heap, and the guard gave her a speculative look, as if considering his next options.

"Sir?" Lev said quickly, and the guard turned.

"What is it, prisoner?" he growled.

He was a muscular man, with a heavy, brutal face, thick eyebrows, and a nose that appeared to have been broken more than once. He clearly had no aversion to using physical force to punctuate his orders.

"I'm sorry, sir," Lev said, keeping his voice as polite as possible. "I think there may have been a glitch on the schedule. I'm not in this shift."

The eyes of the prisoners around him could have possibly burned holes in his uniform. They were probably wondering if he had a death wish, and in all honestly he was wondering the same thing himself.

The guard swore at him, turning away from Jez with obvious reluctance. "Number?" he grunted.

"7592," Lev replied promptly. The guard tapped something into his com, and frowned. He swore again, and grumbled into the com, "We have a glitch. Five prisoners whose assignments got wiped."

Lev let out a breath of relief. Tae's patch had worked.

A moment later, a businesslike woman in a warden's uniform strode over. The prisoners parted to let her through. More people had gathered, until it felt like half the courtyard was watching, and the other half were straining over the first half's shoulders to see.

The warden stepped through them as if she didn't notice their presence. Her manner was collected, her face a calculating calm. Lev recognized her instantly.

Warden Koshelev.

He'd been shocked when he'd found her name on the database, and seeing her made a slight unease start in his chest.

She'd once been a bureaucrat in Prasvishoni. He knew of her, although he'd never met her in person—she had a reputation of calm ruthlessness and brutal efficiency. She saw the world in terms of favours and paybacks, and she was one to always be on the correct side of that ledger. When he'd started in the government, she was on her way to a high position.

Whatever had happened to consign her to acting as warden in a backwater prison, he was very certain that she would let nothing and no one ruin her chances again.

"Call them," she said brusquely "They'll need to be updated in the count. I wonder why the system didn't catch it this morning."

She gave Lev a sharp glance, and he looked down, keeping his expression neutral as the guard shouted out their prison numbers through the wall coms. The warden narrowed her eyes.

"I don't recognize you."

Lev raised his head. "I'm sorry, ma'am. I was transferred in last week from Svalbor. Transfer ship 549. I understand it was delayed."

"Ah. Yes. I wasn't there when they unloaded."

Masha, Tae, and Ysbel had pushed their way through the crowd at the guard's summons, and Jez rolled stiffly onto her side. She was visibly shaking from the electric shock, but she somehow managed a grin.

"Reporting for duty, cap't," she said, pushing herself gingerly to her feet. She dusted herself off carefully as the warden frowned in her direction.

"What happened here?"

"Prisoner refused to follow orders," the guard said sulkily.

"Prisoners," said the warden in a cool voice. "You're getting reassignments." She paused, measuring them. "You two," she said, pointing at Ysbel and Lev, "will be in cell block 15, cell 27. That's the other shift. I'll have the guards escort you. You two," she pointed at Masha and Tae, "can go into cell block 12, cell 33." She paused, and gave the five of them a cold look. "Now. Listen to me. This is my prison. Every cell assignment comes past my desk. Everything you do, I see. And my prison runs smoothly. You've already caused a disruption. Believe me, you don't want to do it again. You behave, everything goes well. You want trouble, I will make certain you find it. Do I make myself clear?"

"Yes, ma'am," Lev murmured.

"And you—" The warden turned to Jez, who was gingerly feeling the bruise on the side of her face and muttering uncomplimentary things about brush pigs with shock-sticks.

"Looks like there's no one to put me with," said Jez, with a sort of reckless cheerfulness. "Guess you'll have to let me go."

The warden's gaze turned icy.

"I suggest we put her in with prisoner 4579," the guard grunted.

The warden looked at Jez thoughtfully, then at the guard.

"I get along with basically everyone," Jez volunteered. Lev shot her an exasperated glare and she winked at him, then winced and swore loudly.

"Perhaps you're right," said the warden in a cool voice. "Very well, prisoner, we'll see how well you get along with people."

Lev groaned internally. He had the sinking feeling this would not end well, either for Jez or for prisoner 4579.

"That would put you in the other shift," continued the warden. "And you will in the future obey orders from the guards, is that understood?"

"Oh, guard? I thought he was a brush pig, that's where the confusion came—"

The guard made to step forward, but the warden put up a restraining hand. He stopped immediately, and Lev raised an eyebrow.

Apparently, she was just as in control of this prison as she said she was.

The warden stepped up until she was looking Jez straight in the eye.

"You," she said softly, "will learn to obey. You'll learn to respect the guards. And you will learn to not make trouble. You'll learn it the easy way, or you'll learn it the hard way. Do you understand me?"

"People have been trying that since I was born," said Jez. "But hell, you might be the lucky one."

Lev closed his eyes for a moment in a sort of horrified resignation.

The warden gestured, and the guard stepped forward, an ugly expression on his face. Before Jez could move, he'd shoved the shock stick into her stomach. Her body jerked for a few moments, until the warden gestured again. Reluctantly, the guard removed the shock stick, and Jez hunched forward, clutching her stomach, breath apparently knocked out of her.

Lev forced his hands to unclench, biting back the vomit rising in his throat.

"Perhaps I will be," the warden said, her voice cool. "In your cell for the rest of the day, no additional courtyard time. That should give you plenty of time to think about things before you meet your cellmate."

Jez narrowed her eyes, but before she had time to say anything, the woman tapped her com and called briskly, "Ansic, Ivanovic, escort prisoner 8859 to her cell."

A moment later, a guard appeared on either side of Jez.

"Hands," said one of them. There was a slightly frantic look on Jez's face, and for half a moment Lev thought she'd fight, but at last, reluctantly, she held out her arms. Lev's shoulders slumped in relief as the guards clipped the magnetic cuffs around her wrists.

"Good," said the warden. "See? You're learning already."

Jez managed to make a rude gesture with her cuffed hands before the guards led her away.

Lev caught Tae's eyes, and they shared a look of mixed exasperation and worry.

Five minutes in, and Jez was already in trouble with the warden.

This had the potential to go very badly indeed.

The scowling guard shoved Lev and Ysbel back into the body of the courtyard. He didn't seem inclined to beat them, but then again, Lev wasn't inclined to mouth off to him. And no one in their right mind would be inclined to get into a fight with Ysbel.

"Behave yourselves," the guard growled. "Warden doesn't like troublemakers." There was a menacing undertone to his words.

Lev ducked his head in response, and the guard turned away. Still, Lev could feel the man's eyes on his back. He shivered slightly.

Thank goodness Jez had been assigned to the other shift.

He shook his head and glanced around, taking in his surroundings for the first time.

This clearly would not be as simple as he'd hoped.

The courtyard area was crowded with prisoners. If he'd had to guess, he would have said there were a hundred prisoners in the cramped yard, but the grounds seemed to have been split into several courtyards, each backing onto the main compound. The wall guns, massive and old-fashioned, loomed over everything, and there were vis-cams every metre or two along the interior walls. Guards stood at the entrances to the compound, each one heavily armed. Even the concrete courtyard floor was covered with what looked like a non-reactive glaze, scuffed and worn but still very effective.

Now that he wasn't obviously trying to get himself killed, the prisoners had moved away from him, although a few still cast suspicious glances over their shoulders. As they returned to what they'd been doing before Jez decided to provide the entertainment, he leaned back against the wall and looked quickly around.

Ysbel was scanning the crowd for Tanya. She'd recognize her family before he would, so he settled back to watch the prisoners.

They mingled in what appeared to be random patterns. He frowned.

Interesting.

There'd be a hierarchy, of course, but it seemed it wasn't something they were making too obvious. The warden clearly wanted her fingerprints on everything that happened here.

Still, there was a pattern behind the randomness, if you knew how to look. And if you had the prisoner list he'd been studying.

And the thing about hierarchies was, it was easy to exploit them. If you knew how to look.

When three loud whistle blasts sounded, he moved to the back of the line, keeping his eyes down so as not to appear threatening. He noticed, with some amusement, that Ysbel had stepped into the centre of the line. No one said a word, or even shot her a dirty look.

Her method of getting into the prison hierarchy seemed to be rather more direct than his. Still, they couldn't all be highly-intimidating mass murderers.

They shuffled agonizingly slowly past the guards counting them off, and into the harsh, flickering orange light and the grimy white walls of the prison proper.

The prisoners ahead of him seemed to know where they were going, so he followed the woman in front of him down a bare, wide hallway, cells lining either side. They passed through two heavy doors, now propped open, into a large, open room that must be the mess hall. It was packed at one end with long, low tables. On the other, a harried-looking prisoner ladled bluish-grey ration-gruel into tin bowls, and across from him a row of deep, utility-style sinks were set back into the wall. From the looks of it, the dish washers would fill the sinks from the other side to do the washing up. The place was so old it didn't even have a cleanser. Or maybe the warden just bought into the government line that work made productive citizens.

He wrinkled his nose slightly at the smell as the line shuffled towards the serving table. He'd forgotten how bad prison food could be.

He took his portion, then glanced quickly around the hall.

There.

He smiled slightly, and moved towards a muscular woman with tattoos running up her neck and into her hair. He sat at the table across from her, and she glowered at him.

"Watch yourself, boy. This isn't your seat."

He smiled slightly and spread his hands in a non-threatening manner. "I came looking for you," he said in a low voice. "I have information you might find interesting."

She glared at him suspiciously. "Who the hell are you?"

"New here," he said, moving closer. He glanced around the room quickly, and leaned forward.

His hands were sweating slightly.

Five of the prisoners behind him were clearly hers, and they were clearly waiting for a signal.

He really, really hated getting hit.

"What is it?" she asked at last.

He cut his eyes around again, and she made an impatient gesture. "Spit it out, or I'll beat it out of you."

"Are you Milojevic?"

She glared at him, and he swallowed. If he'd miscalculated …

"Yes," she grunted at last.

He leaned forward. "Ushakov," he whispered. He hoped desperately that was the right name. "I have information on him."

She frowned. "What?"

"Back at Svalbor. Where I was transferred from. There was a

Blood Riot cell, and one of the members mentioned you. Told me to pass something along." He tried not to let his apprehension show on his face.

If he was wrong, in about thirty seconds he'd be more beat up than Jez.

"And?" she said impatiently. He let out his breath.

"He said he'd heard Ushakov ran this sector, and he said there were rumours that Ushakov's friends on the outside were getting tired of him. Said he's getting shut out, won't be able to run the place much longer. Said it's a good time for a change in the power structure."

"You sure? His friends on the outside are backing down?"

Lev shrugged. "It's what I heard. The Rims are breaking up, new boss rising to the top. Ushakov is old guard."

It was true, to an extent, although he'd added some embellishments. He hadn't found much on the prison set-up itself, but it was surprising how much you could find about prisoners, and their connection to organized crime, if you knew where to look and had access to the information Lev did. And if you could make an educated guess as to who was who.

Milojevic narrowed her eyes at him, but he could see the calculation in them now.

"You better not be lying to me," she said at last. Lev glanced around again, then tapped his fist in the centre of his chest and dropped his hand, index finger pointing outward. He felt slightly ridiculous, but the sign seemed to reassure the woman. She returned it, and he ducked his head, finished his meal quickly, and moved into the line for work detail.

He took a deep breath.

Part one down. Of course, part two was even more likely to get him beat up. But then, he'd just flashed a Blood Riot gang sign in a crowded prison, so there was only so much higher his level of stupid could go.

The guard counted them, cursed at Lev when he seemed unsure of where to go, and shoved him forward. In only a few moments, he was in gloves up to his shoulders, and elbow-deep in greasy water beside a short man with rock-hard muscles and a face that looked carved from stone.

The man glared at him. From his expression, he was contemplating all the different ways Lev could die.

"You looking for a beating?" the man asked softly, once the guards were out of range. "Or maybe you're just stupid. You want to get in with Milojevic, maybe you should pick a work detail where she can protect you."

Lev tried to look nervous.

In all honesty, it wasn't difficult.

"I'm not getting in with anyone," he whispered back. "She recognized me from Svalbor. I transferred in from there."

The man's brows lowered further, and Lev gritted his teeth. He wasn't certain how long his luck would hold, but it may have just run dry.

"What did she want?" he growled at last.

"I don't know if I—"

The man turned to him, and his expression was almost as intimidating as Ysbel's when she was angry.

"She's going to make a play," Lev said quickly. "That's what I gather. They know about what's happening outside."

The man's brow furrowed. "And how do you know what's happening outside?"

"I don't," Lev whispered. "Only what she said." His throat was somehow dry.

The man gave him a hard stare. "And where's she going to make her play?"

"I don't know." He paused a moment, then said even more quietly, "I have a new cell mate. She transferred in with me. I don't know who she's with, but she has pull."

"And?"

"And she told me she's looking for a woman named Tanya. I don't know why. But if someone came to her with the info, I suspect she'd be grateful."

For the first time, the man looked uneasy. "Tanya Fedrova?"

"That's the one. You know her?"

"No. But you hear things. She's the one married to that mass murderer out of Prasvishoni, isn't she?"

Lev shrugged. "I don't know. Me? I'd rather be on the bad side of a mass murderer who isn't here, and in with my cell mate, who is here. If you take my meaning." He cast a meaningful glance in Ysbel's direction. "Anyways, that's what Milojevic seemed to think. My cellmate's been spreading her ask around. I'm guessing she'll be grateful to whoever gets her the information first."

The man glared at him uncertainly. Finally he growled, "I don't know what your game is, boy. But we don't like spies and tell-tales around here. If I find out you're going behind my back, you're a dead man. You'd best watch yourself."

Lev let out a long breath. "I'd gathered that," he murmured wryly.

"What?" the man snapped.

"I said, thank you. I will."

He glared at Lev suspiciously for a moment, then turned back to his own work. But as the work shift ended, Lev hung back a moment. The man, Ushakov, was watching as the other work shift filed past. His eyes followed Milojevic, and his gaze was thoughtful. She didn't look at him, but there was an expression of slight triumph on her face.

Lev allowed himself a slight smile.

Give it a few days, and the guards might be very busy indeed.

That was the thing about hierarchies. They could be exploited. If you knew how to look.

8

Tae, Sector 2, Day 2

The shrill whistle jerked Tae out of his sleep in a panic. He jolted upright on his rough cot, staring wildly around the dim narrow cell, and it took him far longer than it should have to remember where he was, and why. He sighed and rubbed the sleep from his eyes, a dull headache starting in the back of his skull as the orangey artificial lights flickered on down the bare corridor between the cells.

He'd been up most of the night before, trying to hack through the system. He'd had no better luck than he'd had back on the *Ungovernable*.

Hadn't gotten any more sleep than he had back then, either.

This was going to be a long day.

There was no help for it. Before he could make a game plan, he'd need to get a scan of the wiring, and the one thing he'd learned yesterday, other than a reminder of the fact that he really hated prison, was that the non-reactive fill in the bricks completely blocked out his scans.

And the fact that the vis-cams in the cells were so ancient they were mostly non-functional.

He'd passed that on to the others. One thing on their side, at any rate.

When he stepped out of the dim, grungy hallway and into the courtyard, the dry, already-hot morning air hit him like a slap in the face. No wonder they didn't let the prisoners out in the afternoon.

Ahead of him he saw Jez's familiar slouch, and breathed a sigh of relief.

At least she hadn't been killed yet.

She was staring up at the sky, and he could guess at the expression on her face.

"Jez!" he hissed. She turned quickly at his voice, and he bit back a groan. She was sporting a black eye.

"What happened?" he whispered. She grinned, but there was a recklessness behind her expression that frightened him.

"My cell-mate had a little accident last night. Slipped on the floor and knocked herself out. Guards came in, but it was just an accident, so—" she shrugged. "Took her to the medics for observation."

"That?" Tae gestured at Jez's face. Jez shrugged again.

"Hit me in the face on her way down, by accident. It's all fine." She turned and glanced over her shoulder, to where a tall, muscular woman stood at the edge of the courtyard, watching through narrowed eyes. "Well, better run," she said with a wink. "No point in being late for breakfast." She shot the woman a snarky grin and ambled off. He watched her go, worry tightening itself around his chest.

They'd been here exactly one day, and Jez was already spiralling.

He'd told he'd get her out. He'd promised.

And he still didn't have a damn lead into the system.

The woman—Jez's cellmate—glared at him, as if memorizing his face. He ducked his head and tried to blend into the crowd of prisoners. He didn't have time for fights right now. And the woman across the courtyard looked like she wanted one.

To be honest, after spending a night locked in a cell with a pent-up Jez, he wasn't sure he blamed her.

Once he was certain he was out of her sight, he moved over to where he could hang back by the wall. Years of living on the streets had taught him the value of keeping a low profile.

Well, as low a profile as he could, with someone like Jez as a friend.

Still, he'd managed to avoid any real trouble by the time the prisoners started moving towards the long line back into the building. The air had heated noticeably since he'd come out, and sweat was already soaking unpleasantly through his hair. After a lifetime in Prasvishoni, where he'd never once felt completely warm, it was amazing how quickly being too hot became uncomfortable.

Someone bumped into him from behind as he walked, and he stumbled forward, knocking into the prisoner in front of him.

"Hey—" the man began.

"I'm sorry," Tae muttered, brushing himself off. "I'm really sorry. I tripped." He turned to see who had bumped him, and groaned.

The muscular woman stood there, with an unpleasant smile on her face.

"Found you," she said, her voice soft with menace. "Saw you talking to number 8859 this morning. Friend of yours, is she?"

Tae's stomach tightened.

Damn Jez.

The woman grabbed him by the front of the shirt and hauled him close. "I asked you a question, boy."

The rest of the prisoners had moved away, clearing a space around them, and no one seemed to want to meet his eye.

"I—" His heart was pounding in his throat.

The shrill blast of a whistle sounded across the courtyard, and the exodus for the meal line became general.

For a moment, she looked like she was thinking of hitting him anyways. Finally, though, she let go of his shirt disdainfully, shoving him backwards. He stumbled, trying to catch his balance, and she gave him a cold smile.

"We're not done, boy. I'll come find you," she whispered. Then she moved into the line.

He bit back the fear climbing his throat and lowered his head again. Maybe he could slip away.

He didn't plaguing well have time for this.

They filed through the long corridor and into the mess-hall for breakfast, and he kept his head down. Like he always bloody did.

Figure out this system. Get a scan. That was all he needed to worry about. And if he could avoid getting beat up at the same time, well, that was a bonus.

When he glanced up, though, as he ate, he noticed Jez's cellmate watching him. When she caught his eye, she smiled grimly.

Damn.

He swallowed down the remainder of his breakfast and stood quickly, grabbing his bowl, and ducked into a cluster of prisoners.

When he was far enough away that she probably wouldn't find him, he let out a breath and glanced around him at the mess hall.

Nothing here. Even the floor and ceiling were non-reactive, if his com scan was correct. The cooling vents were tiny, hardly big enough to fit his closed fist, and were covered by vent-covers with hair-thin slits. Not ideal for cooling, but certainly good for keeping prisoners from escaping.

Venting system was out then, and maintenance too, from the looks of it.

The whistle blew, signalling the end of meal time, and he glanced around quickly for Jez's cellmate.

She hadn't seen him yet, but she was clearly looking.

Out of the corner of his eye, he saw the man who he'd bumped into earlier. He seemed to be watching Tae as well. Tae almost groaned out loud.

So much for keeping a low profile.

Work detail was the same as the day before—after an eternity of standing in line to be counted, he was prodded through into a wide, low building that looked something like a hangar-bay, but filled with work stations, and much, much too hot.

Their job, he'd learned yesterday, was grinding the edges of manufactured ships parts and packing them away.

He picked a station as far out of the way as possible, and sat down, turning on his grinder and pulling the goggles over his eyes.

Over the noise, he glanced around surreptitiously.

This place wasn't the main compound, but it had to be wired in, to power the grinders. Maybe here there would be a way in.

Someone slammed their hands down on the table, causing the parts in front of him to jump. Tae jumped too, but he knew, before he even looked up, who it was.

His heart was beating far too quickly, and there was a knot in his throat.

The woman gave him a menacing look, and he swallowed hard.

"Listen," he said sullenly, "we were on the same transport in here. That's all I know about her."

"You're lying," she growled. "You'll tell me where she went and where she's hiding from me. And if you don't know, you'll damn well find out." Up close, he could see the edges of the bandage patch on the back of her head, and the grim hatred in her eyes.

His muscles were tight, and he felt slightly sick at the thought of what was about to happen. But he couldn't very well sacrifice Jez. Even if she deserved it.

"I told you. I don't know her," he muttered.

She grabbed his shoulder and jerked him out of his chair, and too late he noticed the two prisoners standing to either side of him. They grabbed him from behind, twisting his arms back painfully. He struggled, but it was no use.

Four other prisoners surrounded them, cutting off the view of the guards.

"You'll tell me, boy, or you'll wish you had," the woman murmured. She drew back her fist, and he turned his head away, closing his eyes.

But the blow didn't fall. He glanced up quickly, throat tight with a mix of panic and relief.

Someone had grabbed the woman by the arm.

"Vlatka. Leave the kid alone."

The woman—Vlatka—narrowed her eyes and jerked her head, and the men holding Tae shoved him forward. He stumbled into a bench, knocking it over, and fell heavily to his hands and knees. He scrambled to his feet and glanced behind him. The two prisoners had grabbed the newcomer—the man he'd bumped into earlier—by the arms. The man swung his body, trying to pull free, and the three of them crashed into the table, jarring it loose. One of the grinders toppled over, falling to the ground with a crunch, and the table fell with it, scattering bolts and shavings across the floor.

And there, under one of the legs where it had fallen—a hole in the floor where the grinder's wiring came through.

No one was watching. The guards were on their way over, but he had time. He could grab a quick scan—

The other prisoners had subdued his rescuer, and Vlatka swung, catching the man in the face. The man's head jerked back, and Tae cursed under his breath.

He needed this scan. He didn't have time for this.

But the man hadn't had to save him …

Shaking his head in exasperation at his own stupidity, he turned and sprinted the few steps back to the fight. He caught one of the men in the ribs with his shoulder, and as the man stumbled backwards Tae grabbed his rescuer by the front of the shirt and hauled him to one side, out of the grip of the other prisoner.

"What—" the man began. "What are you—"

"I'm not going to let you take my damn beating," Tae said through his teeth.

Vlatka lunged for them, and he shoved the man under the fallen bench and rolled under after him. Vlatka dropped to the ground to follow, and he squirmed through the narrow space. On the other side, Vlatka's friends had come around to cut off their escape. But beside them, the grinder was still spinning ineffectually, on its side on the floor. He scrabbled on the floor for something—anything—and someone thrust a bundle of bolts into his hand. Desperately, he jammed the whole bundle into the grinder. It squealed in protest, smoke rising from it as the machinery strained against the sudden load, and he heard guards' footsteps running towards them.

"This way," the man hissed, and pulled Tae behind the table and out beside an empty station. "Sit," he commanded, and Tae did. The man flipped the grinder in front of them on, shoved a bolt into Tae's hand, and dropped into the station next to him, glaring studiously at his work. From behind them, the guards shouted and swore, and Vlatka growled some explanation.

"Don't look up," the man whispered, and Tae didn't have to be told twice.

Someone righted the table, and he bit back a curse. So much for his scan.

At last the guards left, Vlatka and her friends with them, and Tae let out a shaky breath of relief. The man beside him smiled and raised his goggles, and Tae got a good look at him for the first time.

He was tall and slender, probably in his early thirties, with a cultured look about him, despite the rising bruise on his cheek. His expression was pleasant, with lines on his face of someone who smiled more often than not. "Well," he said. "I suppose I should introduce myself. I'm Ivan."

"Tae."

The man gave him a curious look. "You didn't have to come back for me, you know."

"You didn't have to step in."

The man shrugged. "I overheard what she was saying. I don't meet many people who'd risk a beating to protect a friend." He paused. "I have some friends, too. I'll do my best for you, but better watch your back. The guards won't step in until you're hurt bad. And depending on the guard, they might be the ones doing the beating."

Tae nodded, staring at the grinder as it shaved the rough edges off the railing bolt in his hand.

He hated the relief he felt, the guilty thought that maybe there'd be someone on his side for once.

He should feel sick about this. He'd had a chance. Probably the best chance he was going to get, and he'd lost it. He owed his friends, not this stranger.

Still ... he glanced up and shook his head.

He couldn't bring himself to regret going back for him.
Which was probably the whole problem.

9

Ysbel, Sector 1, Day 2

Ysbel downed her breakfast quickly, her eyes roving over the prisoners. It was the beginning of her second day here. She'd known it wouldn't be a matter of stepping into the prison and seeing her long-lost wife, but somehow she'd still hoped—

Every time she caught a glimpse of brown hair, or a slender figure, her heart stuttered. But each time, when the figure turned, or moved, she realized she'd been mistaken.

By the time the meal was over, she felt like she'd aged ten years. Knowing Tanya was here, somewhere, and not being able to see her —it was agony.

Tanya. Olya. Misko. Their names pounded in her brain like a heartbeat.

She'd find them, one way or another. She'd find them and free them if it killed her.

The meal this morning was strained. Groups of prisoners gathered, muttering and casting dark looks at each other, and the line-up for their courtyard time almost turned into a brawl. Their time in the stifling hot morning air of the courtyard felt like the calm before a storm.

Lev had mentioned something yesterday about stirring things up. What had the ridiculous boy done?

The queues for the work lines were just as tense as the ones into the courtyard. The morning heat had done nothing to calm the prisoners' fraying tempers. Ahead of her, two prisoners got into a shoving match, and one of them bumped into her. She turned her flattest glare on the woman, and she stepped back quickly, apologizing. Ysbel gave her a cold smile.

Just as well. She didn't need another murder on her hands at the moment.

She was on cleaning crew today, and Lev was on dish duty again. Judging from his resigned expression, he was not thrilled.

She had to bite back a quiet grin.

It wasn't really funny, when you thought about it. He didn't have to be here, and he was only here because of her, and she still didn't completely understand why.

But at the same time, it was a bit funny.

The guards handed out the rags and buckets, and herded them through to the mess hall. No mops with handles. Probably because they could be used as weapons.

That was too bad. But, of course, almost anything could be used as a weapon if you thought about it hard enough. She should know.

She plunged her rag into the soapy water and pulled it out, dripping.

"Watch what you're doing with that," someone snapped from beside her.

She took a deep breath and turned slowly, and came face to face with a large man with the angry, arrogant expression of someone who was accustomed to being obeyed.

"What did you say?" she asked, without raising her voice or

changing her expression.

"I—" he paused, the look on his face turning to one of slight uncertainty. She felt a grim satisfaction.

"I said, be careful with that. You got me wet." He sounded more sullen than threatening now.

Good. Lev had mentioned the other prisoners seemed intimidated by her. As they probably should be.

She gave a slight sigh.

He'd suggested she perhaps act a little more soft. Easier to get information that way, he'd said. And, if they were going to get Tanya back, Lev said he needed everything they had on how the prison worked.

"Believe me, I don't want to hurt you," she said.

"I … hurt me? Do you know who I am? You couldn't hurt me." His voice grew more strident, and he looked even more uneasy.

"Perhaps you are right," she said, trying to keep her patience. "Of course." Apparently, she didn't have much practice with non-threatening. To be fair, none of the *Ungovernable* crew seemed to fit that description once you got to know them. Still—

"Well then. Stay out of my way." The man's words were probably supposed to be a threat, but they came out as more of a plea.

She bit back an irritated sigh. "I have no intention of getting in your way, you idiot."

He didn't look convinced.

She shoved the wet rag forward on the rough pre-fab tiles. Well. She had questions, and he'd answer them one way or another.

The man had begun mopping as well, and seemed to be trying to move surreptitiously away from her. She caught him with her glare, and he stopped, swallowing hard.

"I have some questions," she said in a reasonable tone. "I was hoping you would help me."

"Questions? I'm not answering your questions." His voice was harsh, but he blinked rapidly and wouldn't meet her eyes.

"I'm looking for a woman. Her name is Tanya. She's about this tall, brown hair, accent like mine. She would be with two children, an eight-year-old and a six-year-old. Do you know these people?"

The man swallowed, hard.

"Do you know these people?" Ysbel asked again, letting her voice go completely flat.

The man winced, then visibly braced himself. "I—"

She stopped mopping and turned to face him.

"I—" his voice choked a little. "I'm sorry. I don't."

He was shrinking into his uniform, as if the drab beige fabric would protect him from her question.

Lev's suggestion was probably a good one, under certain circumstances. But right now, she needed this answer, and Lev's suggestion could go hang.

She let all the expression drop from her face. The man in front of her visibly paled.

"If you are lying to me," she said, slowly and deliberately, "I must tell you. I will find you, and I will take the head from off your body with my bare hands. Do you understand me?"

The man nodded frantically.

"Do you know what I'm in here for?"

The man shook his head.

"Maybe it's time you think about it," she said. "Now. I will ask you one more time. Do you know these people? And remember what I said. And I am not a woman who breaks her word."

"I—I don't know them. I swear it," the man said, sweat beading on his forehead. "I was only transferred in here about six standard months ago, and there are almost two thousand of us here. I know the people in my cell block, because I go to work detail with them and we get counted together. But other than them, I don't know. There are thousands of prisoners. But I'll look for them, if you want. I'll keep my eyes open. I—"

She studied him as he stammered and spluttered, and finally she held up a hand.

"No. I believe you."

He let out a long sigh of relief, his body sagging visibly.

"But," she continued, "I have more questions. I need to know everything you know about this prison system."

He stared at her. "What?"

"Tell me everything you know."

"I—"

"Think hard."

He swallowed. "I don't know much, but I'll tell you what I know. The warden runs a tight ship. Prisoners can't bribe her, but that doesn't mean she's not crooked. This place is a cesspool. There's a payback system, but it all goes back through Prasvishoni. Warden jumps whenever someone back in Prasvishoni says jump. The guards though, some of them you can bribe, if you have something they like."

"That is good to know," she said. "What about inside the prison?"

He glanced around rapidly. "The main gangs here are the Blood Riots and Rims. I'm in the Rims. There's a pecking order, but yesterday something happened. I don't know what. But you best keep your head down. Something's coming down."

She kept looking at him. He squirmed slightly.

"No escape from this place, if that's what you're thinking. Guards all have weapons, but they're keyed in to their personal biometrics.

So even if you grabbed them, you couldn't use them. The wall cannons are the other big weapons, but I've never seen them used. I know they're old. They were supposedly brought in when this prison was built fifty years ago from another prison that had been torn down. I guess there's something funny about their wiring. I don't know what."

She considered him for a moment.

"Alright. Thank you." She paused. "If you find Tanya, please tell me. But please be careful. She has children, and I don't want to frighten them."

He stared at her, seemingly uncertain whether or not to laugh.

"So, what you will do is this—if you see them, or hear about them, you will come and find me at once. But if you do happen to bump into them, you will leave them alone. And the reason you will do that is that me ripping off your head with my bare hands is the kindest thing that I would consider doing to you. What I would do to you if you bothered Tanya or the children would not be a kind thing. Not at all. Am I making myself clear?"

The man nodded again, his face fixed in a rictus grin. She fixed him with her stare for a long moment.

"Thank you," she said at last. "That's all I needed. And I don't think I need to mention that if you speak with anyone about our conversation—"

He shook his head frantically, then grabbed up his rag, scrubbing vigorously at the tiles and leaving a long slug-trail of moisture in the quickest possible line from her to as far away from her as possible.

She watched him go, a frown on her face. She'd known from the beginning she couldn't expect a miracle. It would take time.

But she wanted a miracle. She wanted it so badly it hurt.

That night, when the cell door clicked shut behind her, she

dropped onto her cot and put her face in her hands.

It hurt, missing them, like something vital inside of her had been torn away and she was slowly bleeding out. When she'd thought they were dead, she'd become numb to the pain, because what was pain when you were hardly alive? But now, along with the hope, the pain was back, so fierce and intense it almost brought tears to her eyes.

She wasn't sure how much longer she could stand it.

"Ysbel," said Lev after a moment. "I thought we'd agreed that you were going to try to be non-threatening."

She blinked hard, and looked up. "I did."

He leaned over the bed, raising an eyebrow at her. "Did you? Because what I heard from the other prisoners is that unless someone was actively trying to kill themselves, they should stay as far away from you as possible, because apparently you're a gang boss who's in here for wiping out the entire opposing gang with an ion gun, and half a police force as well. On the bright side, there were a number of prisoners who heard that I was your cellmate and felt so bad that they spent most of the day trying to conceal me from you so that, presumably, I'd live to at least get my fresh air this evening. I think they despaired of my chances of making to tomorrow."

Ysbel gave a one-shouldered shrug. "Well, I did what you suggested. I was very, very unthreatening. I just asked some questions."

There was a long pause. Lev shook his head.

"I—see. And that's all you did?"

"Then I threatened to tear his head off his body with my bare hands."

Another long pause.

"And did that work?" Lev's voice held a grudging amusement.

"Yes." She paused. "It also made me feel better."

Lev leaned back on the bed, and she found she was smiling to herself.

He was an idiot, that boy. A genius, and also an idiot. But … she glanced up at his long legs dangling over the edge of the bed.

He'd seen her drop her head in her hands. She was suddenly certain of it. And she was also suddenly certain that he'd made her smile on purpose.

"Ysbel," said Lev at last. He was laying on his cot, she could tell by the location of his voice.

"What?"

"I'm going to ask you to tell me everything you learned in just a minute, as I assume it was probably fairly thorough, and then we'll call Tae and Masha and see what they have. Masha's apparently been able to get in with a couple of the guards, which should be helpful. We can't talk to Jez, because she has a roommate, but maybe she contacted one of the others."

There was a concern in his tone when he mentioned Jez, which, although likely justified, was a little more than she'd expect between friends.

She smiled slightly and shook her head.

"I'm sure she's fine," she said. "Jez is very smart." She paused. "Well, maybe smart isn't the right word. But she's very good at getting out of trouble." She paused again. "Alright, maybe not as good at getting out of it as getting into it. But—"

Lev's voice was muffled. "Ysbel. I know you're trying to help. But this really isn't helping."

They were silent for a moment. At last he said, "Ysbel? Tell me about Tanya."

There was something in his voice, something she couldn't quite place. Kindness? Guilt?

It didn't matter.

She needed to talk about Tanya. She needed to say her name, needed someone to know her, even just a little.

"I grew up next door to her," she said at last. "We played in the back fields together all the time. My father was a weapons designer, I know you know that, and my mother worked with explosives. But her family were only farmers, and because Tanya's family were farmers, I wanted to be a farmer. I think I was in love with her before I even knew what being in love meant.

We got older, and we had our schooling and our work, and I worked with my father in his shop, and my mother in her lab. And she was working in the fields, because there were six children in her family but still not enough to keep the crops growing. But we saw each other whenever we could. Even after my father died, we still managed to sneak off sometimes. And then, you know, she got accepted to a school in Prasvishoni. And she cried and cried, but I told her she had to go, this was a good opportunity. And finally she left, and I thought maybe my heart had been broken."

She was silent for a moment, lost in the memories. She could still feel the cool of the moonlight on her skin, the breeze blowing through her hair, the tears glowing in Tanya's eyes like jewels.

The feeling that someone had broken a hole in her chest and taken out her heart and torn it in two.

"I worked in the shop with my mother. She was sick, of course. She'd worked with the explosive components all her life, and when she was young she'd never been taught to be careful. She knew it was going to kill her one day, but after my father died, I don't think she cared all that much. But I couldn't leave her, so I stayed. And then she died, and I buried her. But I didn't go to Prasvishoni. Because Tanya was at university, and she was doing great things, I was sure of it, and I didn't want to stand in her way. And then, one day, she knocked at my door. She'd decided she didn't want what the university offered her anymore. She told me she loved me. And that was all she wanted."

She hadn't spoken so many words in years. It felt strange, like something inside of her had broken and the words had pushed themselves out of their own accord. She swallowed, her throat suddenly tight, something burning behind her eyes.

It had been too much. She shouldn't have. She'd trained herself over the past five years not to think, not to hope, not to want. But this—somehow the words had cut her open on their way out.

She wiped at her eyes with the back of her hand.

"Thank you," said Lev quietly, from the bunk above her. And he didn't say anything when she dropped her head into her hands and cried silently, her whole body shaking with it, eyes burning and chest aching.

And maybe, after everything, that was the thing she was most grateful for.

10

Jez, Sector 2, Day 2

Jez surveyed the piles and piles of laundry surrounding them in the claustrophobic, windowless, much too hot room. This was probably the only place in this damn prison that was damp, so of course there was mold creeping up the walls and along the edges of the large metal tubs. Her breath was coming a little too quickly.

She'd seen Tae in the courtyard that morning, which meant the others were still here, which meant they were still going to get out.

Screw this laundry crap. She had to find Tanya.

It was fine, though. She'd be fine. She took a deep breath. "Well, so what do we do?"

The woman standing next to her gave her a strange look, and Jez shrugged. "My bracelet glitched out yesterday. New shift."

The woman looked suddenly wary. "You're that lunatic that got on the bad side of Vlatka, and mouthed off to Zhurov yesterday morning."

"Zhurov?" Jez asked. She remembered mouthing off to quite a few people yesterday morning.

"The guard," said the woman, lowering her voice. "You're either new or crazy. He killed a prisoner last cycle, beat him to death, for calling him weak."

Jez raised her eyebrows, forcing herself to grin. "Must not have had much imagination. I called him a brush pig in a uniform, and said his mom must have been blind because that's the only way she'd have slept with someone as ugly as his dad."

The woman's eyes went wide, and she took a step backwards. "You said that to him? He's going to kill you. Believe me. He'll hunt you down. You'd best learn how things are done here. Zhurov's connected back in Prasvishoni. You got pull there, like Vlatka, like Zhurov, you can get away with anything. And if you don't—" she drew a quick finger across her throat.

Jez tried to ignore the unease coiling in her chest.

He might actually kill her. That was the thing, she'd seen his face. He might have killed her right there in the courtyard, if Lev hadn't stepped in.

She remembered the sick look on his face when the guard had hit her, and for a moment, there was a tightness in her throat.

Damn soft-boy. She could take care of herself, and besides, the very last thing in the entire system she needed right now was to start going soft herself. Especially over a damn scholar.

Anyways, the guard wouldn't need to kill her. She'd either get out, or she'd die from being locked up.

Or, she'd die from her cellmate. That option was looking increasingly likely as well.

By the time they let her out for her evening half-hour in the courtyard, her shoulders ached from shoving the paddle-stick into the bins, and her hands were raw with blisters.

She'd done plenty of hard work before this. But something about how the scalding water slipped into the gloves and made her grip slide on the handle of the paddles seemed designed to tear skin off her palms.

The sky was painted a brilliant orange by the setting sun, and even with the image distorted by the force-field, the sight pulled at her with a longing that was almost pain. She had to swallow hard against it.

Find Tanya. They'd find Tanya and get out. Maybe tomorrow. Maybe today.

Soon.

And then her eyes caught on someone, on the far edge of the courtyard, through a link fence.

A woman. A slender woman, with pale skin and brown hair.

For a moment, Jez couldn't breathe.

It couldn't be.

It had to be.

She looked closer.

Beside the women—yes! Two children, their heads barely visible in the press.

She felt suddenly lightheaded.

They'd won. They could leave. She could get back in the sky and clean the sour flavour of this planet out of her mouth forever.

She took a deep breath. Her hands were shaking, and she felt cold, despite the residual heat of the desert afternoon.

She wandered over casually.

The woman and the children were alone in a small, fenced-off courtyard adjacent to the main yard. The children were racing each other around the small space, and the woman stood watching them.

"Hey there," Jez said in a low voice when she was close enough. "Tanya."

The woman glanced over at her through the fence, frowning. "Who are you?" she whispered, her accent the same heavy outer-rim burr of Ysbel's. "And how do you know my name?"

Jez gave a tight grin, her heart pounding. She'd been right.

"Well," she drawled, "I know your wife."

Tanya's face went suddenly pale. "Ysbel?" She whispered after a moment.

Jez shrugged. "Do you have any other wives?"

The woman looked as if Jez had hit her, her face a sickly white. "My wife is dead."

"Pretty sure she isn't. I mean, unless it's her ghost that keeps threatening to blow me up if I don't stop talking. Look, she wants—"

"I don't know who you are, or why you are lying to me," Tanya said in a low voice. "But believe me, I will find out." She turned, and looked directly into Jez's eyes. "And if I find that you are here to hurt me, or to hurt my children, I will kill you. I promise you that."

Despite everything, Jez was mildly impressed. No wonder Ysbel had married this woman.

The whistle blew, and Jez jumped.

When she turned back around, Taya and the children were gone.

She stood in line to be counted, still stunned.

She'd found Tanya.

Who had threatened to kill her, of course, but still—

She managed to tap her wrist with its hidden com against her thigh. Pilot's code. Ysbel should understand. If she didn't, wasn't much Jez could do. Not like she could call them at night in her cell.

Hey Ysbel, she tapped. *Your wife is hot.*

For a few moments, there was nothing. Then a voice hissed in her earpiece, so loud she almost winced.

"You found my wife, you stupid idiot? Where is she? Why didn't you call me before? Is she alright? Are my babies with her?"

She thinks you're dead. She wouldn't listen.

"Wrist!" the guard snapped, and Jez managed to bump the com to off as she lifted her wrist to get scanned.

She glanced over at the line next to her, and groaned inwardly.

She'd almost forgotten Vlatka. The woman was watching her with a calculating expression on her face and loathing in her eyes.

Tonight wasn't going to be a good night.

Jez was tingling with adrenalin as she waited in line, jiggling her foot against the ground. Once through the prisoner count, Vlatka stepped into the cell before Jez, and for half a second Jez contemplated making a break for it. But the guards were watching her, and something in their cold gaze told her that, although they had no intention of letting her run, they also had no intention of interfering in what was going to come next.

She took a deep breath and followed the woman into the cell. Vlatka turned to her with an unpleasant smile.

The door closed, the lock clicking into place.

If you were going to go down, may as well go down in style. Hardly mattered anymore, did it?

"How's your head?" asked Jez, heart pounding in her ears, stupid grin on her face.

Vlatka grabbed her by the front of the shirt and hauled her forward, an expression of mingled fury and triumph on her face as she drew back her fist.

It wasn't nearly as bad as it could have been. She had to admit it. She'd howled and whimpered quite pitifully, and her cell-mate had seemed entirely convinced that when Jez went down and stayed down, it was because she couldn't take anymore.

Amateur.

Still … she shifted experimentally from where she lay slumped in the corner, and bit back a genuine whimper.

Still, it could have been a hell of a lot better.

She cursed under her breath for a few minutes to relieve her feelings, and glared at the woman lying on the bottom cot.

After the beating, her cellmate had taken a ridiculously long time getting ready for bed. Probably still wasn't asleep.

Jez swore again softly and settled herself gingerly back against the wall, trying to protect the worst of her bruises.

She'd been beat up a lot. She was *good* at being beat up. Because that was the thing—she couldn't seem to keep her mouth shut. When she was a scared 11-year-old, vibrating from adrenalin and the need to move, standing in front of her father, when she was a skinny 14-year-old in Lena's office, her foot tapping nervously, fingers drumming, brain high on anger or nerves or whatever it was, when she faced down Antoni for the first time, and the second time, and the third time, and the fourth time—she couldn't help it. There seemed to be something inside her that wouldn't let her stop, even when she could see the edge, even when she knew that one more word would take her over it. She just kept on.

She glanced around her at the narrow cell walls, that seemed to have crept just a little closer to her every time she looked at therm.

Anyways, being beat up couldn't be worse than this. Nothing could be worse than being locked up. She shivered, winced, swore softly, and dropped her head back against the wall, closing her eyes.

Give it another minute, and she was pretty sure the woman in the bottom cot would be asleep.

She took a deep breath, and then another, and then another.

It would be fine. She'd be fine. This would all be fine.

For a moment she remembered the haunted look in Tanya's eyes when she'd mentioned Ysbel's name, the desperation in Ysbel's crackly voice over the com.

She swallowed hard.

She wondered, for a moment, how it would feel to be loved that much. To love someone that much. To be willing to walk back into prison for them. To never stop loving them, after five years or a lifetime.

Boring, probably. Honestly.

Still, there was something like a lump in her throat.

Finally, when the breathing from the bottom cot was slow and even, Jez pushed herself painfully to her feet.

Her idiot cellmate would be surprised when she saw Jez asleep in the top bunk, rather than semiconscious in the corner.

Jez grinned to herself and touched the scrap of cloth she'd folded into a bag in the laundry.

But not nearly as surprised as she'd be when she put her clean prison uniform on tomorrow and realized what Jez had smeared all over the inside of it.

11

Lev, Sector 1, Day 3

Lev glanced up from his admittedly uninspiring breakfast, and started in surprise.

He recognized, all too well, the swaggering gait and lanky form of the prisoner who was currently being shoved through the mess hall, escorted by three guards.

He swore softly to himself, a knot of worry rising in his throat, and jumped up, grabbing his bowl. He walked quickly in the direction of the sinks, at an angle that would intercept the small procession, while avoiding the small knots of prisoners who were glowering at each other from across the room.

A tense line of prisoners waiting to drop off their dishes before the whistle blew clogged the guards' forward progress, and as one of them went forward to clear the way with her shock-stick, Lev stepped quickly up beside Jez. He looked her up and down quickly, and winced. The bruise the guard had given her was now a sort of dirty purple-green, one eye was swollen almost shut with a deep purple bruise that looked about a day or two old, and she had an angry new bruise in the shape of a fist across her cheekbone.

She grinned at him. "Hey genius-boy," she said in a whisper that did nothing to hide the cocky tone in her voice.

"Jez!" he hissed. "What happened?"

She shrugged, and winced. "Getting transferred. My cellmate threatened to lead a revolt if they didn't move me out."

"Did she do this to you?" It was probably Jez's fault, he knew that, but he couldn't help the irrational anger rising in his chest.

"Yep. Except what the guard did the other day."

He gritted his teeth.

"You should see her, though," said Jez. "She's still in the medics."

"Prisoner! Get a move-on."

"I have a few hours before I meet my new cellmate," Jez whispered as the guard prodded her forward. "Call me on the com. I saw Tanya."

Then she walked forward, and he stared after her, something cold settling in his chest.

He'd seen the desperation in her eyes, under her carefree expression.

Jez was losing it.

He wasn't sure how many more beatings she could take, and if he was being honest with himself, he couldn't picture a scenario where she wouldn't get beat up again, probably multiple times.

He walked slowly to the sink and dropped his bowl into it, then stepped back quickly as the woman beside him turned her glare on the man on his other side.

"Watch it," the man behind him grunted, and he sighed and stepped smartly sideways.

Across from him, a scuffle broke out between two prisoners. A third and fourth prisoner joined in, and then another, then another. Guards waded into the mix, swinging their shock-sticks.

Lev ran his hand over his face.

This was the third today. And it was only breakfast.

His disruption of the prison hierarchy had been—effective, perhaps. But possibly more than he'd anticipated.

This whole thing was going sideways, quickly. Jez was in trouble. They'd found Tanya, but she wouldn't listen. They were split up, he didn't have any more information than he'd had before, and Tae was still hitting walls every time he tried to hack the system. He'd apparently set off a full-fledged gang war. And to make matters worse, when he'd talked to Tae the night before, Tae had seen traces of someone poking around where he'd patched them in.

And they were only on day three.

Someone grabbed him by the arm, and before he had time to react, he was jerked backwards. He fell ungracefully to the floor and scrambled to his feet, biting back a curse.

A bench crashed down right where he'd been sitting, followed a moment later by a prisoner who probably outweighed him by fifty kilos, all of it pure muscle. He ducked instinctively as a fist whipped out over his head.

"Over here!"

He turned. A slight, middle-aged woman prisoner gestured at him frantically. When he reached her, she shoved him into the middle of the line waiting to drop off their food bowls.

"What—" he began.

"You're going to get killed," she hissed. "I don't know what's happened around here, but everyone who hasn't picked a side is going to be killed. Stay out of the way, for the Lady's sake."

He stared at her for a moment. She looked slightly familiar, but he couldn't place her.

"I—thank you." He paused. "But—why do you care?"

She sighed, a mixture of exasperation and weariness. "The same reason I tried to keep you out of the way of your insane cellmate. You obviously don't know how to take care of yourself."

He gave a rueful smile. Possibly she was correct.

She looked away. "Besides, you—remind me of my nephew. Or at least, what I think he'd be like by now. I haven't seen him for a while."

"Ah," said Lev softly. He looked at her more closely. Her face was lined with worry and exhaustion.

Had he done that, with his gang-war?

It wasn't like he had much of a choice. Get in, get Tanya, get out. That was the job.

Still, he couldn't help himself. "How long have you been here?" he asked.

"Ten years," said the woman, her voice very quiet. "I taught at a university on one of the outer-rim planets. But I read the wrong books, and I made the mistake of giving them to my students. And one of them turned me in."

"I—" There was suddenly something hard and heavy in the pit of his stomach.

She must have seen it on his face, because she gave a slight, rueful smile. "It wasn't him. The system made him, and if he hadn't done it, someone else would have."

"I'm—sorry," he said softly. "What's your name?"

"Ykaterin."

He turned, and met her eyes. "Thank you, Ykaterin."

He glanced out at the other prisoners as he dropped his dish in the sink.

How many more Ykaterins were out there, mixed in with the mafia and gangsters and thugs?

He had no chance to call Jez on the com during work, and none during lunch. It wasn't until they shuffled out into the courtyard for their scant half-hour of evening air that he managed to wander into a corner by himself. He touched the com and whispered, "Jez?"

For a few moments there was no answer. Then his earpiece crackled and he heard her voice.

She'd clearly been crying.

"Jez!" Something like panic clutched at his chest. "What happened? Are you alright?"

"I'm fine," she said sullenly, and he heard her sniffle. "It's fine. I just—I have a cold."

He rolled his eyes heavenward and shook his head. "Jez. Listen. If you're in trouble, I need to know about it."

"I'm fine," she snapped. "I just—I don't like being locked up, OK?"

"Yeah." The guilt that had wrapped itself around his chest since he'd agreed to come on this death-mission squeezed. "I'm … sorry."

"Listen. I met Tanya. She didn't believe me about Ysbel, and she told me to leave her alone. She didn't even want to talk, just walked off." She paused. "She threatened to kill me, actually. But at this point, she'd probably have to get in line." A touch of her old snarkiness crept back into her voice.

He sighed. "Jez. That isn't something to brag about. Listen. I'm trying to get us out of here. Tell me everything you can about Tanya."

"Well, she's hot," said Jez in a jaunty voice. "And she could probably kill me if she wanted to. I mean, she doesn't look like it, but she looks at you and you suddenly realize that if she wanted you dead, you'd be dead. I know why she and Ysbel got along."

"This isn't helpful," he said through his teeth.

There was a long pause. "She's been here a long time," said Jez at last, her voice a little quieter. "I don't know if they put her and the kids out with the other prisoners. It's going to be hard to get to her. She's protecting those kids, and I don't think she'll trust anyone but Ysbel. I—she wouldn't believe me, that Ysbel was alive. But—I think she wanted to."

There was another long pause.

"I'm sorry, Jez," he said at last. The guilt coating his throat was so thick that it took him a moment to be able to speak. "We'll get them out, OK? As soon as we can."

"Yeah," she said softly.

He wasn't certain how much longer Jez would last in here. He wasn't certain how much longer he could watch her going to pieces, knowing he'd been the one to drag her into this.

The whistle blew, and he jumped. "I have to go," he whispered. "I —be careful, OK? Just—try not to get beat up again? I'll get you out soon."

"I know," she whispered back, but there was something desperate in her voice. Like she wasn't sure if she believed him.

He wasn't sure if he believed himself.

At last the magnetic lock on the cell door clicked shut.

"Is Tanya alright?" asked Ysbel in a low voice the moment the guard had moved past the door. "How are my children? Did Jez tell you anything?"

He tried to keep his tone light. "She said your wife was hot."

"Yes," said Ysbel grimly. "She mentioned that yesterday. Please tell me something useful."

He sighed. "She's alright, and the children. But—she thinks you're dead. She clearly doesn't trust us, and she and the children may not be in with the rest of the prisoners. It's going to be harder than we thought."

Even if they found her again. But he didn't say it. Ysbel knew it as well as he did.

"She's in the other sector," Ysbel said in a quiet voice. "I can't even go talk to her, tell her." She looked lost, somehow. He rubbed a hand over his face.

"Ysbel. We'll figure this out. It will be alright."

She nodded, but her face was haunted. "I will stop asking about her then, I suppose," she said. "It will have to be Tae and Masha."

He sighed again. "Look Ysbel. We'll find something. We'll all be thinking more clearly in the morning anyway."

"Did she say anything else? Jez, I mean?"

He paused. "She said Tanya threatened to kill her."

For the first time that evening, Ysbel cracked a reluctant smile. "Yes. That's my Tanya."

He splashed water on his face, stripped out of his filthy prison uniform and pulled on the uncomfortable prison pyjamas, and climbed into his bunk. "Goodnight, Ysbel," he whispered.

"Goodnight," she said, and the lower cot creaked as she sat down on it.

He waited until her breathing slowed and evened out, and then waited a few minutes more.

He was exhausted, and his eyes were aching to close, but he couldn't sleep, not yet.

Finally, he sat up cautiously on his bunk and tapped his com. "Tae?" he whispered. "You there?"

"Yes. Masha's here too," Tae whispered back.

"Any luck?"

He already knew the answer, but he had to ask the question.

"I have very little," said Masha. "I'm getting some information on the warden and on what brought her here, which may ultimately prove useful, but unfortunately I've found nothing on Tanya. Except that she is one of the prisoners the warden personally keeps tabs on. Why, I don't know, but I suspect influence from Prasvishoni."

"I have nothing either," said Tae, his voice tight with worry. "I've tried everything I can think of. Apparently the systems here are almost impossible to break through because they're obsolete—they aren't compatible with our tech or our patches. This stuff is so old that the code I write doesn't even read. But we're not going to get three prisoners out of here if I can't hack into the systems."

"Well, at least that gives me something to work with," Lev said at last. "I'll see what I can dig up on the older systems when we have library time. I'm not hoping to find specs or anything, but if I can figure out the basic elements it may make things easier."

"Yeah," said Tae wearily. "It's not like we have a whole lot else to go on. Did Jez find Tanya yesterday? Is that what she was talking about?"

"Yes," Lev replied. "I talked to Jez this evening. She did find Tanya, and Tanya wanted nothing to do with her. I don't know if we'll find her again, and if we do, I don't know that she'll come with us." He paused. "They transferred Jez back to this sector this morning. I saw her walking through. She ... didn't look good."

There was silence on the other side of the com. Lev glanced down at the bottom bunk.

Ysbel was asleep. He swallowed back the acid in his throat.

Masha, to her credit, had said nothing. But that was likely because she knew what he was going to say next.

"That's what I wanted to talk to you about," he said at last in a low voice. "Even if Tanya does come, the best I've found so far are some outdated specs on the internal lock system. Nothing that would help us break out three prisoners out who are set into the prison system, not just patched like we are. So." He took a deep breath, bracing himself for what he had to say next.

Jez. The bruises on her face, the desperation in her voice when he'd spoken to her over the com.

He closed his eyes for a moment.

"We'll go out on the supply ship, like we discussed. We'll bring Tanya and the kids with us if we can. But—I think we need to make our plans with the assumption they're not coming."

Even saying the words made him sick.

Two children, growing up in this place.

He glanced reflexively down at the bottom bunk again.

But Ysbel was sleeping peacefully. She trusted him. When had he ever given her reason not to?

And, of course, she assumed he'd never betray her, because she assumed he was doing this because he cared about her. Because he wanted the same thing she did.

How the hell had he managed to put himself in this position?

"I know," said Tae quietly. "Masha and I have been talking about the same thing. I was hoping we'd have a breakthrough once we were in here. But I have nothing."

"It's more than that," said Masha, her voice cold. "That pilot will get every member of this crew killed soon, if she doesn't get herself killed first. The guards are already talking about her. If she gets into enough trouble, do you think they won't look at her file more closely? Tae, correct me if I'm wrong, but your patches won't hold up under close scrutiny."

"So what needs to happen?" Lev asked at last.

"Get me what you found on the internal locks," said Tae. "I may be able to use that to build a key that will get us out of our cells, at least. If it's just us getting off, I only need to get the five of us assigned to courtyard time when the ship comes in, which should be easy enough, but I'll need to scan the wiring. I—haven't been able to get a scan during the day."

"Can't you use the same patch you used to get us in?"

"No. That patched us into the system, but it doesn't give me any access to the prisoner assignments. I saw a patch of broken wall in the library that may let my scanner through, but I can't get to it when there are people watching."

"I'll send you the lock specs right away," said Lev finally, his voice low.

"Lev," said Masha softly. "You've done your best. The important thing now is to save the team."

"I know."

Lev tapped off his com and lay back on his hard bed, staring sightlessly up at the ceiling.

He couldn't get out of his mind Jez's face, bruised and battered, the limp she hadn't been able to hide.

And he couldn't get out of his mind the sound of Ysbel's silent sobs the night before, as she'd told him about the woman she loved, the woman she'd die for.

He felt sick to his stomach. But then, that appeared to be his new normal.

12

Jez laid on her back on the top bunk, staring at the ceiling and blinking back tears.

It wasn't fair. She'd been fine before stupid Lev called.

OK, maybe fine wasn't the word. But still. Crying when you were all by yourself, locked up in a stupid cell, with every damn bruise on your body throbbing, was one thing. Crying over a com was just pathetic.

She rolled over gingerly and scrubbed at her eyes.

Didn't matter. Anyways, her new cellmate would be here any minute now. Lev had said he had to go, which probably meant they were getting counted and then sent back to their cells.

Sure enough, a moment later she heard from the end of the hallway the click of door locks and the shuffle of footsteps, the muted sound of voices as prisoners shuffled back into their cells.

She couldn't help the twinge of apprehension in her stomach as the noises moved down the hall towards her.

Probably going to get beat up again. Every muscle in her body hurt at this point.

It was her own fault, probably. She knew it. Maybe she could just keep her mouth shut for once in her life.

But the aching restlessness of too long in too small a space was already making her fingers twitch, her body tense to run or fight.

Every muscle hurt, but getting beat up again couldn't possibly be worse than one more second of sitting still and doing nothing.

Then there was a *click*, and the door to her cell swung open.

She pushed herself upright and watched the opening, a tight grin on her face.

Someone stepped through, and the door swung shut behind him, clicking as it latched.

He was a little taller than she was, and maybe a handful of years older. Not muscular, but wiry. He'd be fast, which might be a problem. Still, she was probably faster.

"Hey skinny," she said lazily, even though her heart was pounding. "They grow people small where you come from, or did your mom get in trouble with a rabbit?"

He turned and looked up at her, his eyes taking her in.

"You're one to talk," he said. "You're so scrawny I mistook you for the blanket."

She stared at him for a moment, then threw back her head and snorted with laughter. The movement made her bruised ribs ache, and she leaned forward, swearing softly. The man had a broad grin across his face.

"You must be the one they warned me about," he said, when she'd finished swearing.

"Probably," she said with a smirk.

"I'm Radic."

"Jez."

He nodded. "Nice to meet you. I thought they were going to send me someone to beat the snot out of me, what with the gang-war going on outside."

She raised an eyebrow. "I can if you want."

He snorted. "Looks like you were on the wrong end of the last beating."

"Yeah? Well you should see the person I was fighting with."

She studied him as they talked.

He was definitely bad news. He had a slight scar along the corner of his left eye, and the kind of dangerous grin that meant he was probably full-on crazy.

Still … crazy was something she was good at.

He was watching her too, frowning. "Wait. You're serious?"

"Yep. She's probably still in the medic's. For the second time."

"Who?"

"Vlatka."

His eyebrows shot up. "Oh. They weren't kidding then."

She gave him a cheery grin. "Probably not."

He looked up at her calculatingly. "Well. Jez. How about we make a deal? I don't try to beat you up, and you don't try to beat me up, and maybe we can both get a decent night's sleep tonight."

She slid down from her bunk, swearing loudly when her bruised arm hit the corner of the bed, and stumbled over to the wash basin. She splashed the tepid water on her face and felt around the edges of her bruises gingerly.

The swelling in her eye was starting to go away. That was good. Honestly, the worst part about getting beat up was how damn long it took for everything to get better again.

"Sounds kind of boring to me," she muttered, squeezing her eye shut to see if that would help. It didn't. "Been locked up in here all day."

He gave her a look that was somehow sympathetic. "Hey. I know how it feels."

"How long you been in here?"

He smiled wryly. "Coming up on four years now."

She stared at him, unable to hide the horror in her eyes. He shook his head slightly, face softening.

"It's not that bad. You get used to it."

"Nah. I don't think I'd get used to it," she said, trying to keep her voice light. "Think I'd actually just die."

"No. You wouldn't. Trust me, I thought that way too. It's not that bad though. You figure it out. You learn how to keep yourself entertained."

She smirked at him weakly, fighting back her panic. "That why you were in solitary until they stuck me in with you?"

He gave a slight grin. "Maybe."

"Hey! Quiet in there!" The guard banged on the bars with his shock stick. She scowled, and Radic watched her for a moment. Finally he put his finger to his lips and gestured to the floor. She dropped down, curious, and he reached under his mattress and came up with a bag of gambling tokens and a small bottle of what looked like laundry soap. She frowned at him. He grinned back and pulled off the cap with a flourish. The sharp scent of alcohol that wafted out was strong enough to make her eyes water.

"Where did you get that?" she asked.

He gave her a sly look. "It's not easy. But when you want something badly enough—" He took a swig and handed it over to her. She sniffed it suspiciously.

"Smells like cat piss."

He tipped his head, conceding the point. "Tastes a little like it too."

She took an experimental sip.

He wasn't wrong.

She grinned at him and lifted the bottle in a salute, and took a generous swallow.

It burned all the way down.

"Now," she said, handing it back to him. "You know how to play three blind beggars?"

The game got gradually rowdier as the night got later, and they'd both been roundly cursed by the prisoners in the neighbouring cells by the time the guard strode up to their cell door and banged harshly on the bars. Radic managed to shove the chips and the half-empty bottle under the mattress, and they both jumped to their feet.

"What are you two doing?"

"Couldn't sleep," Jez drawled. The guard lowered his eyebrows.

"Well, you're both on double work shift tomorrow. Maybe that will help. Shut up in there. If I have to come back again, you'll be begging for just a double work shift."

Jez opened her mouth, but Radic said smoothly, "Of course. I am sorry."

"You should be," muttered the guard, turning away. Radic shot Jez a warning look, and she stood very still until the guard was out of earshot.

Then they both doubled over in helpless muffled laughter.

Double work shift was probably better than getting beat up. Probably. Jez grimaced as she dipped her rag into the bucket and scrubbed at an unidentifiable something on the rough corridor floors.

Although, honestly, she wasn't sure the overall effect would be any different. She could already feel the bruises on her knees, and her palms, already raw from her time in the laundry room, were cracked and red.

Radic worked beside her. They'd been working since early that morning, missed the fresh air break and missed breakfast. At this rate, the lunch she'd gambled for the night before wasn't going to do her any good, seeing as two portions of nothing was still nothing.

"You think they're going to just starve us to death?" she muttered, softly enough that the guards wouldn't hear. Radic shook his head.

"They'll give us lunch."

"Me lunch. I won yours last night, remember?"

He gave her a pained look. "Cheat."

She dipped her rag back into the cold, soapy water. "Hey. Easy with the language. You're the one who trades with the guards."

He gave her an easy smile. "You do what you have to to survive here, kid."

"Yeah? So what do you trade?"

He shrugged. "Alcohol."

"Wait, so you just—"

He sighed, and sat back on his heels. "Look, kid. Here's the thing. Do you know how this place works?"

She grinned. "Sure. You mouth off to the guards, you go into solitary. You put your cellmate in the medics, you go into solitary. You—"

He was shaking his head, face serious. "Listen to me. This place belongs to Warden Koshelev. And she wants back in with Prasvishoni. So here's how it works. You have pull in Prasvishoni? You get favours. But you have enemies in Prasvishoni? And they're important? Kid, that happens and they find you dead in your cell. Or maybe beaten so badly you're never going to walk or talk again. This is pay to play—your life is worth whatever the warden says it's worth. So you know what trading with the guards gets me? I stay alive. Because I have enemies in Prasvishoni, and if one of them contacts the warden, well, maybe my good buddy the guard only beats me up a little instead of leaving me dead, because she wants a bottle of my cat's piss next time she's on her way off duty."

"You two! Back to work!" the guard snapped.

They'd almost finished the floor when something made her look up.

The guards in the far corner was watching her intently. It took her a moment, in the dim light, to make out his features.

And then she recognized him.

Zhurov.

She swore softly, something cold settling in the pit of her stomach.

"What is it?" Radic whispered.

"Nothing," she said, trying to sound nonchalant. "Just a guard who doesn't like me."

Radic glanced up where she'd been looking, then looked back over at her, his face suddenly serious.

"The one in the corner?"

She nodded.

He frowned. "Jez. That's not good."

She shrugged lightly, but the cold pit in her stomach didn't go away.

They finished in time for dinner, but they were marched back to their cell without their evening fresh air.

For a moment Jez thought she might cry. If Radic hadn't been walking beside her, she probably would have.

One more night without even a glimpse of the sky. She was going to go mad. She couldn't handle this. She was going to—

"Hey. Jez."

She glanced over. Radic was looking at her with a pitying smile.

She tried to grin back, but it came out weak and shaky.

"Don't let them get to you," he whispered. "You'll be fine."

"Yeah," she said, taking a deep breath. "Yeah. It's fine. It'll be fine."

The guard following behind them as they walked down the empty corridor to their cell stopped at the top of the stairwell, and they heard her speaking to someone.

"Fine," she said at last, "you take them, then, Zhurov."

Jez's heart rate spiked.

She resisted the urge to turn around, but she caught the look on Radic's face.

He was worried.

"Go on," the voice behind them said. It was soft with menace. Slowly, Jez started forward, expecting every moment to feel a shock-stick come down across the back of her head.

All down the long hallway she waited, every muscle in her body tense.

Damn.

She wanted to spin around and hit him before he had a chance to hit her. But Radic's glance held her back.

He was more than worried. He was afraid.

They reached their cell without incident, and the guard beckoned Radic inside.

He hesitated, clearly reluctant. "Zhurov," he said placatingly. "You and me—"

"Get in," the guard snapped.

Slowly, Radic stepped through the door.

Jez was alone in the hallway now. She turned to meet the guards eyes. She was grinning despite the fear twisting in her stomach, despite the adrenalin jangling through her brain.

Not like she had anything to lose. He was going to kill her anyways, she could see it in his face.

"Hey friend," she said. "You miss me?"

He smiled at her, and his smile wasn't at all pleasant.

"Believe me. We aren't friends."

"Oh. Well, fair enough. I don't make many friends with brush-p—"

He backhanded her so hard she staggered into the wall. Then he leaned in closer.

"I could kill you right here. But I'm not going to, not yet. I want you watching over your shoulders, every minute of every day. I want you scared. I want you grovelling. I want you to think dying would be better than living like that. And then—" he lowered his voice even farther, so she had to strain to hear. "And then I'll prove to you that you're wrong. You'll die screaming."

She grinned up at him through her split lip, every muscle in her body tight, brain buzzing with panic and adrenalin. "Guessing you learned how to hit so hard because it was the only way to get people to stop laughing at your face, that right?"

"Shut up!" he backhanded her again, and she barely caught herself on the wall. "Get into your cell before I change my mind."

"Sure, cap'n," she mumbled, trying for another cheeky grin as she sauntered through the cell door.

For a moment, she was sure he'd follow and make whatever beating she'd got from her former cellmate look like a kids game.

Never before had the sound of a lock clicking shut been a relief.

But then he leaned in, his face up against the bars. "Here's the thing, Jez Solokov," he whispered. "I've heard of you. There's a lot of people want you dead, and they're willing to pay. But to be honest, I'd do it just for the good time."

She stared at him as he turned away, heart beating painfully.

How did he know her name?

When he was gone, Radic grabbed her roughly by the shoulders and spun her around. "What the hell, Jez? You remember what I told you? About being patient?"

"Never was good at being patient." She pressed the side of her fist against her lip to stop the bleeding. Radic swore.

"He's going to kill you. He doesn't kid around."

"Really? I thought he was quite the joker."

He stared at her, shaking his head in exasperation. Then, slowly, he smiled ruefully, still shaking his head.

"Guess I'm used to being the crazy one. But I think you may have me beat, kid."

"Just like I did in three blind beggars." She grinned as best she could through her rapidly-swelling lip.

"You cheated."

"I just cheated better than you did."

He sighed. Then he studied her more closely. "What did the guard mean when he said he knew about you?"

She raised one shoulder in a shrug, trying to ignore the way the question had wormed its way into her brain.

It couldn't mean anything. As far as the rest of the system was concerned, Jez Solokov had been dead for the last three weeks.

But for some reason, she couldn't shake the cold feeling in her stomach.

He shook his head and knelt to pull out the chips. "What are we gambling for this time?"

She raised an eyebrow. "Where you get that cat piss last night?"

He looked at her warily. "I have a stash of it. Outside the cell somewhere."

"Want to play for a bottle? I'll stake the rest of the lunches you lost. One win and you get everything back."

He narrowed his eyes. "Fine then," he said after a moment. "But we're playing a game you can't cheat at. Fool's tokens." He pulled out a small cloth bag and shook the tokens into his hand, a slightly smug look on his face. "You still want to gamble, now that you have to play by the rules?"

She raised an eyebrow, trying not to grin. "Guess I'd be a poor gambler if I didn't take my chances."

13

Tae, Sector 2, Day 4

Tae held his breath as the lock on his cell door clicked quietly, but there was no whistle, no sound of blaring alarms.

Slowly, carefully, he cracked the cell door open.

It felt strange, opening the door under his own power and stepping out into the silent halls, lit by the flickering light of a single orange light-bar strung down the middle of the corridor.

He slipped out the door and glanced around quickly.

He had maybe five standard minutes between patrols.

He'd been watching every time the guards led them down the hallway, figuring out which juncture led where. And then, of course, Lev had sent him a map for the entire thing, based off some esoteric thing he'd read somewhere and his two days worth of observations. And, of course, it was flawless.

He had to admit, it did make his life significantly easier. Still ... he was so used to being the one everyone relied on that it felt strange and slightly uncomfortable to rely on someone else's work.

If he'd just done the smart thing two days ago, he'd already have the scans, and be working on getting in.

There were vis-cams set into the walls at regular intervals, but they were just far apart enough that there was a blind spot if you kept directly under them and kept low.

It took an agonizingly long time to reach the stairwell, and he could already hear the guard's footfalls echoing down the empty corridor. He glanced around again quickly and held the lock pick on his com against the stairwell door. When he heard the click of the door unlocking, he breathed a sigh of relief, pushed it open a crack, and slipped through, locking it behind him.

Down one more corridor, and then through the doors to the empty prison library. He held his breath, but the lock-pick clicked and the door swung open. He glanced around, then crouched down in the corner, slipping a small scanner chip into his com.

He moved his wrist quickly along the broken section of the wall, and breathed a small sigh of relief at the faint green glow from the com.

He'd guessed right. It was scanning.

When he got far enough, he sank down against the wall and pulled up the holoscreen.

A map of the wiring rapidly populated the blank screen. He frowned and shook the scanner quickly, hitting the reset button. He watched it closely as it repopulated, something cold and hard in the pit of his stomach.

There must be a mistake somewhere. He must have messed up.

The sharp click of boots sounded in the hallway outside, and he clamped a hand over the com and swore quietly.

The guard. He hadn't been paying attention.

Silently, he slid down against the wall, hoping the pulled-out bench would hide him from view. His palms were sweating, and his heart pounded so loudly that he wasn't sure if he'd hear the guard shout if he did see him.

The boots came closer. He swallowed hard and held his breath. They stopped just across from him. And then, finally, they turned and started down another aisle.

He let out his breath slowly, his head pounding.

When the guard's footsteps at last passed through the doorway and receded down the hall, Tae scrambled to his feet and reset the scanner chip.

It had to be a scanner malfunction. Please, let it be a scanner malfunction.

He passed it over the broken wall again, his stomach a tight knot, a headache pounding behind his eyes. Then he crouched in the shadows and tapped his holoscreen.

He watched, barely breathing, as the information repopulated.

For a long moment he stared at nothing. Then, gently, he placed his hand over his com, and the holoscreen disappeared.

Masha was going to be furious.

When they'd put the wiring in, however long ago, instead of wiring the systems separately, they'd combined them—the prisoner security, the weapons security, the cells security. He'd have to hack through all of them before he could even get on the system.

It was impossible.

And he'd have to do it anyways. Like he always did, because, like always, everyone was counting on him to get this right. And if he failed, if he messed up or miscalculated, everyone would die.

Slowly, he stood. He made his way out the door and down the stairwell, closing the door gently behind him and listening for the lock to click before he moved on.

He was half-way back to his cell when a soft "Pst!" came from the shadows of a cell to his right. He jumped and spun around, hand going to a non-existent weapon.

"It's alright, I won't kill you," said a soft voice. The voice itself was unfamiliar, but the accent was impossible to miss. He peered closer, breath coming quickly.

It was a slender woman, her face indistinct in the flickering orange light.

He could just make out three cots inside the cell, two of them child-sized.

"Tanya?" he whispered through the knot in his throat.

It was impossible.

"Shhh. The children are sleeping."

"What—" he didn't know what to say, and his exhausted brain wasn't being any help, so at last he gave up, shaking his head.

"I've been watching you. You and the woman are friends with that crazy girl, aren't you?"

He didn't need to ask who she meant.

"Why are you hiding from us?" he asked at last. "We've been asking about you for days."

"I know," she said quietly. "But I don't know you. I don't know who you are or what you want. She told me that Ysbel is still alive—I don't believe it. And I need to protect my children, because there is no one else who will."

"So why are you talking to me?" he asked. She paused a moment.

"Because—because on the chance that you did know Ysbel, once, I thought I should warn you. This is not a prison you escape from."

His heart was pounding strangely. "Tanya. Listen to me. Ysbel is here, she's just in the other sector. I can take you to her."

The woman looked at him for a long time. At last she said, "Very well. And if I say I will come?"

"I—" he glanced at his com. It was already morning, and the whistle would blow in the next thirty standard minutes. "I'm not sure

I can set everything up by tonight. But tomorrow night. I'll come to your cell."

She was still watching him. At last she said, "You still intend to try escape, don't you? Believe me, it's been tried. And what happens when they catch you is much worse than death."

"Wha—"

"Do you know about sedation?" she asked quietly.

He felt the blood drain from his face. "They don't still do that, do they?"

"Here? Yes, they do. And with the same old-fashioned tech."

He stared at her, mind spinning.

Of course he'd heard about sedation. It had been all the rage thirty years back, new technology, a way to put people into a painless sleep until a way could be found to deal with them.

Except, it hadn't worked. Except, the people who'd been put into sedation slowly lost their minds. Maybe for the first week after they woke up were alright. Maybe even the first few months. But then the side-effects came into play. It started with their vision—they'd see things that weren't there, terrifying things, that they couldn't escape from even with their eyes closed. Then the ringing in their ears, then the loss of feeling in hands and feet. They didn't die, not right away. They lived years, sometimes. But after the loss of feeling came the pain, phantom pain that it was impossible to treat and impossible to cure. They lived screaming and sobbing until the pain had driven them raving mad. And when they died, they died still screaming.

"That's what they'll do if they catch you," she whispered. "They'll say that it was approved by the government to deal with dangerous prisoners. Maybe it was, I don't know. But if they put you into sedation, you'd best pray to the Lady or whoever you pray to that they never wake you up again."

14

"Tae? Are you on?" Lev whispered into his com once the guards had left from lights out. The prior morning, just before the whistle blew for inspection, he'd gotten a terse message from Tae in pilot's code, but all it said was, 'I have news. Talk tonight.'

It hadn't been a good start to his day. And to be honest, it hadn't been a good day to begin with. The gang situation he'd started had devolved, and he'd spent most of the day trying to avoid getting killed by one side or the other. It was more on the lines of a cold war now, but it wouldn't take much to push it into a full-blown riot. At this point, they needed to get out before there wasn't somewhere to get out of.

Tae's voice was so exhausted it made Lev tired just to hear it. "It's—not good news. I got the scan, but we have some problems."

Lev stared at the com, biting back the sickness in the back of his throat.

"What can you tell me?"

"I—can't hack into the prisoner logs. It was supposed to be simple. But they have the systems hooked up together, and I can't get into one without getting into all of them, and the weapons system is ancient. I've been looking every spare moment. I can't see a single thing I recognize." His voice was sharp with despair.

"It's alright, Tae," Lev said at last, trying to sound less hopeless than he felt. "We'll figure it out. It'll be fine."

"What are you talking about?" Ysbel asked.

He rubbed a hand over his face. "Ysbel. I—"

"You're getting ready to leave without Tanya. Without my babies," she said quietly.

Lev sighed, his shoulders dropping. "Ysbel—"

"I understand," she said. "But I need you to understand something as well. I am not leaving."

"Ysbel, listen to me."

"No. You listen to me. I know you are all here for me. I told you, back on the ship, that I would not ask you to stay longer than a week. But I'm not leaving Tanya and my children. Not again."

"Ysbel. That patch Tae put on. It's not going to last."

She shrugged. "Then perhaps I die. But perhaps I don't. And even if I do, maybe it lasts long enough for me to see them one more time."

"Wait." It was Tae. "I have other news." He paused. "I—saw Tanya. On the way back. She—agreed to come with me, to meet you."

"What?" Ysbel's voice was suddenly hoarse. "You—but I'm in the wrong sector."

"There's a window in the library. The guards use it," he said. "I sent the lock pick I made through to your coms, so we should all be able to open the internal doors." He paused a moment. "Ysbel. I don't know if we can get her and the children out with us. But I'll try."

Lev cut a quick glance at Ysbel. Her eyes were closed, her face cut with pain, and she was leaning heavily against the wall.

"When can I see her?" she whispered.

"Tomorrow night. That's the soonest I could make it work. In the meantime, I'll keep trying to get us through," Tae said. Frustration bled through his tone. "I can't seem to get in. I've tried everything I can think of. I even hacked into the *Ungovernable* to see if I could use her systems and work backwards. Nothing is working. I've never had this hard of a time hacking into anything."

"It's old tech, Tae," Lev said, trying to keep the heaviness from his voice. "It's not your fault. We'll make this work."

"Wait. Is Jez on?" asked Masha suddenly. "The guards told me they'd put her back in solitary."

Lev froze.

"Jez?" he said into the com. He tapped into her direct channel and tried again. "Jez?"

For a moment there was silence.

She hated being locked up. She couldn't stand being locked up. And there was a guard who was hunting her, who, according to Tae, would actually kill her if he caught her.

He found his hands were trembling. "Jez?"

"Hey genius-boy."

He closed his eyes, body sagging in relief. "Jez, what were you—"

"Jez." Masha's voice had ice cracking from it. "Were you even listening?"

"Nope," the pilot said in a self-satisfied voice. "I found some alcohol, and I plan to get drunk, so don't mind me."

There was a moment of disbelieving silence.

Lev dropped his head in his hands.

Leave it to Jez.

"Jez—" he started.

"Leave her," Masha snapped. "She clearly has better things to do. As do the rest of us." She paused a moment. "Tomorrow then, Tae?"

"Tomorrow," said Tae dully.

The com line clicked off.

He sat with his head in his hands as Ysbel dropped onto the cot below him. She didn't speak, and he didn't push her.

Damn that stupid, irresponsible pilot.

He tried to lie down, but he couldn't seem to close his eyes.

"Jez?" he whispered at last into his com. There was no answer.

He sighed, and sat up reluctantly.

This was stupid. He knew it was stupid.

How had he become someone who did stupid things on a regular basis?

He glanced at his com, and a few minute later he slid quietly from his cot. If his calculations were correct, he should have about ten standard minutes to get down the corridor before the next patrol came.

"Ysbel. I'll be back," he whispered.

He cautiously slipped from his cell and, ducking quickly between the shadows cast by the intermittent lights, slipped down the corridors to Jez's cell block.

This was stupid. In fact, this was ridiculous.

Still—

He pressed his com up against the lock to her cell, and the door clicked and swung open. He slipped inside.

He didn't know what he expected to see—Jez laying on her cot drinking straight out of the bottle, maybe, joking and singing drunkenly.

Instead she was huddled in the corner, her knees to her chest and her face buried in her knees. She didn't even look up when he stepped inside and closed the door behind him.

"Jez?" he asked cautiously.

At last she turned, and he was shocked at her face. It was gaunt and tear-streaked, and her eyes were red-rimmed from crying.

"What the hell are you doing here?" she asked dully.

"Jez." He tried to keep his frustration in check. "What's wrong?"

"What do you think is wrong?" Her voice was thick from crying.

"Jez." He knelt beside her. "Look at me. You've got to stop this."

"Stop what?"

He sighed in exasperation. "Mouthing off to Masha. Mouthing off to the guards. Getting into trouble. Getting drunk, for the Lady's sake."

"I haven't even drunk anything yet," she grumbled. "But I'm planning on it." She pulled out a bottle of something and put it to her lips, tipping her head back.

"Jez!" he snapped. "Cut that out. Give it to me."

She lowered the bottle and glared at him, but at last, grudgingly, she handed it over.

He sniffed it, then waved his hand in front of his face, coughing. "Where did you get this? It smells like cat piss."

"Tastes like it too," she muttered, turning back to the corner. She dropped her head down to her knees again, and a moment later her shoulders started to shake.

He sighed, some of his irritation giving way to pity.

"Jez. It's OK. I told you, we're going to get out of here. Just give Tae and me another day."

For a few moments she didn't react, just slumped there, shoulders shaking, but at last she sniffed loudly and looked up, wiping her face on her sleeve.

"I can't do this anymore," she whispered. "I've been trying, Lev. But—" She sniffled again and closed her eyes. "I can't do it. I'm going to try to break out or something, and I'm going to screw everything up, and Ysbel won't get back with T-T-Tanya—" She broke down into wretched sobs again.

"Jez—"

"You don't understand," she sobbed. The panic from the previous days was gone, replaced with a raw hopelessness. "I've been locked up before, back on the prison ship. When I got picked up for smuggling. I—I thought I was going to die. I thought I was going to go crazy. I wanted to die, because it would have been better than being locked up. That's why I broke out. Because I figured I might get killed, but at least I wouldn't be locked up anymore."

"Jez," he said firmly, taking her by the shoulders. "You're going to be alright. I'm right here. I've got you. Look, Tae figured out how to unlock the doors, alright? That's how I got in. You're not trapped."

"Sure as hell feel trapped," she hiccupped.

"Jez—"

She dropped her head again and burst into ragged sobs.

Gingerly, he put his arm around her. The wiry muscles in her shoulders were bunched with tension, and it felt strange, being so close to her when their lives weren't actively in danger. She leaned into him weakly. He froze, but she didn't seem to even notice.

"I hate being locked up," she sniffled. "I can't do it. You want to know why I keep getting into fights? It's because that's better than this. At least then I'm doing something. And you, and Tae, and even plaguing Masha are out asking questions and making plans and I'm just—I'm—" she lifted her hand and waved vaguely around the cell. "I'm locked up here because I can't stop getting into trouble. I'm no good at this. Masha was right. You should have left me behind. I should never have come. Do you know how many times in the last few days I almost tried to run for it?"

"Jez!" He drew back, looking her in the eyes. "You can't. You'd be shot!"

She sniffed. "I know. But maybe I wouldn't. I could try."

"No, Jez! You can't! Just trust me, OK? I promise I won't let anything happen to you. We'll get you out."

"Maybe it would be better anyways," she said in a low voice.

He took her by the shoulders again. "No. Jez, look at me."

Reluctantly, she did.

"Jez. We need you here. I need you." He paused. "I mean, for this plan to work."

He cursed himself under his breath.

Hopefully she was distraught enough she wouldn't notice.

She was still watching him, her face blotchy and tear-streaked, but she looked a little less hopeless than she had a few moments ago.

"Really?" she asked at last.

"Really, Jez," he said firmly.

She gave a tremulous nod.

"OK then," he said.

She sniffled again and wiped her face on her soggy sleeve.

It was ridiculous that he still couldn't seem to look away from her.

He shook his head at himself and made to move. She grabbed his arm.

"No. Can you stay here? For a little bit, I mean?"

He hesitated, then he sighed and nodded. "Sure, Jez. I can stay for a bit."

It would be a good couple hours before the whistle blew for the next count, and he should be safe until then. He turned and leaned his back against the wall. She leaned against the wall beside him, still sniffling, but as her eyes drifted shut, she dipped sideways until her head rested on his shoulder. He stiffened, then he gave a rueful smile and forced himself to relax. He was certainly no innocent, but somehow this lanky, ridiculous pilot seemed to be able to turn him into an awkward fourteen-year-old.

She mumbled something in her sleep and nuzzled her head into his shoulder, and he put his arm carefully around her shoulders to make a more comfortable place for her head to rest. His heart was beating a little more quickly than usual. He rolled his eyes and leaned back against the rough cell wall.

He was just comforting a friend. That was all.

He glanced down at her, her mouth half-open, snoring slightly, hair disheveled and falling over her bruised face, and shook his head.

To be fair, he wasn't usually willing to risk getting caught and shot by guards to comfort a friend.

He wasn't going to be lifting her into her cot, not without getting both of them hurt, and he couldn't bring himself to wake her. Instead, he shrugged out of his jacket and laid it on the floor. As gently as he could, he maneuvered her limp body into position so the jacket formed a rough pillow.

Honestly, the floor couldn't be that much less comfortable than the rock-hard cots.

He stood and pulled the blanket from the cot, spreading it over her, and glanced around the cell.

She'd pulled off her own jacket and flung it into the corner. He reached over and picked it up.

Best to take it with him. They were probably about the same size, and the guards might notice if she ended up with more jackets in her cell than she'd brought in.

He picked it up, slung it over his shoulder, and on second thought, grabbed the bottle to be disposed of before he got back to his cell. If the guards found that, it probably wouldn't end well for Jez, and if Jez found it again, it might actually give Masha an aneurism. Then he took one last look at Jez, lying sprawled on the floor.

Millions of people in the plaguing system …

He shook his head, smiling ruefully to himself, then slipped outside.

It wasn't until he was back in his own cell that he noticed the scrap of a note that had been shoved into an outer pocket in Jez's uniform. He frowned, and pulled it out.

The writing was messy, and whoever it was had been pressing hard on the writings stick.

Solokov. I'm watching you. You turn around, I'll be there. And I will make you sorry. Whenever you're least expecting it, I'll make you sorry.

He frowned.

The guard? It had to be. But how did he know her last name? Masha had wiped their names from every database in the system.

It shouldn't be possible for someone to track her down. And even if it was—why?

He was still frowning as he climbed into his cot.

15

"Tae."

He glanced up quickly. Masha was watching him from the top bunk, her face unreadable. He glanced down at his com and nodded.

Time, then.

"Are you coming?" he whispered.

"Yes." She paused. "How likely is it that we can get out tomorrow?"

He paused.

It was tomorrow, or never.

But he'd spent every second that he could fighting with the system, and there was a block he couldn't seem to get past.

He shook his head, trying not to let his face show his hopelessness. "I'll do the best I can."

She nodded, still watching him with that disconcerting gaze, and he turned away.

His breath was coming too fast, his chest painfully tight.

It was his job to get them out. Every last one of them was counting on him.

And he wasn't certain he could do it.

He unlocked the door, and Masha followed close on his heels as he stepped outside. He glanced up and down the hallway, then started off at a swift walk for Tanya's cell.

This, at least, he could do. That was the first thing. Get Tanya and the kids to Ysbel, and then, when he figured out a way into the system—

If he figured out a way into the system.

He thought he might throw up.

When they reached the cell, Tanya was waiting at the bars.

"Who is this?" she asked without preamble, gesturing at Masha.

Masha gave a bland smile. "I'm Masha. I'm a friend of Tae's, and of your wife."

Tanya gave the unassuming woman standing behind Tae a long look. Tae swallowed hard.

They couldn't mess this up, not now. Please.

Then Tanya raised her chin slightly, and a look of something like grudging respect passed between the two women.

"That is alright," said Tanya at last. "I will come with you."

He pressed his makeshift key up against the lock, and the door clicked and swung gently open.

Tanya hesitated a moment. Then she stepped out, and behind her, two children.

He'd never actually gotten a good look at Tanya before now.

She was slender, but with the wiry muscles of someone accustomed to heavy labour. Her face was lined and worn, and she looked at least as old as Ysbel. The years in prison had clearly taken their toll, but she was still a beautiful woman. Her brown hair was cropped short, but her eyes were large and wistful, and her mouth showed just a hint of humour, long buried.

She didn't look terrifying, not until you looked into those wistful

135

eyes.

There was a steel behind them, unyielding and cold as ice.

This was not a woman he'd want to mess with.

The two children stood silently behind their mother. They were as quiet as shadows, standing almost unnaturally still, only their huge eyes showing any emotion at all. The girl was sheltering the boy, who still had traces of baby fat, and for a moment something caught in Tae's throat.

They looked like the street kids he'd been protecting back in Prasvishoni. With their ragged clothes and their solemn faces, that had seen far too much far too young, they would have fit right in.

Had Caz been able to take his place? Were he and Peti keeping them safe?

He swallowed hard at the lump in his throat, and crouched down on the hallway floor so he was at their eye level.

"Hi," he whispered.

They didn't answer—he didn't really expect them to. He gave them a small smile, then stood to see Tanya watching him, eyes narrowed.

"Follow me," he said briskly, and turned away quickly so they wouldn't see the tears he was blinking back.

They walked silently down the corridors and up the staircase until they reached the library. He paused and tapped his com.

"Lev?" he whispered.

"We're here," Lev whispered back. "Coast is clear. No guards for another fifteen minutes or so. Should be enough."

He nodded, even though Lev couldn't see. Then, carefully, he opened the door. He stepped through to show Tanya it wasn't a trap. Then he stood to one side so she and the children could come through.

She walked like a wary animal, every sense on the alert. The two children followed at just the distance to give her room to move, but close enough that she could grab them if she needed to.

He found himself wondering how they'd learned that so well.

"There, at the back," he whispered. "At the window the guards use to watch the prisoners."

Cautiously, she stepped past him and walked over to the window.

Then she stopped short, and even from where he was he could see her face go white.

"Ysbel?" she mouthed.

He stepped closer.

Through the window he saw Ysbel. She was staring at Tanya, her eyes locked on the woman's face, her own face whiter than Tae had ever seen it. She walked forward, like a person in a dream, and put her hand against the glass. He could see her lips moving, but they couldn't hear the sound.

He shook his head and stepped quickly forward. "Tanya," he whispered, and tapped his com.

She didn't seem even to notice him.

Ysbel saw what he was doing and tapped her own com. "Tanya," she whispered, and Tanya started, seeming to notice Tae for the first time. He held his wrist-com forward.

"Go ahead. Talk. It'll pick it up."

"Ysbel," she whispered, her voice stunned.

"I'm so sorry, Tanya. I'm so sorry." And Tae stared as Ysbel—the woman who had killed thirty-five people without batting an eye, the woman who he'd never seen show more emotion than a twitch of her lip or a raise of an eyebrow—leaned her head against the window and broke down into silent, gasping sobs.

"Ysbel, no. Please." Tanya took two quick steps forward, placing her own hand against the glass in a futile effort to reach Ysbel. "Please. I—don't cry. Please. I've been thinking of you and dreaming of you for five years now. I thought you were dead. I was certain you were dead. I couldn't think of anything else but you. Please don't cry —" and he could tell from her voice that she was crying too.

The children stood back, uncertain. He stepped back to give the two women their privacy, and after a pause, he knelt beside the children.

They turned to look at him with their grave faces.

"My name is Tae," he said, feeling slightly awkward. "What are your names?"

"I'm Misko," said the boy after a moment. The older girl glared at him, then turned her glare on Tae.

"It's not really your business, is it?"

He bit back a smile. "Perhaps not. I'm sorry."

She gave him an icy look, and turned her head away, clearly determined to ignore him.

He gestured with his chin towards the window. Tanya had stepped back, and was wiping her eyes. Ysbel was blinking back her own tears, her face still sickly white.

"Children?" Tanya whispered.

"Go on," he said, gesturing to the window. "Your mother wants to introduce you to someone."

Hesitantly, Olya stepped forward. Then she reached back and clutched Misko by the hand, shooting one last glare in Tae's direction, and pulled them both forward.

Masha had stepped forward as well, holding out her com so the women could talk.

"Olya. Misko." Tanya's voice wavered. "You see this? This is your mama. She's come back. Do you remember her? Or were you too little?"

Olya was staring at Ysbel, frowning. She'd gone a little pale as well.

"Are you sure, Mamochka?" she whispered, turning back to Tanya. Tanya nodded encouragingly, and Olya stepped forward, still frowning. She inspected Ysbel, who stood with silent tears running down her face.

"Hello, sweetheart," Ysbel said, her voice cracking. "I remember you. And I remember your little brother. He was so fat when he was a baby." She stopped speaking, shaking her head, unable to continue.

"I do remember you," Olya proclaimed at last, stepping back. "Mamochka, I remember Mama. She's nice. Can we go see her?"

"I'm sorry, Olya. We can't tonight. But maybe soon, OK?"

Olya frowned, but finally nodded.

"Listen, would you please take your brother and go over to look at a book?" She shot a look at Masha, and the woman nodded in understanding.

"Come, Olya, Misko," Masha said briskly. "I have something to show you." She caught Tanya's eye and tapped her com off as she led the children away, Olya and Misko seeming to have fallen under the spell of her charisma as easily as anyone else.

When they were gone, Tanya beckoned Tae over. "Do you have your com on?" she asked quietly. Tae nodded.

"Then the rest of you can hear me as well," she said. Her voice was still thick with tears, but there was something in it that made him look at her more closely.

"I did not believe you when you said you were here to break me and the children out. I didn't believe that you knew Ysbel. I thought at best it was a joke, and at worst a trap. But now—" she paused, trying to collect herself. "You've done more than I ever could have hoped for. You've showed me my wife is still alive. And for that I will always be grateful. But——" she took a deep breath. "But your plan will not work. We cannot come with you. Get out as soon as you can, and don't look back. Take Ysbel with you, whether she wants it or not."

"Tanya," said Lev, "I appreciate your concern. But if we can get the rest of us out, we can bring you with us. That was the whole reason for this."

"You don't understand," she said quietly. She pushed back her hair to reveal a small white scar on her temple. "You see this? It's a chip they implant in us when we arrive here. I have it. The children have it. Every prisoner here has it, except perhaps for the five of you. And this chip, if I step outside the walls, will send a pulse though my brain that will kill me instantly."

Tae stared at her, and he saw his own horror reflected in Lev's face, and Ysbel's. Jez just looked sick.

"I——" he began. "Maybe I can hack it. Maybe I can shut it off before the supply ship comes."

"That's the other thing," Tanya said quietly. "I have contacts here, and they've told me. The supply ship is coming early. They had an emergency run, and it will be here this morning. It's scheduled to arrive in half an hour, I think. There is no time."

He felt sick. He felt as if someone had punched him in the stomach, and he still couldn't catch his breath.

"Tae," said Lev, his voice a desperate pleading.

"I—don't know," he said at last, his voice unsteady. "Tanya. May I?"

She nodded without speaking, and he stepped forward and inspected the small scar.

It would be a microchip, that would be the only way they could implant. Beside the scar, no external bump—of course not. They couldn't risk the prisoners cutting the chip out. They'd have used a bone-drill and implanted it through the skull, directly onto the surface of the brain.

"I'm sorry," he said at last, his voice sounding strange in his own ears. "I can't. I don't dare try, because if I do one thing wrong, I'll kill her. And even if I did everything right, disabling it without the proper tech—I might kill her anyways. I'm sorry."

"It's alright, Tae," said Lev quietly. "No one expects you to do miracles."

But they had. He had.

"I'm sorry," Tae said again. He felt strange, like he was watching himself from far away. "I couldn't do it in time. Even if I'd managed to find a way, half an hour is too short for me to work the patch in and create a lock-pick for the outside doors." He paused. "Do you know how to get back to your cell?" he asked Tanya quietly.

She nodded.

"When you close the door, it will lock behind you. Masha will warn you before the guards come."

"Tae—"

He tapped his com off and walked quietly out the door of the library, and back down the deserted corridor.

He still felt strangely lightheaded, his legs moving almost without his conscious thought.

He'd failed. He'd failed Ysbel, and Tanya, and those two children who reminded him of everyone else he'd failed back on Prasvishoni.

They'd been counting on him. They'd all been counting on him, because there was no one else who could do what they needed him to do. And in the end, he couldn't do it either.

They were going to die. Worse than that. They were going to be sedated, and it was going to be his fault.

When he reached his cell, he glanced around, lost. It was small, and he almost felt like he didn't recognize it, and he wasn't sure where to sit, or where to stand.

At last he sank down onto the cot, his legs finally refusing to hold him up anymore. He dropped his face into his hands, because he didn't have the energy to hold his head up, either.

It was a while before something small and irritating made him look up. He wasn't sure how long it had been, but Masha wasn't back yet, so it couldn't have been longer than an hour.

His com. It was clicking.

He looked down at it dully, then dropped his head back into his hands.

Click. Click-click-click. Click-click.

Without his conscious thought, his brain caught onto the familiar patterns.

Pilot's alphabet.

T-a-e-y-o-u-i-d-i-o-t-a-n-s-w-e-r-y-o-u-r-c-o-m. You are an ugly bastard and your mother probably washed her face with ship's grease. Hey Tae what do you call it when a swamp rat and a bureaucrat get into a fight? Hey Tae. Come on, you idiot. Answer me. I'm getting sick of tapping all this crap out and I can't think of any more jokes. Also did you know that Lev took my alcohol? If he hadn't, I'd offer you some. Although it actually did taste like cat piss. Hey! Tae!

He sighed and tapped his com, too weary to argue with the force of nature that was Jez.

"Hey!" The pilot's voice crackled over his earpiece. "You took your time answering! I thought I'd get blisters on my finger from all that tapping."

"Jez," he said in a dull voice. "Shut up."

"Nope. Not going to shut up." She paused. "Lev is basically

frantic, but Masha told him to leave you alone. Of course, I don't ever listen to Masha, so I thought I'd call you on the private line. You OK?"

"I'm fine, Jez." He didn't have the energy for this. But nor did he have the energy to get her to stop talking.

She was quiet for a moment. "Hey. Tae. Listen. This isn't your fault."

Finally, for the first time since Tanya had given them the news, he felt something. Anger. Bright and hot and scorching.

"Shut up, Jez!" he snapped furiously. "Just shut up. Don't you get it? You've been killing yourself in here. You've been getting into trouble, and getting beat up, and getting drunk, and do you think I don't know why? I promised to get you out. I told you I would. And I can't. OK? We're stuck here. I failed, and you're stuck here, and Tanya and Ysbel are going to be able to see each other through that damn glass maybe three more times before we get carted off and sedated. OK? You're never going to see the *Ungovernable* again. And it's my damn fault, because I couldn't get you out like I told you I would. Do you get it now?"

For a moment, there was silence on the other side of the com.

Good. He kicked his foot savagely into the corner of the bedpost, the pain of it almost welcome.

Maybe the damn pilot was finally figuring out what had happened. What he'd done.

"Hey, stupid," she said at last. "What, you thought you were supposed to get us out all by yourself? What are you, grand general king of the whole system? Come on. So your thing didn't work. OK, so good thing Lev is here, and Masha, and Ysbel, and me. You got us in, didn't you? You convinced Tanya to come meet Ysbel. So now she's on our side too. You thought you had to do all the rest of it too?"

He stared at the com, frowning in confusion. Had he misheard? He swallowed, suddenly at a loss for words.

She should have been furious. He'd hoped she'd be furious, because the other option was that she'd break down crying, and he didn't think he could handle that right now.

"Tae? You there? Do I have to start tapping crap out in pilot's alphabet again? Because I can. I'm good at it. I can be super annoying if I want to be."

"I know that," he murmured reflexively. "I—but I can't—"

He could almost hear her rolling her eyes. "Come on. Stop being stupid. If you can. Not sure you can help it, I guess. I mean, we can only do what we can do. But still. This is pretty dumb, even for you."

"I—"

"Look." She sounded serious, for once. "Tae. You're really, really good at what you do. I mean, I've never seen anyone who can do what you can do. But—there's only one of you. I mean, no offence, but there's a reason Masha got all five of us together. If she'd only needed you, you honestly think she'd have put up with me?"

She had a point.

"Hey, so I'm going to put you on the general line."

"No, Jez, wait—"

"Hey everyone," said Jez, "got Tae on. Guess he had some stupid idea that he was supposed to save us all, all by himself. But I talked him out of it."

"Tae?" said Lev. Tae had expected anger, or maybe disappointment.

Instead, he sounded almost frantic with relief. "Tae. Are you alright? I would have called, but Masha said—"

"You listen to what Masha says?" drawled Jez.

"Jez," began Masha warningly.

"Too bad I'm not in your sector, right Masha?" she said, the smirk clear in her voice.

"Jez, shut up. Tae. Listen," began Lev.

"No," said Tae, fighting down the nausea in his stomach. "You listen. I'm—I'm so sorry. I'm sorry, Ysbel. I'm sorry, all of you. I thought—"

"You thought what?" Lev sounded honestly confused. "I couldn't find the specs for you. I wasn't expecting you to perform a miracle."

"I—but—"

"You idiot," said Ysbel. Her voice was still hoarse from crying, but she seemed to have regained her composure. "This is not your fault."

"I—"

"Listen, Tae." It was Tanya's voice this time. "I don't know you. I don't know anything about you, except that you let me see my wife for the first time in five and a half years. I don't know these other people, but I do know my wife. And believe me when I say, she would not have assumed that you would do this whole job on your own."

He sat staring at his com, not entirely sure that he could speak even if he wanted to.

They should have been angry. They should have been yelling at him, swearing at him. He plaguing well deserved it. They'd been relying on him, and he'd failed.

Why the hell were they being so nice?

"Tae?" It was Lev again. "Are you still there."

"I—"

There was a moment's pause. "I'm sorry, Tae. I was putting too much on you, and I was doing it because I felt guilty that I wasn't able to do what you needed me to do. That was my fault."

"I—but didn't you hear Tanya? We're not going to make it out. I can't get us out."

There was a moment's pause. Then Masha's brisk, pleasant voice came through the com.

"Then I suppose the rest of us are going to have to start pulling our weight. It would probably be good for you to get at least one night's sleep, since I'm fairly certain you haven't had one since we arrived. I don't know about the rest of you, but I think I could do without a repeat of last time, where you were passing out from exhaustion as we were trying to make our escape."

"Yep. I had to catch you like three times," said Jez. "And, not to be insulting or anything, but you're not the easiest person to haul around when we're running for our lives."

"I—" that seemed to be the only word his brain would produce at the moment.

"Masha's right," said Ysbel. "The rest of us are going to have to start pulling our weight around here. Don't worry, Tae. We'll get us out. I'm certain there's a way." She paused, and for a moment her voice choked up again. "Tae. I—thank you. Thank you."

She didn't say for what. She didn't have to.

Tae swallowed down the lump in his throat.

He still felt somehow unmoored, as if the ground had come out from under him. But—but something that felt like a weight, that he hadn't known he'd been carrying but had been almost crushing him, had been pulled off his shoulders.

He wasn't quite sure what to do with himself. He wasn't entirely sure who he was, if he wasn't the one that every last damn person depended on to fix everything, and make everything work, and save everyone.

But—he felt like he could breathe, for the first time since they'd promised Ysbel they'd save her family.

"We'd best be getting back," came Lev's voice at last. "We'll talk this over from our cells. We're not getting out on the transport ship, so we'll have to think of other options. But we will get you out, and the kids."

Tanya and the kids. Chips implanted into their heads, and he couldn't hack them. But Lev seemed certain that there would be a way, although in fairness Lev had never suffered from a lack of self-confidence. Still … chips implanted into someone's brain. They'd have to have used—

"Wait," he said quietly into the com. He almost couldn't breathe. "Wait a minute."

"What?" asked Lev.

"What if—Tanya, when they planted that chip into your head. What did they say?"

"They told me that if I left the prison walls, it would cause an electric pulse that would kill me," she said, sounding slightly confused.

"OK. OK." His mind was racing. An electric pulse. Everything here was old tech, but this had to be new. At least, within the last fifteen years or so.

"Did they say anything about how long they'd been doing this?"

"No. But I heard from the other prisoners they started this about five years before I got here."

Ten years ago. That narrowed it further.

"And what do they do when people have to transfer between prisons?" he asked. He was almost holding his breath.

"I think they have a device that turns it off. I've seen it when they transfer prisoners before—there's a wand they put up to the side of their heads and input a code. I believe the warden has to request it from Prasvishoni a day or two in advance, and it only works one time. That's all I know. But we can't wait for us to be transferred. They only take it off right before they load you into the ship, and you're guarded the whole time. If you tried anything then, they'd shoot us, and then you. You could not get me out, and you'd lose your chance to escape yourselves."

"No. We can't," he said slowly. "But—Tanya, I'm almost certain I know what tech they used. Here's the thing—if you went out, crossed the walls, it would send a shock that would kill you. If you and the kids went out, it would kill all three of you. But—if two thousand people went out at the same time? Even two hundred? If they all stepped across the line at the same time, the shock that would kill you, or kill all three of you—it would be just a twinge. Not even enough to cause a headache. The system would short out, even if they have capacitors that are much bigger than anything I've ever seen."

There was a long, long pause on the other end of the com.

"So you're saying we break the whole prison out?" said Ysbel at last.

"Yes."

Another pause.

"It could work," said Lev at last, that thoughtful tone mixed with repressed excitement back in his voice, the one that always came when he was thinking hard about a new and interesting problem. "I think that just might be possible. We'd have to come up with a new plan, but—"

"What if I made them weapons?" asked Ysbel suddenly. "I could probably do something with the materials I brought. I meant to make explosives, but I could modify."

"I could help," said Tanya instantly. "We've worked together before."

"Yes," said Ysbel, and Tae could hear the fond smile in her voice. "Yes, we have, haven't we? I couldn't make enough to arm all the prisoners, but after whatever Lev did, it would be easy to start a riot, and then take some guards hostage when they came down to break it up. That may be all we'd need."

"We'd need to be able to pass materials back and forth," said Lev. "There's no way around it. I'll have to think on that. There's got to be a way—"

"I could do it," said Jez suddenly.

"What?"

"I could smuggle stuff back and forth. I mean, I've already been kicked out of a section once."

"Yes, Jez," said Lev patiently. "But that was because your former cellmate was trying to kill you."

"Well, she's still there, isn't she? And on this side there's a guard that wants to kill me. Shouldn't be hard, I'll just have to make sure he tries it in front of one of the other guards." She paused a moment. "One of the other guards that doesn't also want me dead, I mean."

There was a moment's pause as everyone contemplated this.

"Jez, that's a terrible idea," said Lev.

Tae was inclined to agree.

"No it's not. Look, I'm a smuggler, OK? Let me do what I'm good at. If you don't, I'll do other things that I'm good at. Like getting drunk. And getting into fights. And giving Masha an aneurism."

"Jez—"

"Relax, genius-boy. I'll be fine."

There was a momentary pause, and Tae could imagine the look on Lev's face.

He clearly was trying to hide the fact he had a crush on the pilot. Tae wondered if he knew just how badly he was failing.

"Please," said Jez at last, her voice serious. "I—need this."

"Fine," said Lev at last. He was clearly unhappy with the decision. "Fine. If that's our only option, we'll have to take it. But I'll be thinking of ways around that, and if I find one—"

"Trust me, genius-boy, you won't find anything better than me. I'm a damn smuggler, remember?" She was clearly grinning, and clearly enjoying herself.

Tae shook his head, a small smile on his lips for the first time since he'd arrived.

"Alright, this is all very productive, but we need to get back to our cells," said Masha at last, a strange tone in her voice. "If a guard finds us here, all the planning in the world won't help us."

He tapped his own com. "Masha's right. Best get back. Tanya, your cell door—"

"I know. It will lock when I close it." She paused. "Thank you, Tae."

"Yeah," he said. "It was nothing. Don't worry about it."

"It was very, very far from nothing," she said quietly.

"Come on," said Masha. "Time to go. Tanya, I'll leave you with my com. I can use Tae's if I need to communicate."

Masha arrived back in the cell a few minutes later. She gave him a look which he hadn't seen on her face before—almost soft.

"Tae," she said quietly. "I'm sorry. For letting you think this all depended on you."

He stared at her, once more rendered speechless. At last he muttered something incoherent.

She gave him a smile that was almost fond. "Get some sleep, Tae."

And for the first time in a very long time, he did.

16

Jez had been basically an angel since the night before—she hadn't insulted the guards who'd come through for prisoner counts, he'd held her arm up to the bars so they didn't have to come back twice to try to read her prison bracelet, she'd avoided shouting crude words at the prisoners across the hall who looked at her in an odd way, and since lights out, she hadn't sung one single rude song at the top of her lungs.

The effort had almost killed her, but then again—

Then again, the sight of those kids last night, the look on Ysbel's face when she'd seen her wife for the first time—well, she had to make this work. That was all.

Anyways, even being locked up seemed easier when there was finally something for her to do.

When the guards came for the prisoner count the next morning, she stood like a model prisoner, waiting her turn. No one even swore at her before she reached the mess hall, which at this point was a record.

When she got in, she glanced quickly around for Radic. He was standing in the food line, and she managed to bump into him before

151

they got their food. He dropped his dish and swore, turning around to glare at her, before he realized who it was.

He stared at her, then grinned. "You're out."

"Yep," she whispered, with an answering grin. "Hey. I've got something for you, if you're in."

He frowned at her cautiously. "What?"

"Stick-in-the-mud."

"Tell me what it is." His tone was slightly irritated.

"I'll tell you. It might take a few minutes."

He glanced around quickly, then jerked his head in the direction of a table.

When they were sitting, he leaned forward. "What is it?"

She leaned closer. "What would you say if I told you I was breaking out?"

This time he did frown. "I'd tell you you were crazy. There's an acceptable level of crazy. And there's the level that will get you killed. I know you hate it in here. But you can't let them——"

"What if I told you some friends and I had a plan to break everyone out?" She watched his face, grinning.

His reaction was just as gratifying as she'd imagined. His jaw dropped comically, his eyes widening and his face going two shades paler than it had been.

"Wha——"

"Told you it was good," she said with a smirk.

"Kid! That's not good, that's crazy! They're not the same thing, even though I think you think they are."

"Hey. It's not just me. You know Tanya?"

"That woman I told you could take you apart with her bare hands?" His voice was rising now.

"Same one. Anyways, she's helping us."

"Us? Who's us?"

"You know how you were saying you hadn't seen me here before? And you were a bit surprised?"

"Yes, because someone as absolutely crazy as you is usually pretty high on the radar."

"Well, I wasn't here before a week ago. We broke in, my friends and I. Because we were trying to save Tanya. Because she's married to one of my friends."

"She's—wait. Tanya's married to that mass-murderer."

"Yeah. That's the one. Ysbel."

He seemed to have lost the ability to speak. His mouth opened and closed a couple of times, but nothing came out. When he finally did manage to speak, his tone was slightly awed.

"Jez. I thought you were insane before. I had no idea."

"Most people don't," she said cheerily. "So. What do you think? You in?"

"I—" he glanced around him at the mass of prisoners. "You said you'd get everyone out?"

"That's the plan."

"That's impossible."

"Never stopped us before."

He was silent again for a moment, but she recognized the gleam in his eye.

She had him.

"No more prison cells," she whispered. "You want out, right?"

He nodded, in a stunned sort of way.

"Well?"

A slow grin spread across his face. "You know we're all going to die."

She shrugged. "What's life without a few gambles?"

"As I recall, the last time I gambled with you didn't turn out well for me," he said. He was clearly trying to keep his voice stern, but she could hear the familiar mischief sparkling under his tone.

"Yeah, well this time we're on the same team. And if you recall, I always win."

"Because you cheat."

She shrugged and grinned at him. "Anyways, we'll need some things from the guards. How much more cat piss you got?"

"Besides what you cheated off me the other day? How do you even cheat at fool's tokens?" He shook his head, but his grin was almost as wide as hers, and the spark of crazy in his eyes that she'd noticed on their first meeting was back. "I must be insane myself," he grumbled. "Alright, what do you need?"

Jez checked the packet she'd stowed carefully under her uniform.

Hopefully it was in a place she wouldn't get hit.

Well, with luck, she wouldn't get hit at all. Although that might take a hell of a lot of luck.

She straightened her jacket, put on her jauntiest grin, and sauntered out into the courtyard.

Her heart was beating far too fast.

She shouldn't be so afraid of the stupid guard. That's all he was, a guard, and she'd had plenty of people mad at her before. Hell, Antoni had been mad at her before, and he was a lot bigger than that brush-pig over there.

But something deep inside of her whispered that she should be afraid. That she should be very afraid. Because true, Antoni had been angry at her before. And he'd beaten her up before. But he'd never actually tried to kill her.

This guard clearly intended to.

She swallowed hard. Didn't matter, she'd be fine. She had no intention of letting him try.

He was already glaring at her across the courtyard. She strolled casually in his direction, glancing around as if she hadn't caught sight of him yet.

Three other guards were standing on the other side of the courtyard, but they were looking in the opposite direction.

That wasn't ideal. Still, she could shout pretty loudly if she had to.

The guard was still watching her, his eyebrows drawn threateningly. He seemed irritated she hadn't noticed him yet.

She wandered a little closer, still looking everywhere but at the guard. At this point, if she'd dripped water on his uniform, it would probably have started steaming.

She paused only a couple meters from him.

"Solokov," he hissed. She glanced around innocently.

"Solokov!" he snapped, a little louder.

She shrugged, and looked back up at the sky.

"Jez!"

This time she did turn around.

"Oh, hey!" she said with a grin. "You still around?"

"I told you. I've been watching you. And I will be watching you."

"Did you tell me that?" She shrugged. "Must have forgotten."

His face was flushing dark, his eyebrows lowered so far she could hardly see his eyes underneath.

"Maybe you need a reminder."

"Guess I do," she said. "Course, that would depend on you being able to remind me anything. Honestly, the only thing I remember when I see you is why I've always thought brush-pigs were the ugliest —"

"Damn you," he snarled, grabbing for her. She slipped out of his grasp, and he swung his shock-stick. It caught her hard beneath the ribs, knocking the breath from her. She staggered backwards, gasping for air, and he stalked forwards after her.

She glanced desperately backwards. The other guards hadn't noticed anything, and she couldn't scream, couldn't even make a sound—

He lashed out again with his stick, and this time she managed to fling herself to one side. It missed her by centimetres.

"Help," she gasped, choking in a breath. "He's trying to kill me."

Damn. It wasn't nearly loud enough.

He grabbed for her again, and she jumped back, but not quickly enough. He caught her by the shoulder and jerked her forward.

She drew a breath into her bruised lungs and screamed as loudly as she could.

"Shut up," he hissed. "Not so tough now, are we?" He drew back his fist, and she screamed again, a pathetic wail that made the entire courtyard turn and look.

It was too late. He was going to break her damn face, he was going to kill her—she closed her eyes and turned her head away and waited for the blow.

It didn't come. Instead, a stern female voice snapped, "Zhurov! What's going on?"

The hand on her shoulder released, and she collapsed into a pathetic heap.

"Zhurov. Warden doesn't want more paperwork."

Jez glanced up quickly. Zhurov was glowering at the new guard, but didn't seem inclined to push his luck. At last he turned and stalked off across the grounds.

Jez stayed where she was, her muscles shaking with relief. She felt inconspicuously under her prison jacket to make sure her package hadn't broken.

"You, prisoner," said the guard, without any noticeable thawing in her tone. "Aren't you the one who keeps getting into trouble?"

Jez raised her face and managed a grin. "Nah. I'm basically an angel."

The woman was glaring down at her, tight-lipped. "Listen," she said. "You picked the wrong guard to mess with. I'll switch you into the other sector, because I don't want the warden after me when you die, and she has to deal with the high-ups." She leaned closer. "But this is the last time. Lady have mercy on your soul if you end up back here again."

Jez got slowly to her feet, brushing herself off, and fought back a shiver.

She guessed the Lady had better get busy, then.

17

Tae, Sector 2, Day 7

"Guard!" hissed one of the prisoners, a young woman named Anya. Tae grabbed a handful of long, thin pipes and shoved them into a packing crate, then snatched up a bolt and bent over his grinder. His hands shook slightly.

Behind him, the prison guard's footsteps approached, and slowed. He closed his eyes and took a deep breath to steady his nerves. But the footsteps resumed their pace, continuing on down to the end of the table.

Tae blew out a breath of relief and glanced over. Ivan, in the station beside him, winked.

"Not bad, as long as you have an early alarm system," he whispered. He bent and pulled a handful of pipes back out of the packing box, and held the edges up to the grinder, and Tae managed a slightly shaky smile.

He wasn't used to trusting people. He really wasn't used to people helping him, especially people he didn't know.

But if they were planning on breaking out an entire prison—Ysbel had been right. They weren't going to pull it off on their own.

Tae lifted a pipe out of the box and held the edges up against the

158

grinder, sheering off the non-reactive coating, then held them just close enough to heat the metal without grinding it all the way off. He pushed gently against the grinder surface, bending the ends in on themselves until he'd closed the end off completely, and a sharp sliver, shaved partially off, protruded from the inside, then he set it off to cool.

It was ingenious, really. Ysbel was making sealed cartridges, with the two explosive components separated inside the cartridge. Drop the cartridge into the smaller pipe, so that it fit snuggly but couldn't fall through, jam the smaller pipe into the larger closed off pipe, with its internal spike. The spike penetrated the cartridge, the components mixed, and suddenly you were firing a primitive, but highly lethal, heat gun.

Leave it to Ysbel to come up with a weapon that would be so deadly, and so very easy to mass-produce.

"You're good at that," Ivan muttered, looking ruefully at his own pipe.

"Just smooth down the smaller pipes," Tae whispered. "Leave the bigger ones to me and Anya."

"Because you're techies?"

Tae gave a small smile. "Considering there's nothing else for us to use our skills on, since this damn system is too old to hack." He dropped the cooled pipe into the box and pushed it under the table. Ivan caught it with his foot and shoved it farther.

"Guard!" Anya hissed. Tae swore and shoved the pipe he'd just picked up back underneath a pile of bolts.

The guard stopped behind them. "I saw you'd finished a box," he grunted. "Give it here, I'll take it back."

Tae and Ivan looked at each other.

"Quickly!" The guard tapped his shock stick against his leg impatiently.

Slowly, Ivan bent and pulled the heavy box from under the table. The guard pulled a small antigrav from his belt and bent to fasten it onto the box.

Ivan's face was pale.

He had a right to be. When they opened a box of bolts for inspection and found it filled with makeshift pin-guns …

Tae was gritting his teeth so hard his jaw ached. Five seconds was all he needed—

One of the prisoners across the table from them dropped a sheet of metal with a loud clang. The guard started and glanced up.

Tae stooped, touched his com to the antigrav, and typed something quickly. As the guard turned back, he dropped to his knees, feeling around on the floor.

"Sorry," he muttered, "dropped my piece."

The guard shook his head and reached for the box. He tried to lift it, swore, pulled off the antigrav, and hit it against the table. He frowned at it, shook his head, and moved off, muttering about the damned ancient tech in this place.

Ivan, face still pale, shoved the box back under the table with his foot. A moment later, there was a scraping sound as someone pulled the box out of sight. Tae watched the prisoners across the table from him closely. Someone dropped a tool and bent to retrieve it, and someone else bumped into them. There was a small scuffle, some swearing, and then the prisoner who was in charge of dolling out the parts to be ground rolled her cart past.

And the box was gone.

Tae let out a breath and caught Ivan's eye. Ivan shook his head ruefully.

"Quick thinking."

Tae smiled reluctantly. "I guess we'd better get to work to have a box of actual parts ready in case the guard comes back." He paused. "Your friends are fast."

Ivan returned his smile.

"I'm in prison for organizing protests. Doesn't sound like much, I know, but in this system—you'd be surprised at how many large, bulky items you have to get past officials in order to stage an effective protest. Those will be in Tanya's cell before lunch."

They'd chosen her cell because it was larger than most, with three people, and least likely to be inspected by the guards.

Tae smiled reluctantly. "At this point, I wouldn't even question."

"Speaking of which, how did your smuggler friend smuggle this many boxes of plumbing pipes over here?"

He sighed. "I don't think she did. I think she smuggled distilled alcohol over here, and her fence set up the deal."

"Ah." Ivan said, smiling slightly. "Not a bad idea, really. I'm not sure why we didn't think of something like that when we were on the outside organizing protests." He picked up another pipe and held it to the grinder. "Speaking of which," he said, in a voice barely audible over the whine of the machinery. "I've been thinking. We need to deal with the weapons on the walls."

Tae closed his eyes for a moment, feeling the beginnings of a headache at the back of his head. "I've been working—"

Ivan shook his head. "No. That's not what I meant. I told you, no one has successfully hacked into the weapons system in this prison, and believe me, they've tried. But if your plan is going to work, the guards can't be able to break up a riot with the wall guns."

Tae sighed.

That was the one problem they hadn't been able to solve. The problem that, again, would depend solely on his ability to hack into a system that was impossible to hack into.

"But listen." Ivan bent closer. "I've been watching since I got here. I guess you could say it's a holdover from my protest days—you need to know if the officials have a way to just kill you all outright, or if they're going to have to come in and arrest you." He paused and put down the pipe he was working on, tracing a rough map into the metal shavings on the worktable top. "See? Right here. In every compound. If we could get the doors open between the compounds, then right here is sheltered from the guns."

Tae stared for a moment. "I—are you certain?"

"Where the guns are now, in the towers—see? They can't use their full potential range of motion, because they're set into the tower doors. Unless they can move them out, but you told me—"

"I can't promise anything," said Tae slowly. "I can't get into the system. But I haven't seen any path for commands for moving the guns, only for bringing them online, aiming, and firing."

Ivan gave a satisfied smile. "That's what Anya said as well. She's been poking at the weapons system since she got here three years ago,"

Tae breathed out slowly, feeling lighter than he had in a very long time.

For the first time since he'd met Masha—no, for the first time since he was fifteen, and Kira had died and he'd become the de-facto leader of the starving band of street kids back in Prasvishoni—they had a plan that didn't depend entirely on him.

18

Lev, Sector 1, Day 8

Lev stared at the eight-year-old over the holoscreen.

She stared back at him.

She was clearly better at this than he was.

He glanced over to one side, and shook his head in slight irritation. Why was it when Tanya needed a baby-sitter, she immediately thought of him?

"What's your name?" the girl asked at last. From the unimpressed look in her eyes, he assumed she'd given up on leaving any meaningful conversation-starting to him.

"I'm Lev," he said.

Tanya and Ysbel were sharing notes over Ysbel's com about the weapon preparation. Misko was asleep.

Which left him, apparently, to babysit Olya.

He hadn't been around someone who wasn't an adult since he'd gone into university at age thirteen.

"My name's Olya," she said.

"Hello, Olya," he replied, since some reply seemed to be expected.

How did you talk to eight-year-olds?

"So, Olya. What did you do today?"

She looked at him as if he was stupid.

In fairness, it was a stupid question.

"I did the same thing you did. We're in prison."

"Ah."

"And what did you do today, Uncle Lev?"

He frowned. Uncle? That was new. Still, Tanya would have had to tell them something.

"I thought you already knew what I did today."

"Of course I know!" she said in exasperation. "But Mamochka says I'll get in trouble if I listen to what she and Mama are saying. So I guess I have to talk to you. And you don't have anything to talk about."

"Well. Why don't you tell me something you want to know about?"

She frowned at him for a moment, thinking.

"Can you tell me what it's like to fly?" she asked at last, a little wonder in her voice. "I haven't flown. At least, Mamochka said I did when I was very small, to get here. But I don't remember."

He smiled. "I have a friend you should meet sometime. Her name is Jez. She loves to fly. When we get out of here, maybe she'll let you come sit in the cockpit."

"Do you ever sit in the cockpit?"

"Sometimes."

He felt a sudden longing to be there again, Jez humming to herself, badly out of tune, as she worked the controls, the calm emptiness of space around of them, how everything felt peaceful. Or, at least, as peaceful as anything felt when you were in close proximity to Jez.

"Well, I do want to fly a ship," said Olya at last, decisively. "But what I really want to know is how they work. And why they can fly so fast, and what kind of fuel they use, and how you go through a black hole. And how the gravity in a black hole works, also. Because I know how gravity works, but Mamochka said it's different there, and it bends time or something, but she couldn't explain it to me. She told me to stop asking questions."

"Well," said Lev, trying to keep the amusement from his tone, "I might be able to answer a few of your questions. If you'd like. But what are you going to tell me in exchange?"

She paused for a long moment. "Do you know I can get to the other section through the library?"

He stared at her. "What?"

She looked smug. "I can climb through. I found it last year."

"Olya." He could hear the excitement in his own voice. "This is important. Where did you get through?"

She gave him a skeptical look. "First, you have to tell me about black holes."

By the time Tanya and Ysbel finished their conversation, and Tanya's face appeared in Tae's com, Lev had almost talked himself hoarse. Olya, however, was looking ever-so-faintly impressed.

"Goodbye, Olya," he said. "It was a pleasure talking with you."

"You're actually kind of smart," said Olya grudgingly. "Goodbye, then."

He hit the com and turned to Ysbel. He couldn't hide the smile on his face. "Ysbel. I think your daughter just solved a whole lot of our problems."

Ysbel was already asleep when something clattered against the bars of the cell. He jumped, his heart rate spiking, then the lock clicked and a dark figure slipped through the door.

"Hey genius-boy," Jez whispered, and he sagged back on the cot.

"What the hell are you doing here, Jez?" he hissed.

"Just got back," she said with a grin. He looked at her more closely, and frowned suddenly.

"Jez? What happened to you?"

"What do you mean, what happened?"

She was holding one arm with the other, as if to keep it from moving. He swore, worry twisting in his stomach. "How badly are you hurt? Did you break it?"

She shook her head. "It's not broken. Just sprained a bit."

"Jez—" He shook his head and slid down to join her. Ysbel stirred in her sleep, and he lowered his voice. "What happened?"

She shrugged, apparently unconcerned. "Same thing as always. I brought the laundry soap Ysbel needs to manufacture the explosives." She dropped a bag onto the floor.

He dropped his face into his hands, swallowing back his anger. "Did your old cellmate do that to you?"

"She wanted to do a hell of a lot more." He could hear the smirk in her tone.

"Jez." He didn't raise his head from his hands. "You're going to get killed. And for some crazy reason, I have no idea why, I'd really, really like to keep you from getting killed."

She leaned up against the wall beside him. "Hey, genius-boy," she said, her voice a little more gentle than it had been. "It's fine. I'm fine. See? Nothing broken. You think I haven't gotten beat up before?"

He sighed and finally looked up at her. "Jez. I talked you into coming on this stupid job. I agreed we could do it. I brought us all here. And if you get killed, I'm never going to stop feeling guilty about it for the rest of my life, OK?"

She was looking at him strangely, as if she didn't quite understand his words.

"Lev?" she said at last. He met her eyes. She was frowning a little, and without her customary smirk, he could see the strain in her eyes, the hint of fear hidden behind her expression.

"Listen, Lev. I—I'm sorry. I'm crap at being locked up. It's not your fault. But at least this is something I can do."

"What? Get beat up?" he exploded. "Jez, for heaven's sake—"

"No, stupid, smuggle stuff. Getting beat up is just a side effect." She tried for a jaunty grin, but it faltered. "I—never had someone worry about me getting beat up before. Guess I didn't think about it."

"Well, I do, OK?" he said.

"Yeah."

Neither of them spoke for a few moments. She was still watching him, and he couldn't seem to pull his gaze away from her. "Jez," he said at last. His voice wasn't working quite the way it should. "We have to think of a better plan. I've heard rumours. That guard is going to kill you. The warden won't stop him. Now that your back here, how long do you think it's going to take before he comes to find you in your cell? You're in solitary, Jez. You don't even have a cellmate he has to distract."

"I don't know," she said quietly. She gave what was clearly meant to be a carefree shrug. "Anyways, there's only a couple days left. Figure I can stay out of his way until then."

"Jez—"

She turned away quickly. "Listen, I have to do this. It's the only thing I can do, OK? It's the only thing I'm good at."

"It's not—" he began, then he shook his head. There was no point in arguing the point. "I'm just worried."

"I know," she whispered. "I—thank you." She stood abruptly and turned away from him, fumbling at her wrist for the button that would activate the lock-pick. She stepped out, then turned and glanced back before she closed the cell door behind her, but when he met her eyes she turned quickly away.

He waited until after her footsteps disappeared down the hallway. There was something tight in the pit of his stomach, and he swore steadily to himself under his breath while he waited.

What the hell had gotten into him?

He was supposed to be logical. He was supposed to know what to do, and what was an acceptable risk. Except now he couldn't trust himself anymore. Was he worried because he should actually be worried? Or was he worried because that damn pilot had got him inside-out and upside-down?

He swore again, a little louder, to relieve his feelings, then, shaking his head, he slapped his com, calling a private line to Masha and Tae.

"What is it, Lev?" Masha answered, in her usual clipped, pleasant tone.

"Masha. We have to think of a better solution. Jez is about to get killed, and I can't seem to talk her into any sort of caution."

There was a moment's pause. Then Masha said in a wry voice, "Tae just spent the last half-hour haranguing me about the same thing. He seems to think that Jez is in imminent physical danger."

Tae's voice came through his earpiece. "She is. You didn't see what happened today. I almost thought the guard wouldn't get there in time. Why the hell does she always have to pick fights with the biggest, meanest person she can find? If she comes back here, she's dead." He sounded half exasperated, half worried.

"And we—may have more problems than that," said Lev slowly.

"I'm not sure if I've told you yet, Masha, but apparently there is someone looking for Jez from before."

He quickly told her of the note in Jez's pocket. When he'd finished, Tae swore softly.

"What kind of trouble has she gotten into now?"

"I'm sure she's gotten into a whole lot of trouble in her lifetime," Masha replied. "That's not what I'm worried about. I'm worried about how whoever it was tracked her here."

"That would mean they'd somehow managed to go back behind Masha's system-wipe," said Lev. "That should be impossible."

"Should be," said Masha. "But apparently, it isn't."

"More to the point at the moment," Lev said grimly, "that guard is hunting her, and now she's back in his hunting grounds. He's going to kill her, and I don't think at this point he's going to be willing to wait nicely until we've made our escape. We've got to do something."

"Yes. I'm aware of that," said Masha. "I've been thinking it over. As much as I hate to admit it, we probably can't afford to lose Jez, at least not at the moment. It would take me a significant amount of time to find someone who can fly like she can."

"Also, you'll never find someone who can make your stupid plans actually work like I can, or put tech together like Tae can, or blow things up like Ysbel can, and I promise you, there will be vacancies in all those positions if anything happens to Jez," he said through his teeth.

Masha sighed. "Unfortunately, I'm aware of that, Lev." There was a moment's pause. "I've been thinking about it. I believe I have an idea."

19

Ysbel surveyed the rag-tag group of prisoners arrayed in front of her, maybe thirty in total.

They surveyed her back, warily.

They were a motley bunch. Mostly political prisoners. Still … Tanya had vouched for them, like she had for Radic and Ivan, and she supposed that was good enough for her.

She would have preferred the organized crime bunch, but apparently they were too busy trying to kill each other to have time for an escape attempt.

Not that they wouldn't be doing their part. If Lev and Tae managed to get them out of their cells in large enough numbers and close enough proximity, they'd provide the riot all on their own.

"Alright," she said at last. "How many of you have held a weapon before?"

Three hands went up.

She sighed heavily.

It was late, and they were gathered in an empty room in the library. Lev had assured her they'd be safe for at least an hour. She kept glancing at the window behind her, involuntarily, as if perhaps she'd see Tanya standing there with the children.

But no, Tanya was working, and she needed to be too.

"Alright then. Show me how to hold this." She tossed a dummy pin-gun at one of them.

They all jumped aside in panic. Finally, gingerly, one of them bent to pick it up.

Ysbel looked at them through narrowed eyes.

"Listen, you useless bunch. You'll have to stop acting like I'm going to throw an explosive at you. Otherwise we will never get anywhere."

"Are—are you going to throw an explosive at us?" asked a timid voice from the back.

"No," she said patiently. "If I wanted to kill you, I would have taken the cell block down while you were still inside your cells. I could have, if I'd wanted to. And I didn't. So, see? There is nothing to fear from me."

None of them looked convinced.

"Alright, you." She pointed at the woman with the makeshift weapon. "I showed you how to fire it. It's just like a heat-gun, but it will have a wide, short range instead of a long narrow one. Now you show me."

The woman raised the mock gun with trembling hands. Ysbel shook her head in disgust.

"No. Give that to me."

She took the weapon from the woman, spun it around, and pointed it directly at the woman's belly. The woman froze.

"There. You see? You don't have to aim very well, because at this range, I would melt a hole the size of my shoulder in whatever this is pointing at. As long as you're not aiming for a leg or an arm, that will take whoever it is out. Even if you are aiming for a leg or an arm, my experience is that someone whose limb has been melted off is thinking about something other than trying to fight back. Now." She took two steps backwards. "At this range, I will not melt all the way through anything, but I will cause a serious burn that will cover her whole torso, and possibly hit the person beside her as well, if they're close. It will not kill her instantly, but it will certainly make her question her choices." She took four more steps backwards.

"Now. From this range, I will be giving her third-degree burns over her entire body. The beam here is wide enough that it will catch at least one person standing on either side of her, if they're standing close. So you have to be a little careful at this range. You see, it's now weak enough that there is no melting skin, which is not ideal for us, but—" She shrugged. "You must remember, I am making all this with very limited materials. So I am not able to do nearly what I'd like. Now." She stepped forward and handed back the mock weapon to the terrified woman in front of her. "You see? Very simple. Now, let's practice."

It wasn't an unmitigated disaster, she admitted to herself grudgingly as the terrified prisoners filed out of the library an hour later. They had actually seemed to catch on to the concepts fairly quickly. Still—

"This is the problem with trying to get an armed revolt going with a bunch of political intellectuals. In a prison made up of political prisoners, you would think I would get at least one assassin or a terrorist," she grumbled as she rejoined Lev in the cell. He was glued to his com, scanning some sort of information he'd pulled up, like he'd been doing since the guard left. He glanced up.

"You got them all locked back in?"

"I think they locked themselves in to get away from me," she grunted. He raised an eyebrow.

"I did tell you that they were intimidated by you."

She snorted. "Terrified is probably the better word. Every time I made a movement, they practically hit the ground."

He seemed to be trying to hide a smile.

"It's not funny," she grumbled.

"It is a little funny," he said, managing with clear effort to keep a straight face. She rolled her eyes.

"Alright, it is a little funny. This is what I get from working with your kind of people. I don't think any of them have killed a single person in their lives."

"Some people would look at that as a good thing," said Lev mildly. "At any rate, Jez's friend came to talk to me over lunch. He said he knows some people, and I've asked Tanya to vet them. If that goes through, I'm guessing you'll have exactly the kind of people you want to train."

Ysbel glared at him. "You think I want to train people who would be friends with Jez? On purpose? Without any sort of coercion? What kind of lunatic do you think I am? I think I prefer the stupid intellectuals."

This time Lev did grin, and he slid down from the bunk. "How is it coming? Really?"

She shook her head. "Pin-guns take almost no skill to use. As long as they can keep from killing each other when they're aiming for the guards, I think we should be fine."

He nodded. "That's good." He glanced down at his com. "I've been going through all the information I have, but it's not going to be enough. At some point, I'm going to have to get the chip with the guards' schedules on it. We need everything to run smoothly, and the only way for that to happen is if we know exactly where the guards will be when, and exactly when the shift changes." He shook his head. "Tae and Masha and I are still working on how to make that happen. But we still have a few days."

"And Jez?"

"Still alive, anyways, which is honestly surprising. "

"Good." She paused. "She was right, you know. If you use that girl for what she's good at, she's very, very good at it."

Lev gave a small smile. "Who knew that annoying everyone who's big enough to beat her up would be a skill we needed?"

"Well," said Ysbel, "in fairness, that is how she escaped last time."

He chuckled softly, shaking his head. "Alright. Well, I still have some information to go through, but you should get some sleep. You'll be training prisoners again tomorrow, probably in two shifts."

He was right.

She wasn't sure if she'd manage to sleep, though.

"You know," she said quietly as she lay down, "my Tanya hasn't changed at all. She's gotten older, perhaps, like I have. But she's just as beautiful as she was the last time I saw her."

"She is a beautiful woman," said Lev softly. "I can tell how much she loves you."

"Her hair is short," she said. She closed her eyes, picturing Tanya's familiar face. "I will miss her long hair, I think. Of course, if she wants her hair short, she is still beautiful. I would love her if she were bald. But I loved her long hair." She paused. Talking like this hurt. She'd known it would hurt, and she hadn't done it in so long.

But they were so close now. Only a few more days.

"And the children." Her voice cracked slightly. "I didn't think they'd recognize me. It's been so long. They were only babies when I saw them last. But—" She paused, swallowing hard. "Do you think she really recognized me? Do you think Tanya talked about me enough that she really knew who I was?"

"Well," said Lev, with a faint smile in his voice, "she certainly was giving me the stink-eye, and Tae too. I think she must have recognized you, or else she liked you the moment she saw you. Tanya said you were Mama, and she knew who she was talking about right away. She must have talked about you frequently."

She nodded, unable to speak for a moment.

Little Olya. She was older, but the determination in her face was just the same as it had been when she was a three-year-old.

"I imagine Tanya had her hands full with that girl," she said at last. "We both did, back when—" She broke off suddenly, choking on tears.

Lev, in the bunk above her, was silent.

"You know," she said at last, in a low voice, "my children grew up in this place. I will have them back soon. But they grew up in this stinking part of hell, and I lost them for five years. We will get them out. And then, one day, I will kill the person who sent them there."

There was another long silence.

"I suppose whoever it is would deserve it," Lev said at last, quietly.

The next day, for the first time, as she started on her daily work shift, she noticed the glances the other prisoner were shooting in her direction were not only terrified. They were looking at her with some curiosity, and even grudging respect.

She frowned as she worked.

She avoided people, as a general rule. Tanya liked them, but she liked them better from a very far distance.

Still … there was something surprisingly pleasant about the camaraderie of that day's work shift.

Maybe the stupid political prisoners weren't so bad after all.

And maybe it felt more gratifying than she'd imagined, knowing they'd be breaking these people out of the hell-hole they'd been trapped in for however many years now.

She was standing in line for the prisoner count prior to their dinner meal when a guard stepped through the line of prisoners and tapped her on the shoulder. She turned slowly, and the guard took a small step backwards.

"Um. Prisoner," he said, in a voice that was ever-so-slightly nervous. "Please come with me."

She frowned and cast a quick glance over her shoulder at Lev. Or at least, to where Lev should have been standing.

He was gone as well.

A sudden knot tightened in the pit of her stomach.

They couldn't afford something going wrong. Not now. Not when they were so close to the end.

The guard led her down a long hallway and into what looked like the guards' office. "Have a seat," he said, gesturing to a low chair. She sat cautiously, noticing as she did so that he'd stepped back and was covering her inconspicuously with his weapon.

She could possibly move fast enough to get it away from him.

But probably not.

The door opened a moment later, and the warden stepped into the room.

"Prisoner 1554," she said brusquely.

"Yes, ma'am," Ysbel grunted in reply.

The warden placed her hands on her desk, leaning forward to look Ysbel in the face. "I've been hearing rumours. There are things going missing. Production is going down. And it turns out, there's something funny about your records. Yours, and four other prisoners who came in with you. I don't like complications in my prison. Do you understand me?"

"Yes," said Ysbel. She kept her face expressionless, but her mind was racing, her muscles shaky.

Damn.

Tae had warned them the patches wouldn't hold forever.

She didn't need them to hold forever. Just a few more days.

"I am sorry," she said after a moment, her voice relentlessly steady. "I don't know anything about this."

The woman narrowed her eyes, but Ysbel had had years of practice in keeping her face blank.

"Someone has been trying to hack into the system. Believe me. It's been tried before. It won't work."

Ysbel said nothing, and after a long, long moment, the warden sighed and straightened.

"Very well," she said at last, gesturing for the guard. "You may go. But," she paused, and gave Ysbel a meaningful look. "If you know something about this, I'm warning you. It will go better for you if you tell me now than if I find out on my own."

"I told you," said Ysbel sullenly. "I don't know what you're talking about."

"I hope, for your sake, that's true," said the woman in a level voice. "But if for some reason your memory gets jogged, I believe I could arrange—" she paused delicately. "Some benefit for you if you were to tell me what you know."

Ysbel didn't deign to answer, despite the cold fingers constricting around her heart, just sat staring at the woman with her flattest gaze until at last she sighed and turned away, waving her hand at the guard as she went.

"Prisoner," said the nervous guard. "If you'd stand, please—"

She stood, and followed him out of the room and down to the mess hall, where the others were already eating. She cast a quick glance around the room. Lev was back, his face cut with a frown. Had they taken him to be questioned as well? And what in the system had Jez been up to?

The knot of worry in her stomach didn't ease, not during their evening break in the courtyard, not during the time they waited for lights out, not as she poured cartridges, her fingers working the familiar materials almost unconsciously.

"Lev?" she asked at last. "You weren't in the line for prisoner count at dinner."

He glanced up, his face preoccupied. "No. I wasn't. They asked me in for questioning."

"Questioning? For what?"

"I don't know." His voice was troubled. "They wanted to know if I knew the four of you. They wouldn't tell me why."

"They told me," she said quietly. "Apparently, someone's noticed what we're doing."

Lev stopped what he was doing. "What?"

"They've noticed supplies going missing, and production going down. And the warden said she's noticed someone trying to hack into the system."

"That's not good," said Lev softly. "That's not good at all."

20

"Jez!"

She started, jerking her vision from the distorted view of the sky through the force field. One of Radic's friends gestured to her frantically. She glanced in the direction he was pointing, and swore softly.

Zhurov was walking in her direction across the crowded courtyard.

She glanced around quickly, then slipped into the meal line. Her heart was pounding.

She was pretty sure the other guards wouldn't step in again.

The entire endless prisoner count she couldn't keep her hands still, fingers drumming restlessly against her thigh. She ducked her head, trying to blend in, and held her breath as they shuffled through the line and past the food tables.

She just needed to keep out of sight a couple more days. That was all.

Still—she let out a breath of relief as she sat down at a work table in the back. That actually hadn't been so hard. And besides, Radic's people were looking out for her. It would be fine.

A shadow fell across her table, and before she had time to react, a heavy hand came down on her shoulder. She swallowed, tasting a sick fear in her throat, and glanced up.

Zhurov stood over her, and he was smiling.

"Jez Solokov," he said softly. "I think you'd better come with me."

Damn, damn, damn.

She grinned up at him, narrowing her eyes, muscles shaky with adrenalin. "Nah. Think I'll stay right here."

He tightened his hand around her shoulder and jerked her to her feet. "Get up."

"Hey now," she managed as he dragged her upright.

"Jez," Lev hissed in her earpiece. "Yell for the guards."

For a moment she hesitated. But it was Lev, and for some crazy reason, she trusted him, so she opened her mouth and shouted as loudly as she could. Zhurov twisted her arm up behind her back, hard enough that tears came to her eyes.

"Shut up, Solokov," he growled. "No one's coming."

And then there were three pairs of running footsteps, and someone shouted breathlessly, "Let her go, Zhurov."

He tightened his grip on her arm, and she gasped in pain, and then he shoved her to the ground. She scrambled to her feet, but Zhurov wasn't watching her anymore. He was glaring at the other guards, one of whom whispered something in his ear. His face darkened with rage. She couldn't hear what the other guard was saying, but from his urgent tone and frantic gestures, it must be important. She rolled her shoulder gingerly. Nothing broken, that was good.

Zhurov turned his attention back to her, his glare speculative.

"Go on, Zhurov," one of the guards whispered. For a moment she thought he might protest, but then he stalked off.

"Should have known you were a plant, you damm plaguer," he muttered as he brushed past her. "Don't think that will keep you safe."

She stared after him.

"I'm very sorry, uh, prisoner," one of the remaining guards said to her. There was an infliction on the word 'prisoner.'

"Ask to be transferred," Lev's voice murmured. "Trust me."

She took a deep breath and straightened, brushing herself off. "I want to be transferred," she said flatly.

What the hell. Couldn't be in much more trouble than she was in now.

To her shock, the guards looked nervous. "Of course. I'll arrange that right away. Looks like one of our guards has something against you. Wait here, we'll be right back. I'll make sure he's assigned off the floor for the rest of the day."

She contented herself with a haughty look, since she had no damn idea what was going on.

"What the hell?" she whispered into com when the guards had turned away.

"Turns out you're not a prisoner after all. You're a plant from Prasvishoni. Come to check up on how the warden's running the prison. Masha stayed up all night forging the forms, and Tae hacked them into your file, just a little hidden. The warden discovered them this morning." There was a familiar smug tone to his voice. She stared at the wall in shock for a moment.

"Masha?" she said, when she'd recovered her voice. "Thought she'd be happy to see me killed."

"She's—had a change of heart. For now." There was a slight amusement in his tone. "But I don't know that Zhurov will let your new identity stop him from trying."

She stared down at her com for a moment, then looked up to find where Lev had been watching her from.

She couldn't see him.

Still—the knowledge that he was watching was strangely comforting. Even if he was a soft-boy.

"How many times are they going to inspect?" Ivan whispered to Tae as he bent over his machine.

"I have no idea," Tae whispered back.

The guard walked slowly down the row behind them. Tae tried to work steadily, tried not to let his impatience show.

They were short an entire batch of Ysbel's gun parts, and he'd only managed three pipes in the last two days.

Masha had been right. They were looking for something. If they had time, he would have told Ivan to leave it. But Tanya and the kids were being transferred in five days, and they didn't have time to lose.

"We're not going to make it," Ivan said in a low voice, once the guard had gone past. "Thank the Lady your friend smuggled the laundry soap yesterday. They have guards watching there too. They've been asking questions."

"I know," Tae muttered. "But we don't have an option at this point. We have half the guns we planned for, and we planned for the bare minimum we need."

Ivan nodded grimly.

Tae glanced up furtively. The guard was at the end of the line now, and was bent down, inspecting one of the stations. Carefully, without taking his eyes off her, Tae pulled a segment of pipe out from under the bolts. He held it up against the grinder, waiting as the rough surface tore off the non-reactive coating and began to heat the metal underneath. The grinder jolted and caught, and jerked the pipe out of his hand. He swore and grabbed for it, but it was too late. It had caught between the grinder blade and the base. The grinder squealed in protest, and Tae jerked at the pipe. The guard at the end of the row looked up, frowning, and started towards them.

Tae swore, wrestling with the pipe. "Look away," he hissed at Ivan. "No point in them getting both of us."

"Tae—"

His hands were slick with sweat, and he swore softly. The guard would be there in moments.

What would he say?

At least he could claim he was the only one doing this. That he'd taken the soap as well. But they'd ask where he'd stored it, and—

Behind him, there was a loud clatter. He winced, then glanced up quickly.

The guard was sprawled out on the floor, swearing creatively.

And over her stood … Jez?

"Sorry," said Jez. She was grinning widely, and didn't look at all sorry.

She glanced over her shoulder and shot Tae a wink.

Ivan elbowed him, and he turned back to his grinder and yanked one last time at the pipe. It popped free, and he sucked in a breath and shoved it back under the pile of bolts.

Behind him, Jez was helping the guard to her feet. The guard stood, wincing, and, limping heavily and muttering swearwords under her breath, started off.

Tae shook his head in reluctant admiration. Trust Jez to know how to trip someone hard enough to disable them.

Behind him, Jez tapped her com. "Hey tech-head," she whispered. "I'm basically a celebrity around here now, so don't worry about the guards. I'll keep them busy."

She sauntered off in the direction the guard had gone. Tae pulled the pipe back out from beneath the pile of bolts, still shaking his head.

Maybe Masha's idea had saved Jez from Zhurov, but it looked like the payoff was going to be she'd irritate so many people, from prisoners right up to the warden, that they'd kill her and hide the body just to be rid of her.

"The woman you were protecting when we first met?" asked Ivan, amusement in his tone.

"You have an older sister?" Tae grumbled.

Ivan frowned. "I—yes."

"And did she irritate the crap out of you?"

"I—suppose she did. Sometimes."

"Think of that, except times ten," Tae muttered, turning back to the grinder. "There was a reason Vlatka wanted to beat her up."

"I'm—beginning to see that," whispered Ivan, with a small smile.

21

"No," said Ysbel flatly from her bunk. "It is not happening."

Lev sighed. "Trust me, Ysbel. I don't want this either." He leaned his head back against the wall. "Masha, we've got to think of something else. This is a terrible idea."

"We have exactly two days left, Lev," she said, her pleasant tone coming through his earpiece. "If you have a better idea, you can let me know."

He shook his head. "She's a kid. We're not using a kid."

"That 'kid' is about to be transported to the Vault, if you recall, unless we can find a way to get her and the rest of us out of here," said Masha, her voice sharp.

He sighed. "It's not my decision. Talk to Ysbel and Tanya."

"Not happening," said Ysbel.

"Wait." It was Tanya. "Ysbel. My love. You are right. This is dangerous. But we have to do something, and Lev can't get in there on his own. If he's caught, we're all as good as dead. I don't like it any better than you do. But—I think it's our only option at this point."

Ysbel hesitated, clearly torn.

185

"Believe me," said Tanya softly. "I'd do it myself if I could. I would do anything to protect these children. To protect you. But I can't."

Ysbel gave a deep sigh. "Alright," she said at last. Then she turned to Lev. "You will bring my daughter back. You will bring her back safely. Nothing will happen to her, and you will be fully responsible. Do you understand me?"

He sighed. "Yes, Ysbel."

"Good. Because if you come back without her, or if she's hurt, even a tiny little scratch—"

"I know. You'll blow me up, or pull my head off with your bare hands, or take out my tongue and stuff it down my throat and choke me with it. I understand."

"Good." She paused. "I hadn't thought of the tongue one. That's a good one, though. I think I'll save it."

He shook his head.

He wasn't a hundred percent sure why he'd ever agreed to this.

"Alright. So, now that we've settled how we'll kill me if I mess up, shall we get going?"

Ysbel stood. "Tanya. We will meet you in the library."

Five minutes later, they'd gathered on opposite sides of the glass.

Olya was with them. She was looking quite smug.

"Alright, Olya. Where's the opening you found?" Lev asked resignedly. Olya, looking very self-important pulled free of her mother's hand and walked over to one of the lower of the clear panes, over in the corner. She pushed against one corner, and a moment later it popped open.

Lev glanced down at the 8-year-old. "Can you get through there?"

"Yes. If I suck in."

Tanya came over quickly and knelt beside her daughter, hand on her shoulder. Lev could see her knuckles, white with the effort of not squeezing too hard. His own heart was beating too quickly.

But they'd talked it over again and again.

They had the weapons. Masha had spoken to the prisoners in charge of starting the riot. The only thing they were missing were the guards' schedules, when they went on and off duty.

The chip would be in the warden's office, and Tanya had been there before, with the children. She knew what to look for, and how to tell where the cameras could see. Lev didn't.

But, Olya did.

So Olya was going to come with him.

Tanya picked the girl up and hugged her for a long moment.

"I'm fine, Mamochka," came Olya's muffled voice from Tanya's shoulder. "Let me go."

At last, reluctantly, Tanya released her. Olya squirmed through the gap, and he pulled her the rest of the way through. Then he knelt beside her.

"You alright?" he asked.

She nodded.

"Are you scared?"

She gave him a long-suffering look and shook her head. Then she held out her hand. "Here. Aunty Masha said to give this to you."

He took the chip from her. Masha had spoken to him earlier over the com—she wanted him to leave it on the warden's desk, and he knew Masha well enough to know that asking for an explanation would be a waste of breath.

"Alright then." He paused. "Your Mama's here, too. Do you want to see her for a minute before we go?"

For the first time, the girl's face showed apprehension. "Yes," she said at last, but her voice was slightly uncertain.

"It's OK," he said quietly. "She'd be really happy to see you, I think."

Olya looked at him, her face slightly pale. "Do you think she'll like me?" she whispered. "She hasn't seen me since I was basically a baby. Like, even littler than Misko."

"I think she'll love you," said Lev gravely, speaking around the knot in his throat.

Slowly, Olya turned towards the back of the room, where Ysbel was standing quietly.

"I'll hold your hand if you want," Lev whispered, standing up. She reached up and took his hand, and there was something about the smallness of her hand in his that made the knot in his throat grow a little more.

"Come on," he whispered. She nodded, and they walked forward.

When he was halfway there, Olya slipped her hand from his and started walking a little faster. Ysbel knelt, so she was at eye-level to the girl, and a few steps away from her, Olya broke into a run. She collided with Ysbel, and Ysbel caught her and stood, clutching the girl to her chest. Tears pricked at Lev's eyes.

He brushed them away in irritation. He had work to do tonight, and getting sentimental wasn't going to help.

Ysbel and Olya were still clutching each other, as if each was a drowning swimmer and the other was a life raft. They didn't speak—they didn't seem to need to.

He looked away quickly, but on the other side of the glass, Tanya was weeping as well.

He shook his head wryly, and wiped his eyes again with the back of his hand.

So much for that.

Finally, Ysbel lowered Olya to the ground. The girl still clung to her neck, her arms clasped like ships clamps.

"Mama missed you," Ysbel said, voice thick. "But you have to go. I don't want you to get hurt."

"You don't have to worry about me," said Olya, her face still pressed into Ysbel's shoulder. "I'm very smart."

"That's what Lev told me," she said, a smile in her voice. "But even very smart people have to hurry if they want to get done before the guards come back. Go on. Mamochka and I will be waiting for you when you get back."

For a moment, Olya didn't loosen her grip. At last though, reluctantly, she let go.

"I missed you, Mama," she whispered.

"I missed you too. More than I can say," Ysbel whispered back, giving her a brief squeeze. "Now. You go and show that silly Uncle Lev how to get into the guards' office. OK?"

"OK," Olya whispered. She turned slowly, as if she didn't want to let Ysbel out of her sight. Then, she walked briskly back to Lev. "Alright, come on. I'll show you what we're doing," she said, and marched off down the hall.

He glanced back at Ysbel, whose face had gone hard once more. She ran a finger meaningfully across her throat. Lev sighed and nodded, then followed the eight-year-old into the corridor.

There was nothing about this situation he liked.

Olya moved quickly, and he had to walk fast to keep up with her. She glanced behind her every so often, giving him exasperated looks every time he fell too far behind.

He found himself speeding up just to avoid her annoyed glares.

They walked left from the library, around a corner, down a long hallway, and around another corner. She stopped abruptly, and he almost ran into her. He was rewarded with another glare.

"We have to get through that door," she whispered. He nodded, and activated the lock pick. He held it up, waited until the lock clicked, and then gently pushed open the door.

"Alright," he whispered. "I don't know where I'm going after this. Your Mamochka said you knew where the cameras were, and how to get around them. So I'm going to have to follow you. But—" he gave her a wry look. "Your mama said she would take my head off with her bare hands if you got hurt. So please try not to get hurt."

She gave him a speculative glance. Finally, she gestured for him to come closer. He knelt beside her, and she whispered, "You have to stay right behind me, OK? I'll try to keep you safe, but I can't if you're going to be stupid." She paused. "And, try to be careful. Because you told me about black holes yesterday, and you didn't have time to finish."

"I will," he said gravely.

She gave a decisive nod, and gestured him to his feet.

"Follow me," she whispered.

She was surprisingly light on her feet, for a kid. She moved quickly and quietly, and didn't hesitate over her steps. Lev was hard-pressed to keep up with her.

One step forward. A pause. A quick dash to a door frame. Wait. One step to the left. Another. A third. A pause, and then another dash ahead.

He would have liked to study the setup as they went, but he was too occupied trying to put his feet down where Olya had put hers to get a good look at the cameras.

He'd just have to trust her, and hope she wouldn't kill them both. Although, he thought wryly, if she were to only hurt herself, she'd end up killing both of them anyways.

At last they made it to the door of the guards' room, and she gestured impatiently at the door.

"Quick," she hissed. "You have about three seconds."

He fumbled with his com, heard the lock click, and shoved the door open. They tumbled inside, and he pushed it closed behind them, and they both leaned against the door, panting. Finally, Olya turned to look at him. She had a supremely self-satisfied look on her face.

"I told you I could do it."

"You did," he said, with a slight smile.

The kid didn't lack self-confidence, at any rate.

Then again, he'd been told the same thing.

He stood cautiously, brushing himself off, and glanced around the office. The desk itself was fairly clean, but there was a mug and a pair of handcuffs, a couple papers, and some old information chips of some sort scattered around on the top of it. He dropped Masha's chip on the desk, and picked up the others gingerly. Presumably if they'd been left sitting on the desk they weren't coded with heavy security, but you couldn't be too careful.

"Tae," he whispered into his com. "We're in. How comfortable are you on the security blockers on our coms?"

"You shouldn't set off any alarms," Tae whispered back. "I programmed a write-around spoof into the coms before we came, so it should fool any security protocol permanently if it's not actively tracked, and temporarily if it is."

"Thanks." He slotted one of the chips into his com and tapped the holoscreen on. It flipped up, glowing a faint green, and he scrolled quickly through the information.

Nothing too important here, just some prisoner schedules.

The next chip contained meal schedules, the third a schedule of pick-up and drop-off of supplies.

That would have come in handy earlier.

Now, though, he was looking for something else.

He tried Tae's lock-pick on the desk drawers, and they clicked open.

A few more chips, but not what he was looking for.

He straightened and glanced around. They were running short on time. He had maybe fifteen minutes, and it would take him some time to get the files open and flip through them. Yes, he had a photographic memory, but he had to actually look at the documents first.

Behind the desk was a small cabinet. He opened it. It contained, among other things, a handful of chips, but when he slid each of them into his com, none of them were the guard schedule or the grounds map.

He swore quietly.

"My Mamochka said you shouldn't say words like that."

Lev jumped. He'd almost forgotten about the girl.

"What are you looking for?"

He sighed. "Olya. I'm sorry. I don't have time to talk right now. Could you please wait quietly? I'll be done soon."

"OK. But can you tell me what you're looking for first?"

"Olya—"

"I'm very good at looking for things. Mamochka said so."

He sighed and bent down to her level, since apparently it was the only thing that would shut her up. "Olya. I'm looking for a chip that would have the information about guards schedules. It should also contain a compound map, and some information about the wall cannons and the towers. OK?"

She nodded cheerfully. "OK."

He stood and went back to his search, shaking his head.

Ten minutes, maybe.

If he didn't find it, he'd have to come back again tomorrow night, and they were already low on time. They couldn't plan the time of the riot without the schedules, and if they didn't get that—

"Is this what you're looking for?"

He jumped again. The damn kid was quieter than he'd expected.

She was holding out a chip. He frowned.

"Where did you get that?"

"Over there." She pointed upwards, and he saw a small door he hadn't noticed, swinging open on its hinges.

"What—"

"You said you were looking for a chip with the guards' schedules and the map of the compound," she said patiently. "So it had to be somewhere where the guards could get it. And since the guards don't have chip slots in their coms, they'd probably have to scan it in as they walked past, so it wouldn't be in the desk, obviously. And the door over there goes out to the grounds, so I thought it must be in one of those cupboards up there." She shrugged, as if it was self-evident.

He stared at her.

He could, he supposed, have figured that out himself. Should have, probably.

"Was I right?" she asked.

He slipped the chip into the com. An overview of a long line of figures and diagrams popped up on his holoscreen.

He looked back at Olya and raised his eyebrows.

"Good job," he said. "I think you found it."

"Are you going to steal it?"

"No. They'll notice. We need it back exactly where you found it."

"I'll put it back," she said. "I know exactly where it goes. I was watching when I took it."

And, he realized, she probably had been.

He turned back to the screen, scanning quickly through the pages. There were three-hundred-some-odd, and he scrolled through them as rapidly as he dared.

Finally, when he was certain he'd be able to recall the information he needed, he pulled the chip back out and handed it to Olya.

"Here," he whispered. "Put it back, and then let's go."

She had just closed the cupboard and was turning around when he heard the faint 'click' of a lock from the other side of the room.

He grabbed Olya by the arm, panic jolting through him, and pulled her down beside him, ducking behind the desk.

The door swung open, and the ancient artificial lights flickered stubbornly to life.

Lev held his breath, hoping the whining buzz of the overhead light would be enough to hide the sound of their breathing.

There were unhurried footsteps on the hard floor. They crossed over to the desk and stopped.

Lev could see the guard's boots through the thin legs of the desk. The bulk of it concealed them for the moment, but if the guard bent over or took one more step

The guard yawned, and there was the sound of someone groping around on the desk.

Had he put everything back where he found it? He was fairly certain he had ... He glanced down. Olya was watching him with large, slightly frightened eyes. He tried to give her a reassuring smile, but he wasn't sure it worked.

The guard mumbled a curse, and the desk creaked as he heaved himself up to sit on top of it.

Lev clenched his teeth.

If he looked behind him, to where he and Olya were crouched

behind the desk, he'd kill them.

The guard yawned again, then crossed one leg over the other and leaned back. Lev could see the back of his head now, his fingers curled loosely around the edge of the desk, his weigh back on his hands, and as he leaned back, the light caught on a familiar silhouette.

Lev cursed silently.

It was Zhurov. Of course it was Zhurov.

Another glance at Olya told him she'd figured out the same thing he just had.

They were going to die.

"Damn," the guard muttered to himself, "plaguing night shifts. I must have left it in the damn drawer."

The guard shifted his weight on the desk, and Lev's heart jumped into his throat. He clenched his teeth.

He could get Olya out. The door to the compound was still locked, but if he threw himself forward and dragged her along, he could get it unlocked and shove her through before the guard was able to grab him.

He'd be beaten to death, of course. Not a proposition he really wanted to think about. But he'd get the kid out.

Looking down at her, he realized that even without Ysbel's threats, he'd have done it.

He caught the girl's eye and mouthed silently, *I'm going to push you out the door. When you get out, run as fast as you can. Don't wait for me.*

She frowned at him.

The guard's weight was on the edge of the desk now, heavy boots just above the floor.

She shook her head, her face set in determination. Then she grabbed his arm and lifted it to the desk drawer.

He was too surprised to resist.

The lock clicked softly as it touched his com, the sound hidden by the noise of the guard straighten his uniform.

Olya! No! He mouthed.

She ignored him and slid the drawer open a crack, then reached her small hand into it.

Lev sat frozen, not daring to move.

He could still grab her, get her out the door—

She pulled her hand back, fist clenched tightly.

The guard slid off the desk, and Olya flung her handful of chips. They scattered across the floor at Zhurov's feet, as if he'd knocked them off as he stood, and he swore, bending down.

"Damn warden, leaving her damn chips everywhere," he grumbled.

Olya grabbed Lev's sleeve and tugged him towards the door. He rose cautiously into a crouch and followed her.

They were in full view of the guard now, but his head was down, his meaty hands scrabbling on the rough floor for the tiny chips.

Lev touched his com to the door handle.

It clicked, and for half a second Zhurov shifted, as if he was going to look up. Lev put his hands on Olya's shoulders, ready to shove her through and slam the door behind her.

The guard turned back to the chips.

He gestured at Olya, and she slipped through the door. He followed, hardly daring to breathe. He pulled the door silently closed behind them, thanking the Lady, the Consort, all the Saints, and whoever it was who kept the hinges greased.

Then he followed Olya in a silent sprint down the corridor.

They didn't stop running until they reached the library and had closed the door behind them.

He looked at the girl.

She was looking at him.

They stared at each other for a moment. Then they burst into silent peals of laughter, bending over and clutching their stomachs. Finally, Lev sank down against the wall, wiping tears of mirth from his eyes.

"You're pretty smart, Olya," he whispered.

She smiled, in that self-satisfied way of hers. "Well, you're probably pretty smart too," she conceded. "But that was a pretty dumb idea to throw me out of the door and stay inside. You probably would have gotten beaten up."

"I probably would have," he said gravely. His muscles still felt weak at the thought of what would have happened to him—worse, what would have happened to Olya if he hadn't gotten her out in time. "But I suspect your mama would have done worse if I'd come back without you."

"You wouldn't have left without me," she said, her voice confident. "I know you wouldn't have. That's why I went with you. That's what I told Mamochka, and Mama."

He just looked at her for a moment.

"How did you know I wouldn't leave you?" he asked at last, quietly.

She shrugged. "Because when I asked you those questions about the black hole, you didn't tell me to be quiet. You listened to me. And you bend down when you talk to me. I think it's silly, but people who don't care about kids don't do that."

"Ah." He had to swallow hard at the strange lump in his throat. "Well. I'm glad we didn't have to find out who would have been beat up. Shall we go back to your mama and Mamochka now?"

She cocked her head to one side, studying him. "OK. We can go back," she said finally. "But you have to tell them that I was the one who found the chip."

"I will," he said, and despite everything that had happened that night, he found he was smiling.

He was still smiling after Olya and Ysbel had made their tearful goodbyes and they'd gotten Olya back through the partition to Tanya, after they'd finished their brief conference and made their way back to their cells.

"Thank you," said Ysbel, when the cell door had clicked shut behind them. "For bringing me back my daughter."

He smiled a little wider. "Ysbel, you have an extraordinary daughter," he said. "I don't think I'd have gotten back here without her, to be honest."

Ysbel smiled back, and for a moment, just a moment, he thought that they understood each other perfectly.

It took him almost an hour to scan through the documents in his memory, trying to parse out the information that they needed. Then he hit his com.

"Tae, Masha, Jez. Are you there?"

Three "yes"'s of varying degrees of exhaustion, worry, and cockiness came back through the com.

"Listen. We're going to want to stage this in the morning, right around the time they let the first shift out for fresh air. The second shift will just be starting breakfast. On our side, Radic is going to get the riot started. He said at this point, it's only a matter of getting people in the same room at the same time. What's the set up for your sector?"

"We'll pass the weapons into the cells tomorrow night, in between the last two prisoner counts. Our people will take two each, and leave the weapons for your sector under the dish sink, like we discussed."

"And I'll start a fight," said Jez. "I'm good at starting fights." There was a dangerous excitement in her voice he hadn't heard there in a long time. He hadn't realized how much he missed it. He smiled to himself.

"Yes, Jez. Thank you. We're all aware of that."

"Once the guards step in to rescue her, we start taking hostages. You'll need to have your hostages by that point as well, and get the guards to open the external locks to the courtyard. We'll get the locks between the different compounds open, and that should make the brawl even bigger. Ivan will direct the hostages back to where the wall guns won't reach us, and then we're home free."

"How many guards on the floor tomorrow morning?" asked Masha. Lev closed his eyes for a moment, picturing the document.

"We're aiming for right at the shift change. So—" he paused, calculating the numbers in his head. "Depending on timing, there will be roughly fifty guards per sector. Once trouble starts, they'll send in everyone they have, which will end up at closer to one hundred, maybe one twenty, again, depending on timing. It will be vital to get the first fifty guards in each sector locked down as soon as possible."

"Good," said Masha. "Ysbel. The prisoners know how to use the weapons?"

"As much as they can be," she grumbled.

"Tanya?"

"I will echo my wife. Most of these people are intellectual political prisoners. Most of them are not used to weapons. Except, of course, the ones who want to kill Jez, and the ones who, thanks to Lev, want to kill each other." She paused. "Are the rest of you aware, by the way, of what Jez did to Vlatka?"

"Do we want to know?" asked Tae.

"Maybe not," conceded Tanya.

Lev paused for a moment, thinking. Was there anything he was missing?

There probably was, honestly—he hadn't gotten a full night's sleep in two weeks. But hopefully it wasn't anything too important.

There were a few moments of silence. Finally Masha spoke.

"This is going to be dangerous. There are more unknowns than I like in a job like this." She paused. "But if I were to pick a crew, this is the crew I'd pick. If anyone can pull this off—"

"You did pick us," Jez pointed out helpfully.

There was another silence. Finally Lev said, "Tomorrow, then."

"See you on the other side," said Jez, in a jaunty tone. "I'm going to bed."

Her com clicked off, and one by one, the others' did as well.

Lev lay back on his cot, but he couldn't fight the faint unease that had settled into the pit of his stomach.

Just over twenty-four hours.

22

For the fourth time that day, Ysbel ducked her head and tried not to catch the eyes of the guard.

There were more of them than there usually were. She didn't have the schedules that Lev had, but there were more guards than there should have been.

She shook her head, trying to push back her unease. They'd been stealing supplies steadily since for over a week. Most of it, she hoped, hadn't been noticed, and Jez had done a frankly excellent job at distracting their attention, but they were suspicious about something.

She didn't like it. Still, it couldn't be helped, not when they were trying to pull the plans together on such short notice. They only had to last until tomorrow morning. Then this would be over. They'd be free.

She'd be able to see Tanya, not in her memories, not through a glass, but Tanya, in person. She'd be able to hold her. For the first time in five years, she'd be with her wife again. Even the thought brought the ache of tears to her eyes. She shook her head resolutely.

Enough time for that tomorrow. Today, she had to make sure everything was perfect, and she had to keep out of the way of the guards.

Her heart was pounding, her chest tight.

"Prisoner 1559."

She jerked her head up. A guard stood in front of her. Behind the guard, one of the prisoners was shaking his head helplessly.

"Yes?" she said, looking up slowly, forcing the emotion from her expression. "What do you need?"

"You dropped something," said the guard, his face cold. She glanced down, heart pounding.

Her mop lay on the floor, beside the bucket.

"I'm sorry," she said. "I was startled when you called me. I won't stop working again."

"Good," said the guard. "See that you don't."

There was something unreadable in his voice, and the knot in her chest tightened.

Only one more day. Only until tomorrow morning. That's all she needed.

By the time they were led back to their cells, her hands were almost shaking with nerves.

Her hands never shook. That would be a dangerous trait in someone who manufactured explosives.

But she'd never played for stakes this high before. Not when her own life was on the line, not ever.

Tanya. Olya. Misko.

After the guards called lights out and the final prisoner count of the evening was finished, Ysbel waited until the guards' footsteps had faded down the hallway. Then she tapped her com.

"Tanya," she whispered. "You have all the weapons ready?"

"Yes."

She had to know about the weapons. But she would have called anyways, just to hear that voice.

She choked back her tears. "Are—the children alright?"

"Yes. They children are fine." Tanya paused. "They can't wait to see you. Olya has been talking of nothing else since two days ago." She paused again, and Ysbel could hear the emotion in her tone. "I —can't wait to see you either."

"It's been a long time," said Ysbel.

"Tomorrow, my love."

"Tomorrow."

She tapped off her com.

They'd done the impossible. In one week, they'd managed to make enough weapons to arm the prison, they'd planned and prepared for the largest prison break in the system's history.

Only a few more hours, and then it wouldn't matter what the guards found out.

23

"Get up! Now!"

Jez jerked awake and dropped off her cot into a half-crouch before her brain had time to figure out what in the hell was happening.

All the lights in the cell block had switched on, and she blinked against the brightness. Had she overslept? Damn, she couldn't have overslept, today was the day they were getting out. She couldn't have

—

"Arms on the wall!" A guard slammed a shock-stick against the bars of her cell door. "Now!"

So much for whatever the hell Masha had done to her record.

She glared at him, trying to slow her racing heart. "What the—"

"Get your hands on the wall or I'll shoot you right now," the guard growled.

For a moment, she was tempted to take her chances. But—they were too close. She couldn't risk their whole plan.

Even if it meant they'd take her.

She took a deep breath, and bit back the surge of panic. It would be fine. If something happened, Lev and Tae and Ysbel and the others would get her out. She wouldn't be locked in here forever.

She swallowed hard, then, fighting every single instinct in her body, she turned around and placed her hands on the wall.

The lock clicked and her cell door swung open.

"You're no plant, are you?" the guard said softly. "You had us going for a bit there. But looks like your luck ran out."

Something had gone wrong. Very badly wrong.

"Hey, bastard," she said with a grin. "Get bored and come looking for me? Hate to disappoint, but you're not really my type."

The guard who stepped through didn't bother to respond, just grabbed her arms.

She almost turned around and hit him. She almost tried to wrestle the gun away from him and turn it on the two guards who stood at the door, covering them. Even though it was almost certain to fail.

It was worth a try, though, right?

Or, it would have been, if it wouldn't have ruined their entire escape plan.

She let him wrench her hands down behind her back, wincing at the pressure on her bruised arm, and then secure them with cuffs.

"Alright, prisoner. Move." He grabbed her by the shoulder and turned her around, shoving her towards the cell door.

A sick feeling in her stomach told her there may not be a plan anymore.

The guards shoved her down the corridor, towards the mess hall. There was no one else out in the corridor, and the air was cooler than it ever was during the day. Must be close to the middle of the night.

"Hey. You may as well tell me what's going on," she said, trying to keep her voice reasonable. "Not like I'm not going to figure it out at some point." She paused. "Wait. Let me guess. You've letting me go for good behaviour."

"Shut up," the guard behind her snapped. She managed a grin.

At least she wasn't losing her touch.

They reached the mess hall. The door was open, and a handful of guards with drawn weapons stood on either side.

Jez scanned the room quickly as she stepped through the door, then drew in a sharp breath.

In the centre of the room stood Tanya, and beside her, the two children. Their faces were confused and terrified, and they were huddled close to their mother.

And on the floor, in front of her, sat a large pile of black cylinders Jez recognized instantly.

Her stomach tightened with dread.

They'd found the guns.

The guards jerked on her cuffed arms, and she stumbled to a halt.

Beside her, Lev was kneeling on the hard floor, hands locked behind his back, gun pressed to the back of his neck. His expression was grim, and a large bruise was rising across the side of his face. She felt an entirely unexpected surge of anger.

How dare they? He was a soft boy, not a fighter. She'd plaguing well—

Lev caught her eye and shook his head firmly.

She glared at him.

Then she caught a glimpse of Ysbel. She was struggling ineffectually against her cuffs, and it took three guards to hold her back. A magnetic gag had been clipped across her mouth, but even from under it Jez could hear her muffled cursing.

There were tears running down her cheeks, and Jez swallowed and looked away quickly, feeling sick to her stomach.

Across from her, Tae and Masha stood, cuffed and guarded.

Masha's face was almost expressionless, but there was something hard and hopeless in her gaze. Tae had dropped his head to his chest, as if he, too, couldn't bear to watch what was about to happen.

The warden strode into the room a moment later, and came to a stop before Tanya.

"So," she said. "It appears we've tracked down our thieves."

"I'm not sure what you're talking—"Masha began, but the guard standing next to her backhanded her across the mouth.

"You'll talk when I say you'll talk, and not before," he snapped.

"Really?" Jez said. She couldn't help herself. "Because from what I see—"

The guard beside her didn't even bother to hit her, just pulled out a gag and slapped it across Jez's face.

It was a bit insulting, actually.

Lev looked almost relieved, which was even more insulting.

As if she couldn't make good decisions about whether or not to talk without someone actually gagging her. He just didn't appreciate —

She glanced back at Ysbel, and broke off the thought.

"The weapons were found in this woman's cell," the warden continued, gesturing to Tanya, as if there had been no interruption. "It took us a while to track it down. But, we were fortunate." She smiled, but it was the thin smile of a predator. "Someone tipped us off. And sure enough, when we went to prisoner 4572's cell, we found exactly what we were told we'd find. And," the guard leaned forward slightly, clearly enjoying the moment. "We also found something interesting in our system. The five prisoners our informant pointed to, who had all experienced the same system-glitch two weeks ago. For, it appears, the same reason. Because none of you were supposed to be here."

She shook her head slightly. "It was a clever patch. But we would have found it eventually."

Jez tried to point out that the five of them would have been long gone, along with the entire population of the prison, by five hours from now, so their finding it eventually would have been a bit redundant. With the gag stuck firmly across her face, thought, she couldn't do more than grunt. Which, as a method of insulting communication went, was somewhat lacking.

"So." The warden put a hand on her hip. "What do you have to say for yourselves?"

"I—" Masha began, but Tanya raised her head.

"It was me," she said quietly.

Jez's stomach twisted in sudden horror. Ysbel's eyes widened, and the woman struggled more frantically against the guards holding her.

"I managed to send out a signal and called them here. They were old co-workers of mine. They came because I asked them to, and I offered them plenty of credits."

One of the guards holding Ysbel brought his shock stick down hard across her back, and she fell forwards, unable to use her hands to break her fall. Tanya closed her eyes briefly, then she looked away from Ysbel and fixed her eyes on the guard. "You can take them if you'd like," she said with a shrug. "I don't care. But don't think they'll be able to tell you what you want to know. The plan was mine."

For a moment, there was silence. Then Lev managed to lift his head high enough to catch the guard's eyes. "She's lying," he said through his teeth. "I thought of this plan."

Tanya narrowed her eyes at him. "You are not getting paid. You may as well stop."

"It's true," said Tae, his voice low. "It was us. I hacked the patches into the system to get us in, Lev made the plan."

Ysbel had stopped struggling for a moment, and even through the gag obscuring her face, Jez could see the desperate relief in her expression.

"Let prisoner 9877 go," said Lev, his voice level. "We used her because there was more room in her cell to store the weapons, and she moves around more freely because of the children. She probably thinks she's going to get some sort of leverage from claiming the idea for herself, but she had nothing to do with this."

The warden was looking from them to Tanya, a slight frown on her face.

"Tell me, then, why would you break into a prison?" she asked, her voice heavy with skepticism.

"Because I bankrolled them," said Masha, her pleasant voice sounding eminently reasonable. "For reasons too long to go into, I have a personal grudge against the administrator of this prison on Prasvishoni. I thought it would embarrass him if I could stage a prison break here. Even if I wasn't successful, it would be a stain on his reputation."

Jez turned to stare at her.

Masha? She knew the woman would risk her life for them, probably because she needed them. For something. Jez wasn't certain what, and, to be honest, didn't really care. But for Tanya?

"If that's the case," said the woman, eyes narrowed, "tell me the name of the administrator."

"Lubos Devic. He has an ex-husband and three children, who live with his ex but visit him on the weekends. He speaks a little too loudly, and has a habit of tapping his fingers against the table when he's agitated."

"And his favourite drink is a red nova, with ice," broke in Tanya. "Please. Enough showing off. You will not get paid, even if you parrot back to me everything I told you to get you to do this job."

"That's enough," said the warden. "No one is getting any sort of credit for this. I do not reward criminals." She turned to Tanya. "If you were the one who planned this, then tell me—how did you get these weapons?"

"I made them," said Tanya. "I can tell you the exact design." She avoided Ysbel's eyes. "Pick up a weapon, please. I will explain it to you."

Jez closed her eyes for a moment, swallowing hard against the sickness creeping up her throat as Tanya spoke. The woman sounded so convincing that Jez half-way believed her herself.

"Very well," said the warden at last. "You know too much to be nothing but a fence, like these others claim. So, I'll believe you."

Ysbel threw herself forward again, and the guard shoved the shock-stick into her ribs. Jez winced in sympathy. Ysbel's body jerked on the floor until finally the guard pulled the stick away with a disgusted look on his face. Olya whimpered and buried her face in her mother's legs, and Misko started crying.

Jez glanced guiltily at Tanya. The woman stood with her head up, eyes straight ahead, but a tear ran down one cheek. Tanya brushed it away hurriedly.

"So," said the guard. "I will lock these five up and decide how to deal with them later. You, however, if you have the capacity to plan and execute something like this, are too dangerous to leave in the prison population."

"I do not want to go to the Vault," said Tanya in a low voice, "but I will go."

"No." The warden shook her head. "You won't. I'm afraid you're too much of a risk. I have someone starting up the machine now, and it should be ready in a few hours. I'm sedating you. The children as well," she added, almost as an afterthought.

Tanya's eyes grew wide. "No! The children did nothing."

The warden shrugged, her face cold. "I'm sorry. But they're not old enough to be in here on their own, and I can't have them running around unsupervised. Really, this is better for them as well."

"No! I will find someone. There are plenty of people here who would—"

The warden cut her off with a brusque gesture. "I've made my decision."

"No! Please! I'll—"

The warden gestured, and a guard stepped forward with a gag. He snapped it across Tanya's mouth, and her protests were suddenly muffled.

Misko was wailing, and Olya began to cry as well, awful, helpless cries that suddenly made Jez remember what it was like to be eight years old and afraid.

Her stomach twisted.

She jerked sideways, twisting her arms out of the guards' grip, but before she could do anything more, something hit her across the side of the head and she staggered, momentarily stunned.

Lev, too, was struggling, and Tae was fighting the guards holding him. Even Masha momentarily managed to pull herself out of the guards' grip before they grabbed her again. Ysbel, on the ground, was sobbing, her shouts through the gag sounding like the cries of a wounded animal.

But it was too late. The guards led the struggling Tanya out the door, and shoved the frantically-crying children behind her.

24

When they shoved Jez back into her prison cell, she hardly had the energy to fight. They unclipped her handcuffs, and for half a second she thought that maybe, the moment they left, she'd use Tae's key to open the cell door, she'd find some way of getting to where Tanya was, she'd—

The guard swung the cell door shut, and the lock clicked into place.

"Don't bother," he called through the bars. "The warden changed all the locks. You won't be getting out of here before we have a chance to decide what to do with you."

She tested it, of course. The moment they were out of sight, she strode to the door and pressed the button on her com.

Nothing happened.

She spun around and kicked at the edge of the cot as hard as she could, swearing. There was a cold that had started in the pit of her stomach and was spreading slowly outward, until she felt like she was sitting in a ship where the temp control had gone, and every part of her had gone numb.

The only thing she could see when she closed her eyes was Ysbel's face, Tanya's face, the only thing she could hear was Olya's terrified whimpers.

It wasn't fair. They'd come here to save them, and they'd made it worse.

Sedation.

She kicked the cot again, and swore louder, but her voice sounded weak and choked.

The stupid thing was, she hadn't even cared at first, at least, not much. She'd been so damn stir-crazy that all she'd wanted was to get out again. But then she'd met them. She'd seen Ysbel's face, when she'd seen Tanya again for the first time in years. She'd seen those damn little kids, their solemn faces and their mischievous eyes.

And now she'd killed them.

Well, it hadn't been just her. It had been whichever of the damn prisoners had betrayed them. But the kids were as good as dead. So was Tanya.

So was Ysbel, probably. She'd never seen someone look the way Ysbel had looked when her family was condemned to death in front of her. For the second time.

She dropped down onto the cot, because for a moment she thought she was really going to throw up.

And the thing was, it wasn't just Tanya and the kids.

Radic. He'd actually been her friend. Of everyone in the whole damn prison, he'd actually been her friend. He'd worried about her, played tokens with her, tried to keep her from getting hurt. In his own way, of course, which was kind of a stupid way, but still. The look on his face when she'd told him they could get him out. He hated being locked up almost as much as she did. And now he wasn't getting out either. If the guards had tracked the five of them down, they sure as hell were going to find him, and Tae's friend, and the prisoners who had helped them.

Locked up here for years, all of them. She'd thought she could actually do something about it.

It wasn't fair. None of this was fair. The damn warden, and the damn guards, and the damn system that locked people up for stupid things like protesting and reading the wrong damn books, none of it was plaguing fair.

She was going to be locked up forever, of course. So were Lev and Tae and Masha and the rest of them. Maybe sedated too. Thing was, she hardly had the energy even to care.

She tapped her com to the general line.

"Hey, Tae," she said dully.

For a long moment, no one responded. Finally Tae came on. He sounded like he'd been crying.

"Sorry Jez. There's no way I get us through these locks before they —before Tanya—" he stopped, his voice choking.

"Yeah. That's what I thought. Not your fault," she said dully. "Thought maybe I could break out, get away from the guards. I've done it before, right? But then I couldn't."

No one spoke for a while. At last Masha's voice came through the com.

"I've thought this through. Unless we can find a way to get one of us out, I—" she paused, and for the first time she could remember, Jez heard actual emotion in her voice. "I'm sorry. I wish I had better news."

"I'm sorry too," said Lev quietly. In the background, from his com, Jez could hear Ysbel's quiet sobs.

She slapped her com off.

She couldn't listen to it anymore.

She stood and paced in a small circle around the cell. How many hours did they have? She'd never seen a sedation machine, but she'd heard of them.

Once Tanya and the kids were sedated, the guards would almost certainly come for them.

She'd probably care about that, soon.

Finally, she sank back down onto the cot, head in her hands. She winced at the pressure on her sore arm, but she didn't even have the energy to swear.

She gave a half-smile.

Wouldn't Vlakta be mad that she wouldn't get a chance to beat Jez up again.

Wouldn't that damn Zhurov be mad. Maybe he'd be one of the guards taking her up to be sedated, and she could get in a few more good insults before she went under. Could happen. He was on shift right now.

The thought was almost enough to make her grin, just for a moment.

Then she froze.

No.

No, no, no. Nope. It was a terrible idea. She was definitely not going to do it.

No. The truth was, it was a brilliant idea.

But she couldn't stop the hot fear spreading through her stomach like an acid wash, cutting away at the numbness.

Her heart was beating too quickly. She swallowed hard, but she found her hands shook as she tapped the com.

"Hey," she said, trying to keep her voice steady. "Think I may have figured out a way to get us out of here."

"What is it?" Lev answered immediately, and practically over top of him Ysbel said, "If you can get us out, pilot—" her voice was desperate.

"Well, see," said Jez, trying to grin despite the fear creeping up her limbs. Dumb to be afraid. They were going to be sedated anyways, probably. "Well, see, I have a good friend here."

"Radic got out? How did he——" began Tae.

"Nope. Not him. Got another friend. He really, really wants to see me, I'm pretty sure. In fact, I'm pretty sure he'd make a special trip just to have some one-on-one time with me. And I saw him in this sector, when they were hauling me back to my cell."

There was a moment's pause. Then Lev swore violently.

"No, Jez. That's a terrible idea."

"It's a brilliant idea, genius-boy."

"Zhurov will kill you! Now that you have no protection—he'll kill you. He's been wanting to since the day were got here."

"So?" she shrugged. "Not like he's had any luck so far."

"Jez. Lev is right. He's going to kill you." It was Tae this time.

"But here's the thing. I bet I could steal his key while he was trying. He likes to get up close and personal, I've noticed."

"If you're dead, that won't do any of us any good." Lev was clearly trying to keep his voice reasonable, and failing badly.

"He might not kill me. Anyways, bet he'll have heard of what happened this morning. He'll want to save me for the sedation."

Probably.

She clenched down on her fists to keep her hands from shaking.

"And then what?" asked Masha quietly. "Assuming you're correct, Jez, and he doesn't kill you, and you manage to steal his key, then what?"

She paused. She hadn't really thought farther than that.

A small voice inside her whispered that after the guard got through with her, she wouldn't be up for doing much of anything.

Certainly not breaking Tanya and the kids out of their cell.

"I don't agree with this," said Tae, his voice strained. "I don't agree with this at all. But, if she could get the key to me, I could program it into our coms. It should be enough to get us through the doors."

"There are guards," Lev said bluntly. "You think we can just walk by them?"

"I could take care of the guards." Ysbel's voice was barely audible, and hoarse from tears, but there was something in it that made Jez shiver.

"Ysbel—" Lev began.

"I will not kill them all, if that's what you're worried about," Ysbel said, although Jez wasn't entirely sure she believe her. "I will only threaten them."

"Ysbel. They have weapons. We don't. You used up all your materials on the pin-guns, and the guard confiscated them."

"Perhaps. But I have this."

There was a pause.

"What are you going to do, hit them over the head?" asked Lev at last. "That's the dummy gun, isn't it?"

"Yes. But they don't know that." For a moment, Ysbel sounded a little like her old self. "I think if I threaten them with this, they will get out of the way. If Tae has the key, we can lock them into the cells."

"We can't take their weapons. They're coded to the guards' DNA. So the dummy weapon's all we'll have. You want to break out of prison with a fake weapon?"

"No," said Ysbel. "I want to break even farther into prison, get Tanya and my children, and possibly kill the warden. I want to take down this whole bloody, corrupt place. It's long overdue. And then I intend to break out of prison. With a fake weapon."

Even Jez was impressed at this. She raised her com. "Hey. Ysbel. That's actually pretty hot."

"Piss off, Jez. I'm still married."

"Yeah, well—"

"Piss off, Jez."

"Jez. I can't believe you're encouraging this," said Lev through his teeth. "This whole scheme is ridiculous."

"You're just saying that because you didn't think of it," replied Jez with a smirk.

"No, I—You know what, never mind. I can't believe we're having this discussion." He sounded on the edge of desperation, and for a moment she remembered the bright bruise across his cheek and felt something like sympathy tighten in her chest.

He was a soft-boy. He wasn't supposed to get beat up. He wasn't supposed to be desperate.

He certainly wasn't supposed to be desperate worrying about her.

She swallowed down something in her throat.

"Lev," said Masha at last. Her voice was still calm, but there was an undercurrent of something—fear? Worry? Jez wasn't sure. "While I share your assessment of the situation, it appears to me we have two options—Ysbel's admittedly-risky plan, or waiting to be taken away to be sedated."

"Risky?!?" snapped Lev. "That's not risky. That's suicidal."

"No," said Masha quietly. "Doing nothing is suicidal. This, at least, is a chance."

"I'd be scared of Ysbel. Even without a fake weapon," Jez volunteered. "That's why I like her so—"

"Jez. Shut up."

There was a long moment of silence.

Jez's hands were shaking. She leaned up against the cot, trying to steady herself. Whatever Lev said, this was the only option, and they all knew it.

But—the look on Zhurov's face. The hatred in it. The helpless feeling that evening, when Radic had been shoved into the cell and she'd been alone with the guard in the hallway. He could have done whatever he wanted. He'd known she'd known it, and he'd wanted her afraid.

And despite her bluster, deep down inside, she had been. She'd been terrified, and panicking, and so, so afraid.

"Anyways," she said at last, into her com. Her voice shook slightly. "You'd better figure something out. I'm calling my buddy over."

"Jez! No!"

"Sorry, tech-head."

"Jez—" Lev's voice was shaking too. "I—Masha's right. This is our only chance. But I—you—"

"Relax. I'll be careful." She tried to grin, but she knew he could hear how scared she was. Probably they all could.

"Jez," said Ysbel, in a low voice. "I—I will owe you everything for this."

"Well, better be prepared to pay it."

There was a pause. "I won't kiss you."

"You said—"

"Shut up, Jez."

She took a deep breath. "Well, guess I better make Zhurov's day," she said, in what she hoped was a jaunty tone. "Call you when it's over."

"Jez—"

She tapped her com off and closed her eyes for a moment.

Nothing to it. It'd be fine. Just another beating. She could handle that. Had plenty of practice in the last two weeks. Like drinking. You had to work your way up to it.

She took a deep breath, the another.

It'd be fine. Nothing to worry about.

Still, her legs were trembling slightly as she walked over to the bars.

"Hey!" she shouted. "How do you tell a prison guard from a brush pig?" She waited a moment. "Don't know? Well, to be honest, nor do I."

He should be patrolling this corridor. The routes had probably changed with everything that had happened that morning, but still, he should be there.

"How long do you think it took your mom to figure out she brought the wrong kid home?" she shouted. "And you think she ever felt sorry for the poor brush-pig sow trying to raise a human baby along with the rest of her litter? Hey, I have an idea. You unlock me, and we can go look for the rest of your family!"

There were footsteps coming down the hall now, heavy and purposeful. She swallowed back the bitter taste in her throat. Her stomach was knotted so tight it hurt.

The guard rounded the corner, and she caught a glimpse of his face.

Zhurov.

She swallowed again, tapped her com, and whispered, "Got him. Don't call me."

She tapped her com off as he strode up to the door.

Adrenalin flooded through her veins.

She was going to die. She was definitely going to die this time. And she couldn't stop grinning.

"Hey ugly," she said. "Like my jokes?"

He came close to the bars and pushed his face up against them.

He had an ugly grin on his face.

"Hello there, Jez," he said softly. "Don't think I don't know what you're doing. You're a coward. You don't want to be sedated, and you thought you could get me to kill you first. Your friends who are looking for you—they said you were all talk."

Her heart pounded against her chest. This had to work. He had to come in.

"At least I can talk," she drawled "Some of us, not going to mention names, mostly just grunt. Don't you agree?"

His grin faded. "You think you can taunt me into coming in to kill you. But I'm not that stupid."

"Could have fooled me," she said. "But don't worry, brains aren't everything. They say space-jellies don't even have brains, and they seem to do just fine." She paused, cocking her head to one side. "'Course, they look better than you do. Smell better, too. But can't have everything, I guess."

His eyes narrowed.

She grinned, every muscle in her body tense.

"But here's the thing, Solokov," he whispered. "The thing you didn't think about. I don't have to kill you to make you hurt. And believe me, I know so many ways make you hurt."

"Oh, so there is something you know," she said. "I wondered why they kept you around. Figured it wasn't for your personality."

The lock on the door clicked open.

She had him.

The thought sent a mixture of panic and another shot of adrenalin jolting through her body.

He stepped through, closing the door firmly behind him.

She took an involuntary step backwards, and he smiled. The look was ugly on his thick face.

"I can hurt you without killing you. But sometimes—" he shrugged. "Sometimes I make mistakes."

She swallowed hard.

His smile broadened, and he cracked his knuckles.

Jez stirred. The movement sent lighting bolts of pain lancing through her body and crackling through her brain.

Everything hurt.

No, hurt wasn't the word. It was somewhere beyond hurt, somewhere so far beyond that her brain was struggling to make sense of what had happened to her body.

She couldn't breathe. That was a problem. Some twinge of self-preservation inside her head pulled at her, and, with what seemed like far too much effort, she managed to turn her head to one side and spit a mouthful of blood out onto the floor of the cell. Even that effort made the walls of the cell dance around her.

But she was breathing now. That was good. She knew she was, because of the stabbing pain in her ribs at every shallow gasp.

She closed her eyes and let her head loll back against the wall.

She must've been unconscious before. This seemed like a good time for a repeat performance.

No. There was something she was supposed to do.

What was it?

Didn't seem to matter, since her vision seemed to be fading anyways.

Ysbel. Tanya. Radic.

She blinked, trying to force the encroaching blackness back.

Even blinking hurt.

The key! That's what she was supposed to do. Had she—and then she realized one hand was clenched into a fist, and inside the fist was something small and sharp that cut into her palm.

Slowly, she opened her hand and glanced down, without moving her head.

Inside her palm sat a small key-chip.

She slumped back against the wall in relief, and took quick stock of her injuries.

One eye was already swollen shut, and her nose was puffy and sticky with blood. There was something wrong with her mouth, and a throbbing knot of pain on one side of her jaw. Broken, probably. She probed gingerly at the inside of her mouth with her tongue, tasting blood. She still had all her teeth—that was a bit of a surprise, to be honest—but her lips were split wide open, and dripping blood down her chin. Broken ribs, how many she wasn't sure, but also wasn't sure it would make much difference. Mostly it just felt like someone was trying to stab her with a rusty spike every time she took a breath. Her left arm—she glanced down, and wished abruptly that she hadn't.

She was pretty sure it wasn't supposed to bend like that.

Wait. She still had her com.

With much more effort than it should have taken, she reached her good arm over and tapped the com button.

"Miss me?" she mumbled.

Hell. She sounded like crap.

To be fair, she also felt like crap.

"Jez!" Lev sounded frantic. "Are you OK?"

"Define OK." She had to pause to spit another mouthful of blood.

"Jez." It was Tae this time. "Listen. Did you get the key?"

"Got it." Her words were so slurred that she wasn't sure he'd understand.

She could hardly understand herself at this point.

"OK. Can you unlock your door and get to my cell?"

"Yeah." It hurt too much to talk. "Coming. Minute."

"Alright. I don't want to rush you, but we have maybe an hour left. We need to get going."

"'K."

It was actually quite amazing how many words you could say without moving your mouth. She should remember that. Might come in handy one day.

Her head had dropped back against the wall, her eyes drooping shut.

"Jez. Can you hear me?"

She managed a grimace of annoyance. Whoever it was needed to shut up and leave her alone.

"Jez!"

"Mmm," she mumbled.

"Jez. You have to get up. Can you get up?"

Ysbel. Ysbel and Tanya.

She forced her eyes back open.

Get up. She could get up. Of course she could get up. What kind of a lightweight did they think she was?

The biggest problem with a broken jaw was that it seriously impeded her ability to swear. And getting her bruised body to its feet in the prison cell was an event that demanded swearing, and yelling, and probably some mild-to-moderate blasphemy. But somehow she managed, and stood, bracing herself against the wall, the world swimming around her.

OK, so the floor wasn't going to stand still. That was alright. She'd been drunk plenty of times. She could do this.

She held onto the wall with her good arm, and made her wobbly way over to the cell door.

The guard had thoughtfully closed and locked it when he left.

Damn.

Now she'd find out if this had been worth it.

Painfully, she rested her shoulder against the wall. Her hand holding the chip was shaking.

This had to work.

She hadn't prayed in years. She hadn't prayed since her parents had kicked her out of their house when she was fourteen, and she sure as hell hadn't meant it for years before that.

But, she supposed, if there was a time she could use a prayer, this would be it.

"Lady," she mumbled, clutching the chip in her shaking fingers. "If you're up there—" she swallowed blood. "You plaguing well owe me one, you bastard."

On reflection, maybe it wasn't the best prayer, as prayers went. But it sure as hell was sincere.

She lifted the chip to the lock.

The lock clicked, and the door swung gently open.

She sagged against the wall in relief, her vision dancing with pain.

She'd done it. She was out.

25

Tae, Sector 2, Day 12

Tae wondered, in a small corner of his brain, how long it would take him to wear a groove in the floor of his cell. Surely he should have by now.

Where was Jez?

She'd sounded like hell. She'd sounded like she was on the verge of passing out.

Why had they all agreed to this plan?

Of course. Because it was the only damn plan they had.

He shook his head in frustration, and went back to pacing.

She had to be **OK**. She had to be. She was the most irritating, annoying, frustrating person he'd ever met in his life, she was constantly getting on his nerves, she seemed to know exactly what to do to make an already unbearable situation worse, and he knew, with absolute clarity, that if anything happened to her he would never get over it.

This must be what having siblings was like.

Masha was seated on her cot, head dropped in her hands, her posture one of contained exhaustion. She raised her head to look up at him.

"She'll be fine," she said. Even he could hear the worry under her tone.

He swore violently under his breath.

She shouldn't have run into any guards. Surely Zhurov would have made sure there was no one else on the floor when he beat her.

Still—

He ran his hands over his face and swore again, louder this time.

He almost didn't hear the click of the lock. And then the movement of the door swinging open made him start in surprise.

"Hey tech-head."

He jerked the door open and stood for a moment, staring. Jez swayed in the doorway, then slowly toppled forward. He caught her before she could fall. "Masha," he called through gritted teeth. "Get over here."

"'M fine," Jez mumbled. "Don't need Masha."

She was clearly not fine.

Masha was across to them in two strides, and when she saw Jez, her face went grim.

"I don't have a first aid kit."

"Don't need—kit," Jez mumbled. "Get the damn doors—" her voice trailed off.

Tae cursed. "Masha, I need help."

Masha had already crossed to Jez's other side, and gently lifted the pilot's unbroken arm over her shoulder. Jez whimpered softly, and somehow that sound scared him more than anything else so far.

"Hang on, Jez," he said. "Just hang on. We'll get you out of here."

"Thought—I was the one—got you out."

He rolled his eyes reflexively. "Fine. Just give me the key." He reached down and took the bloodstained chip from her trembling hand.

Damn. Damn, damn, damn. His own hands were shaking.

"Jez. I've got something for the pain," Masha was saying in a low voice. "Can you swallow? Come on Jez."

He wiped the blood off as best he could and slipped it into his com. He pulled up the holoscreen, and let out a quick breath of relief.

He was in. They had their lock-pick back.

It took him only minutes to set the key into his com, and to send it out to the others.

"Lev, Ysbel," he whispered. "We're in. Key on your com. Meet us at the library. This key should open the connecting door."

"How's Jez?" came Lev's voice immediately.

"She's—" He glanced over at the pilot, who was sagging against Masha, somehow managing to swear without moving her mouth. Even looking at her made him feel sick to his stomach. "She's—not good."

To be honest, he wasn't quite sure how she was upright and conscious.

"Can we leave her in the cell? Lock her in?"

"No," said Tae firmly. "She'll be killed. Do you know how many people in this prison would love to settle old grievances with her if she's helpless? And if that guard sees her—"

He glanced at Jez again, and tightened his lips. He was going to have a score to settle with Zhurov if he saw him again.

"Alright. We'll bring her along then," said Lev, and the tone in his voice told Tae that Lev's thoughts were traveling down paths similar to his own. "We'll see you shortly."

He slapped his com off and turned back to Masha and Jez. He bit back the sick rising in his throat and gently put his arm around the pilot, trying not to bump her broken arm.

"Jez? Can you walk? We have to go."

"Yeah," she mumbled. "'M fine."

She sounded about half-conscious.

He glanced over at Masha, who gave him a worried glance in return. Then, supporting Jez on either side, they made their slow way towards the library.

They'd just damn well better not run into any guards, that was all.

26

Ysbel's hands were shaking again.

This was a terrible habit. Trembling hands could get her killed.

But she couldn't seem to stop them.

She'd watched Tanya and her children die in front of her once, five and a half years ago. And then she'd watched it a second time, her wife and children dragged off to a horrible death as she lay helpless and bound on the floor.

She'd thought it would kill her.

She'd wished it would kill her.

And now she was free. She hefted the dummy pin-gun in her hand.

They would wish they had never laid a hand on Tanya. More than that. They'd wish they'd never heard Tanya's name.

Ahead of her, Lev walked swiftly down the corridor, glancing around for any sign of guards. Even in the dimly-lit hallway she could see the tension in his posture.

That stupid, wonderful pilot.

She'd sounded bad. And Tae had sounded sick.

Ysbel shook her head slightly, something between guilt and gratitude tightening her chest.

It didn't matter what Jez did from now on. It didn't matter how much she talked, or how many terrible jokes she made, or that she could never sit still not even for one single second.

Ysbel owed her a debt she could never repay.

They'd get Tanya and the children. And then they'd take down the prison.

She was slightly surprised at how glad the thought made her. She hadn't been lying, back there in her cell. Somehow, in the two weeks she'd spent here, she'd discovered that she did care about the fact that there were these crazy, soft political prisoners locked away in some hole at the end of the system, trapped in a system of bribery and political favours and death to those who didn't matter.

She stepped through the library door after Lev, tightening her grip on the dummy gun.

"We're here," Lev whispered into his com, his voice strained.

"Open the connecting door," Tae grunted, and Ysbel stepped past Lev and held her com to the lock. It clicked, and she pulled the door open.

Tae and Masha stood there, both liberally smeared with blood, and supporting a half-conscious Jez between them.

Ysbel bit back a curse.

She'd seen a lot of injuries in her day. You couldn't work with explosives and not see injuries. But this was different. There was something sick and deliberate about Jez's injuries, the bruise-coloured fist-marks on her face, the way her arm was broken, like it had been twisted until the guard could hear it splinter, the blood clotting and hardening down her face.

She glanced at Lev.

His face had gone completely bloodless.

She'd never seen him furious before. She'd seen him irritated, yes, angry—but this was something different. There was a cold, hard rage in his expression that almost made her take a step back.

"How is she, Masha?" he asked through white lips.

Masha shook her head. "I can't tell, not without a kit. I gave her something for the pain, which isn't going to help how coherent she is."

Jez raised her head. "'M fine. Told you that."

One of her eyes was swollen completely shut, and both lips were split, but she somehow managed something that almost looked like a smirk. Then her eyes went unfocused, and she slumped against Masha.

"Come on, Jez," Masha said in her steady voice. "We have to keep going."

"We can't let her rest somewhere?" asked Lev in a strained voice. Tae shook his head helplessly.

"Where? Where can we leave her where we'll be sure she's safe, and we'll be sure we'll be able to come back for her?"

Jez managed to raise her head again. "Can't plaguing—rid of me that easy," she slurred.

Lev gave a tight shake of his head. "Alright then. We don't have time to lose. Let's go."

"Let me," said Ysbel, stepping in front of him.

She patted the butt of the dummy gun grimly.

This was just one more score she had to settle with these prison guards. And the thing was, she was good at settling scores.

They met the first guard a few steps down the hallway. He took one look at their grim faces and Ysbel's weapon and went for his gun.

"I wouldn't."

At the tone in Lev's voice, the man hesitated.

"Of course," Lev continued. "I'd love to have an excuse to hurt you right now."

There was something frighteningly cold in his voice, and Ysbel glanced at him with new respect.

Slowly, the guard raised his hands.

She'd imagined, when she planned this out, that the gun would have to frighten the guards. Apparently, Lev in this mood was all she needed.

"Hands on the wall," Ysbel grunted. The guard complied. She disarmed him quickly and efficiently, cuffed him with the cuffs on his own belt, and pulled off his com, dropping it on the floor and crushing it beneath her boot. She glanced around, her eyes coming to rest on a supply cupboard.

"Just shoot him," said Lev, voice slightly distant, as if he'd already grown bored of this entertainment.

"I'd like to save my ammunition, I think," she said, gesturing inside the cupboard with the barrel of the dummy gun.

The guard obeyed, with remarkable alacrity.

She closed the door behind him, then brought the makeshift gun butt down on the handle. The thin metal twisted and buckled under the pressure, and she smiled grimly to herself.

They met the second and third guard around the next corner, and left them locked in a bathroom. They seemed relieved to have a locked door between them and Lev. The fourth, fifth, and sixth she brought along, cuffed together in a chain.

Wouldn't be a bad idea to have a bit of a human shield.

"Next passageway to your right, then up the stairway. If they're holding them for the sedation machine, that's where they'll be," said Lev, in that cold, emotionless voice. She cast a glance back over her shoulder.

This version of Lev was one she would not want to get on the wrong side of.

She shoved the three guards ahead of them down the hallway in an awkward half-waddle, prodding them with the barrel of her gun whenever they tried to slow down.

"If you need a break, Ysbel, kill them," said Lev from behind her, just loud enough that the guards could hear. "I'm sure we'll find more."

They sped up noticeably.

"You could just shoot them in the leg," he continued, almost conversationally. "The shock of the burn would likely kill them eventually, but you could get them to keep going for as long as we need them to."

They sped up more.

They met another guard on the stairs, who took one look at them and tried to run. Ysbel pointed her dummy weapon, and he halted dead.

On Lev's suggestion, she left him handcuffed around the door, laying on the floor, his body bent awkwardly with his hands on one side and his legs on the other, and the cuffs connecting them through the hinges. It was a surprisingly practical and effective solution, except for the fact that any person in their right mind wouldn't have thought of it. It required a certain capacity to view the human body as having the potential for much more malleability than it at first appeared.

She smiled tightly to herself. Perhaps she could get used to this new Lev.

Behind her, Jez mumbled something incoherent as she stumbled up the steps, and Lev's face grew more frightening.

Then again, perhaps not.

Then they were in the passageway, and at the end of it was a door.

Ysbel's breath was coming fast and shallow, her heart pounding so hard she thought it might break her ribs.

But this time, her hands were completely steady.

There were guards in the hallway, three of them, and they turned quickly as the prisoners and their hostages burst out of the stairwell. Ysbel shoved the three handcuffed guards ahead of them, their bodies forming a rather effective shield, and the guards by the door, their weapons half-way drawn, hesitated.

"I could shoot them," said Ysbel conversationally, "or I could shoot you from between their shoulders, so that you'd shoot them while trying to protect yourselves. But you won't know which I'll choose unless you finish drawing your weapons. So," she gestured pleasantly with her mock gun. "Go ahead."

"Please, do," said Lev, something deadly in his voice.

The guards looked at one another, and then back at the five of them and their hostages.

Then, slowly, first one, then another, placed the weapons in their hands gently on the ground and stepped away from them.

"Wise move," said Ysbel. Lev stepped around her and kicked the guns out of the way, then cuffed the guards' hands behind their backs with more force than was strictly necessary, and pulled off their coms.

Once the guards had been dealt with, he paused for a moment, propping his arm against the wall and leaning his head against it. He took a long breath, then another. Then he turned, and even in the state he was in he managed to give her a slight smile.

"Well, Ysbel?" he asked quietly. "Are you ready to see your wife?"

She wasn't sure she could breath. She wasn't sure if her heart would be able to keep beating. She wasn't sure if it would even matter.

She gave a slight nod.

"Aright," he said. "I'm going to unlock the door and step back. I don't know what's in there, so shove the guards in first. There are enough of them they'll take most of the fire, I imagine."

The calm calculation in his voice was somehow even more frightening than his earlier anger.

She met his eyes. He held his com up to the door, and the lock clicked. Then he kicked it inward and stepped back.

It was almost embarrassing how quickly the guards inside dropped their weapons and allowed themselves to be handcuffed.

And there, on the other side of the room, a small cell with walls that were transparent reflective glass. And inside them, a slender woman with short brown hair, arms around two children, who had their heads buried in her lap.

For the first time in her life, Ysbel thought she might faint.

She was aware, distantly, of Lev shoving the guards into their seats and cuffing them, of Masha, spattered with blood, disentangling herself from Jez for long enough to come take the gun from Ysbel's nerveless hand.

"Go on," Masha whispered.

Ysbel stepped forward, feeling like she was walking in a dream. She held her com up to the door, and as the lock clicked, Tanya looked up for the first time, reflexively pushing the children behind her. Her face was tear streaked and set. Then she saw who it was standing there, and her eyes widened.

"Tanya," Ysbel whispered. Her voice didn't seem to be working properly. "Olya. Misko. Hello, my loves."

Slowly, Tanya stood. She took two steps forward, as if in a daze, and reached out her hand.

"Ysbel?" she whispered.

And for the first time in five and a half years, Ysbel pulled her wife into her arms, clutching her so tightly she wasn't sure if her arms would be able to let go.

Tanya dropped her head against Ysbel's shoulder, and Ysbel clung to her. Her arms were shaking, and she could hardly see through the tears in her eyes. For the first time since that awful day five and a half years ago, she felt whole.

She heard dimly, in the background, alarms blaring, voices shouting over the prison coms.

Then Lev stepped into the room.

"Ysbel. Tanya," he said grimly. "Looks like our time is up. We'd better go."

27 🐿

Lev, Day 12

Lev stepped back into the guard's room, glancing around quickly. Masha was covering the door with their fake weapon, and Tae, face grim, was holding Jez upright.

He cursed silently. Every time he saw her, the cold anger burning in his chest grew just a little more intense.

He should never have agreed to this. He should—

There was a sound behind him, and he turned. Ysbel and Tanya were bringing the two children, very gently, out of the tiny walled-in compartment. Olya was looking around, blinking, eyes still swollen from crying, but when she saw him, her face lit up.

He cursed again.

And that's why he'd agreed. Because he hadn't had a choice.

"Ysbel. You take Olya, I'll take Misko," said Tanya, lifting the boy into her arms. Ysbel nodded, holding out her hand, and Olya grabbed it.

From outside the room, alarms blared, lights flashing through the crack in the door, muffled shouts and commands coming through the prison coms.

He sighed. No one could say that they didn't do things with style.

"I'll take the gun," Masha said, and Lev nodded, crossing quickly to Jez and Tae.

"Jez," he said softly, not entirely sure of his voice. "I'm going to put your arm around my shoulder, OK?"

She glanced at him blearily, and his stomach twisted at the sight of her bruised face.

"Hey genius-boy," she slurred.

"Don't try to talk," he said, biting back his anger.

There would be plenty of time for that later. Right now, they needed to get out.

"Tae," he said quietly.

Tae nodded, and shifted Jez's weight onto Lev. Her angular body was limp, sweat and blood soaking through her prison uniform.

"Just a minute," Tae whispered. "I'm pretty sure there'll be a master key in here."

Lev shifted his arm gently around Jez's waist, trying to hold her somewhere it wouldn't hurt, but even that movement made her gasp in pain.

He froze, and closed his eyes for a moment.

Someone was going to damn well die for this.

Tae returned a moment later, a grim smile on his face. "There was. If the guards wanted trouble, they have it now. I opened every damn cell in the prison."

"Ready?" said Masha, her voice somehow still calm.

"We're ready," Lev said, voice slightly choked.

"As ready as we're going to be," grunted Ysbel. She leaned over and kissed Tanya briefly on the lips.

"Get a room, you two," said Jez indistinctly.

"Jez. Shhhh," he whispered.

"Alright." Masha gave them one last quick look, then kicked the

239

door open and stepped outside.

"We're clear for the moment," she called back. He glanced at Tae again, and they half-dragged the stumbling Jez from the room. Tanya came next, carrying Misko, and then Ysbel and Olya.

"One moment," said Ysbel. She let go of Olya's hand and stepped back into the guard room. She returned a moment later, tucking something inside her prison jacket.

"Alright," she said. "Let's go."

They started off down the hall, Masha in the lead.

Before they reached the bottom of the first flight of stairs, they began to catch glimpses of the chaos below them. Clusters of guards ran past the stairwell, too intent on whatever they were doing to even notice the rag-tag band of bloody, desperate-looking prisoners on the stairs above them. He glanced at Tae, who had a grim smile on his face.

Apparently the master key had worked, then. Although to be fair, they hadn't been overly subtle about their own escape attempt. Presumably if you locked up a sufficient number of guards someone would notice them, in closets and bathrooms and around door-frames—alright, that one may have been a little extreme. But he'd been quite angry at the time.

He glanced over at Jez's bloodied face and clenched his teeth.

No, he was still quite angry.

She caught her foot on a step and stumbled and gave a small whimper of pain, and his heart almost stopped. Tae caught his eye, his own face drawn with worry, and for a moment Lev was certain that they were thinking exactly the same thing.

If Zhurov happened to show his face, it would be something of a competition as to who got to him first.

They reached the bottom of the stairs and, after a quick glance around, Masha beckoned them forward.

The corridor was empty for the moment, and they hurried down it.

A group of guards sprinted round the corner and almost ran directly into them. Masha pointed the dummy gun in a no-nonsense way, and Ysbel gestured them into one of the empty prison cells.

Good. The prisoners weren't just sitting around, at any rate.

The guards glanced from her to Masha to Jez to Tae to him, and obeyed.

Masha locked them in with the key on her com, and they continued forward.

The alarms were so loud he could hardly think, worming inside his brain and sending a dull, pulsing throb across the back of his skull.

"Were are we going?" he shouted to Tae. Tae shrugged.

"Suggestions?" he shouted back.

Another group of guards pounded around the corner, only to be intercepted by a hard-faced Ysbel and a gun-wielding Masha, and directed into the nearest cell. Once the door had locked behind the guards, Masha fell back slightly so she was walking only a step in front of Jez.

"Whatever's going on, it buys us a chance," she said. "We can't get Tanya and the children out without killing them, but perhaps there's a chance we can hide them until we find a solution."

"Just keep going," shouted Lev. "We'll figure it out as we go. Sounds like the guards are pretty distracted as it is."

It wasn't a good plan. But then, they'd passed the point of good plans a long, long time ago.

Jez stumbled again, head sagging forward. She gave a gasping moan that turned his stomach and slurred out a choked curse.

"Can't—"she muttered, voice shaking with pain.

"Do you have any more painkillers?" he asked through clenched teeth. Masha shook her head grimly and pulled something small and white out of the inside pocket of her jacket.

"I'm going to regret this, I'm certain of it," she said.

"If we can keep Jez conscious and on her feet until we're through this, Masha, I quite honestly don't give a damn."

She dropped the pill into his hand, and he turned to Jez.

"Jez. Come on. Open your mouth."

Her face was drawn, her eyes dull with pain. She shook her head.

"Can't," she muttered. "Hurts."

Her jaw hung at a slightly unnatural angle, and he bit back another wave of nausea.

"Come on, Jez," he said quietly. "It's small. Can you try?"

She looked at him with dull, pleading eyes, and he could feel her body trembling under his arm.

"It's OK, Jez," he whispered. "Just open a little." He paused. "This is what Masha gave you earlier."

She managed to raise an eyebrow slightly, and the corner of her mouth twitched in what was probably supposed to be a grin. He gave a rueful answering grin.

"Come on. This is probably the only time Masha will be offering you drugs."

She managed to open her swollen lips a crack, and he pressed the white tablet into her mouth. She bit down on it reflexively, her head sagging.

"Come on," Ysbel growled. "We don't have time to waste."

"I know," he said shortly. "I'm doing the best I can."

The endless, blaring alarms felt like spikes drilling into his head through his ears, and he clenched his teeth in frustration.

If he could only have two minutes to actually think.

"Our best option is going to be out through the courtyard," he shouted. "If we can get around behind the cell block, there may be some places there we can take cover. There are equipment sheds, and they'll check them, but it may give us something to work with."

Masha nodded, and they set off again at a stumbling run towards the courtyard, he and Tae half-carrying, half-dragging Jez between them.

They ran into three more knots of guards on their way out the door, and left them in various empty cells, but now he was seeing prisoners, too. The noise of voices was growing louder, shouts and yells and the sound of fighting.

Ysbel grabbed one of the prisoners as she ran past, and the woman spun around, hands coming up in a defensive position. Then her eyes widened.

"It's you!" she gasped. "We thought they'd killed you."

"What's going on?" snapped Ysbel.

"Someone unlocked our cell doors. Ivan said it must have been Tae. He got us together, and we're all in the courtyard. Like we planned."

"But you don't have weapons."

The woman gave a sharp shake of her head. "We don't. But they're much more disorganized than they should be, and it took the Rims and the Blood Riots about five minutes to start fighting, and now there's a full-on gang war in the courtyard. I don't know what happened, but the warden hasn't stopped us yet. We have a chance. We figured we may as well take it."

Ysbel let go of her. The woman straightened.

"I'll let them know you're coming," she said with a grin. Then she dashed off down the hallway.

Lev and Tae stared at each other, and from the corner of his eye, he caught the slightest hint of a satisfaction on Masha's face.

For the first time since the guards had jerked them awake out of their cells that morning, he felt an actual smile on his face.

Tae was grinning back at him, his expression a mixture of disbelief and relief. "They actually—"

"I think they're doing it. I think they intend to break out, weapons or no weapons," he said.

Jez raised her head slightly. The painkillers seemed to have kicked in—she looked just as bad as she had before, but some of the sharp desperation was gone from her eyes.

"We getting out then?" she mumbled.

"Yes, Jez," he said, and he couldn't keep the relief from his voice. "It looks like we're getting out."

There was a shout, and the sound of a scuffle from the hallway ahead of them.

"If we survive that long," he amended.

By the time they broke out into the courtyard, whatever organization the breakout may have originally had had devolved into a full-out brawl. Prisoners were shouting and fighting, guards were screaming through the coms and running along the walls, shouting to each other.

He scanned the scene quickly. At a closer glance, the prisoners seemed to have been formed into two or three loose bodies, and they were concentrating themselves into the corners Ivan had pointed out, where the angle of the towers would make it impossible for the wall-cannons to reach them. That, at least, was good. But the key to the plan had been the guards they'd take as hostages.

It appeared they had no hostages, or if they did, it was only one or two. He'd counted on at least fifty or a hundred.

He swore to himself. They'd locked up a dozen guards on the way in and out, but it was too late to go back and get them. And a quick glance at the walls told him that the guards, no matter how unprepared the breakout had caught them, were getting back into position in a depressingly-efficient manner. It would be a matter of minutes before they'd have their long-weapons drawn, and the prisoners would have no choice but to surrender.

"Come on," he shouted to Tae, and dragging the stumbling Jez between them, they pushed forward. Ysbel broke a path for them through to the courtyard, and a moment later they were in the open air.

"We outside?" Jez mumbled, voice sounding vaguely interested. "'S nice."

"What the actual *hell* happened to her?" came a familiar, strained voice. He glanced up to see Radic, a smear of blood across his face and a broken shock-stick in his hand, standing in front of them.

"Long story," said Lev grimly.

"Is she—dead?"

"Do I look dead?" Jez slurred.

They all turned to look at her.

"Yes," said Radic after a moment. He turned to Lev, face a mix of anger and confusion. "What's going on?"

"You tell me," said Lev. "Jez got us out, and we got Tanya and the kids out, and then we came out into this."

"We're not doing well," Radic said grimly. "We don't have weapons, we don't have hostages. They should have shut this down long ago, but something's happened, and they don't seem to be organizing. Even so, there's too many of them, and they have too many guns."

Lev glanced up at the wall. "I give us maybe three minutes before they start firing on us."

"Suggestions?"

"You should try that stuff Masha has," Jez mumbled dreamily. "Better than your cat-piss, I'll tell you that."

"Other than that suggestion," said Radic. "Although," he glanced around, his shoulders drooped in despair, "that may turn out to be the best option, honestly." He shrugged helplessly. "We don't have weapons. That's what's killing us. Ivan is trying to keep everyone out of range of the wall guns, at least, but that will only last until they get their long-guns set up."

Lev glanced across the courtyard, then up at the walls.

Already, the guards were setting up the tripods.

He shared a hopeless look with Tae.

Then Masha strode through the crowd towards them. Somehow, people stepped out of her way, politely, as if they'd suddenly realized it would be a shame to not let this nice, friendly woman through.

Or maybe, he thought, they saw the cold glint in her eye, and realized it would be a Very Bad Decision not to let this woman through.

She pulled out her makeshift gun as she reached them, gave Lev a meaningful glance, then stepped in front of Jez, levelling her weapon at the sagging pilot.

"Stand back, or we kill the plant," she shouted.

For a moment, the noise around them faded. Radic stared at Lev, and Lev gave a quick shake of his head.

"I mean it," Masha shouted. "We're already half-way there. Stand down!"

The guards on the wall looked at each other in confusion. The prisoners stared at them as well, and moved inconspicuously away.

Lev couldn't blame them, to be honest. There was something terrifying about Masha's air of competence, and the businesslike way she held the dummy gun.

"They know she's not a plant, don't they?" Radic whispered to Lev. Lev shook his head again.

"I—think so. But the shifts just changed. Maybe word hasn't been passed on yet."

Behind them, he heard someone scrambling through the crowd of prisoners. He glanced over his shoulder, and swore.

"It's Vlatka,'" he said through his teeth. "Radic—"

Radic managed to catch the furious woman before she could reach the half-conscious Jez, shoving her back.

"This is not the time," Radic growled.

"Better hurry, I'm not going to be able to hold them off for long," said Masha, her voice hard and businesslike. "The other prisoners aren't too happy there was a plant in the middle of us."

A couple of guards started down the stairs from the walls. More stood as if not entirely sure what to do.

"Get her back," Masha shouted to Lev.

He glanced at Tae, who shrugged helplessly, and they started pulling Jez back into the crowd of prisoners.

Off behind them, the situation between Radic and Vlatka had devolved into a full-out brawl.

One of the guards reached the courtyard floor, and someone shouted from the wall, "No! Don't go in there! She's not—"

Another guard reached the floor. Up on the wall, Lev caught sight of another guard's furious face. She was shouting something to two guards in front of her. They nodded, grabbed two more guards to accompany them, and pounded down the steps, presumably to stop the first three guards who were already on the ground.

Lev turned back to the fight behind him. "Go!" he hissed at Radic. The man pulled himself back from the fight, glanced around quickly, and nodded his understanding. He jerked his head at a handful of other prisoners, and they spread out to the sides around where Lev and Tae supported Jez.

"What's—" Jez began groggily.

"Not the time for it," Lev hissed. She turned a fair approximation of a glare on him.

"I'll shoot her! Stay back!" Masha shouted.

"Why's Masha shooting me? What'd I do?" she mumbled. "Must've been good."

"Jez, shhh."

The guards spread out, focused grimly on Masha, weapons drawn.

"I'll shoot her," Masha snapped, holding the dummy gun to Jez's head.

Behind the three guards stalking towards Masha, the four guards the warden had sent had reached the ground and were pounding towards them.

The moment they were close enough, Lev caught Radic's eye and gave a faint nod.

Radic grinned. He gestured to the other prisoners, and they sprang forward, grabbing the guards around their necks or by their gun-arms and yanking their hands behind their backs.

"Cuff them," Radic shouted, then grabbed one of the guns and swung it, hitting the guard he'd just disarmed in the temple. The man collapsed, and Radic hoisted him up by the arms and pulled him backwards into the crowd.

More guards were pouring down the stairs now, weapons drawn, but the prisoners were using their hostages to their advantage, and the guards pouring onto the field didn't dare shoot.

Atop the wall, guards were shouting instructions that, it seemed, no one could hear, and other guards were frantically retracting the stairs.

But it was too late.

Lev glanced around quickly.

There were no armed guards on the ground any longer. Every one had been disarmed and cuffed with brutal efficiency, and were now being guarded by a knot of prisoners each.

And, looking at their faces, he realized that they wouldn't need weapons to threaten the guards' lives.

Slowly, the shouting on the walls died down, and the courtyard gradually stilled as well.

He held Jez closer, pulling her weight onto his shoulder, relief making his legs weak.

Masha smiled broadly. She tossed the dummy gun to Ysbel, who caught it expertly in one hand, her other still holding firm to Olya.

"Now," Masha called up to the guards on the wall. "It looks like we need to sit down and have a talk."

28

Ysbel looked around the courtyard, smiling broadly, then glanced down at the little eight-year-old who's hand was still clasped in hers. Olya was grinning as well.

Somehow, they'd pulled it off.

Somehow, impossibly, they'd pulled this ridiculous suicide plan off.

Tanya met her eye, and for a moment, Ysbel thought her chest might break open from the happiness flooding through her.

"We'll need you to drop your guns," Masha called. "I'd hate for something to happen to these guards."

Ysbel glanced around again, impressed despite herself by Radic and Ivan. They'd managed to gather the groups of prisoners into two loose knots. In the front were the hostages, and behind them, shielded by the hostages from the long-range guns of the guards and out of reach of the wall cannons, they were impossible to hit.

Tanya came close, and Ysbel leaned in and gave her a lingering kiss, blinking back tears.

They'd done it.

It was the noise that alerted her. For a moment, between the noise of the prisoners and the noise of the guards, it hardly registered in her brain, the metallic scraping, grinding sound from the walls.

Then she looked up. Her whole body went cold with horror.

Tanya followed her gaze, and drew in a quick breath.

"Masha," said Ysbel, just loud enough to be heard. "Lev. Tae. I think we miscalculated."

Masha glanced over at her with just a hint of irritation, then followed her gaze.

Lev was already staring, grim-faced, and Tae looked like someone had punched him in the stomach.

On the walls, the towers were pushing apart as the guns rolled forward, creaking on the thick rails.

"Manual," Tae whispered. "No wonder I couldn't hack them. They're manually-operated." He swore bitterly. "I should have guessed. I should have thought of that."

The warden strode out onto the walls.

"Stand down, prisoners." Her voice was tight. "Release the guards, or so help me, I'll have those who are left of you cleaning up bits of your friends off the grounds for the next week."

The cannons, on their new trajectory, were pointed directly at the mass of prisoners.

Ysbel's whole body felt sluggish with a sort of sick horror, the blood thick in her veins, her heart struggling to pump, her muscles struggling to react.

She swallowed down the bitter despair coating her throat, forced her lungs to breathe in.

"Masha. We'd best stand down," she said quietly.

Masha glanced behind her at where Lev and Tae were supporting the bloodied Jez, then over at Tanya and the children. Her gaze lingered on Misko for a moment, and Ysbel was surprised at the softness in her face.

She turned to Radic, who had come up beside them.

"Ysbel says stand down," she said quietly. Radic nodded. His face was pale. He turned to the prisoners behind them.

"Go ahead," he said, just loudly enough to be heard in the now-silent crowd. "Let them go."

Slowly, the prisoners stepped back from the guards. The guards, hands still cuffed, gathered in a small knot.

"Stay back," the warden called. "If anyone comes within three metres of them, I'll order the gunners to fire."

No one moved as the stairs were let down again, and a group of grim-faced guards came down. A handful of them held their weapons on the crowd as the others pulled the handcuffed guards back to safety.

They didn't retreat up the ladder with the others. Instead, more guards came down to join them. The expressions on their faces told Ysbel that whatever was going to happen next, it wasn't going to be good.

"Olya," she whispered. "I need you to do something for Mama, OK? I need you to stand behind me. I need you to keep your eyes closed, OK sweetheart? I don't want you to look." She bent down and looked into the girl's small, stubborn face, pale with fear.

"Olya. Mama and Mamochka will try to keep you safe. Do you understand me?"

Olya nodded, her face still pale.

"I love you, Olya."

"I love you, Mama." Her voice was almost inaudible.

Tanya had come to stand beside them. She lifted Misko down off her hip. "Olya, my sweet. You need to watch your brother. Can you do that for me? Just like we do on work shift?"

Olya looked between Ysbel and Tanya and nodded solemnly.

"And Misko, you listen to your sister. Alright? Just like in work shift."

Misko nodded, clutching his sister's hand.

Tanya kissed them both on the forehead. Ysbel did the same, running her hand over Misko's soft hair, something thick in her throat.

Her children.

She blinked back tears as she turned back.

She was side by side with Tanya, their bodies shielding the children. Tanya slipped her hand into Ysbel's and Ysbel squeezed it tightly.

"I love you," she whispered.

"I love you too," Tanya whispered back. "I have always loved you."

She glanced up. Masha had moved closer as well, adding her body to theirs. It wouldn't do much, not if the guards started shooting. But still, the sight of it made a lump rise in her throat.

Lev had moved closer too, with Jez leaned awkwardly against his shoulder.

She frowned. Where was Tae?

Then she saw him, a few meters away. He had his com up, and was typing into it frantically. She shook her head fondly.

He wouldn't give up. He wouldn't ever give up. Two weeks of trying to hack into the wall cannons with no success, but he wasn't going to let them die without trying one more time.

"Well," she said softly. "I suppose that we have lost for good this time. We don't even have our crazy pilot to break out and save us anymore." She paused. "I am sorry. I'm sorry I brought you into this. But—" she swallowed back tears. "But I will die here, with my wife and my children, and—and with my friends. For that, I thank you."

"Sorry we didn't do a better job at all this," said Lev quietly, giving her a wry smile.

Masha said nothing. But there was a look on her face that told Ysbel more than Masha probably wanted her to know.

She looked up again. The guards were starting towards them.

She squeezed Tanya's hand one last time. At least this time, they'd die together.

She supposed, in the end, that was all she could ask.

29

Jez looked around her with bleary eyes.

Apparently, they were all going to die.

Nothing new there, really.

It was hard to care too much at the moment. Whatever had been in the white pill that Masha had given her had granted her a sort of serenity. It still hurt—everything still hurt. She wasn't actually sure that there was a muscle in her body that didn't hurt. On the other hand, she cared a lot less, which was probably a good thing. Considering.

Behind her, Tanya and Ysbel stood side by side. She smiled fondly.

If they were all going to die, it was kind of nice that at least those two'd get to die together. Ysbel would probably appreciate that.

She was upright, somehow, and she couldn't quite figure out why. By rights, she should be on the ground. If her injuries hadn't done it, whatever Masha had given her sure as hell would have. But she was standing.

Oh. She glanced over. Lev stood beside her, looking ahead at the approaching guards, grim-faced. His arm was around her loosely, and she was leaned up against his shoulder.

It was kind of nice, actually. If she was going to die with somebody, she was suddenly glad that it was going to be with this soft scholar-boy. There was something about him.

And, the nice thing was, she didn't have to think too hard about it, because they were, in fact, both going to die.

Although, she thought vaguely, if they didn't die, it might be nice to be leaned up against him one day when she wasn't either beat up or completely smashed. Or, in this case, both.

She'd have to think about that, if they survived this.

The guards stalked towards them, faces grim, weapons drawn. The other prisoners had mostly drawn back, but, to her gratification, Radic stood alongside them. So did Tae's buddy, Ivan.

Although, come to think of it, she couldn't remember seeing Tae lately. She was pretty sure that at some point he'd been helping Lev hold her upright, since her legs didn't appear to be functioning anymore, but he wasn't there now.

She glanced over just to make certain.

And then, pushing through the guards, came a figure that was far too familiar. Even in her state, something cold and sick grabbed her chest when she saw him, and beside her she felt Lev stiffen.

Zhurov grinned at her with his little, beady, brush-pig eyes. There was something savage and triumphant in his expression.

"Hey there," she said, her words slurring with a mixture of split lip and Masha's painkiller. "Glad you came. I didn't have enough ugly in my morning yet."

He scowled. Beside her, Lev gave an exasperated sigh. "Do you have to?" he whispered.

"Yep." She tried to grin, but it was harder than it looked, since her lips seemed to have swollen to at least twice their normal size, and there was something wrong with her jaw.

She shrugged philosophically.

Hardly mattered now.

The dull 'boom' from outside the walls hardly even caught her attention.

The same couldn't be said for the guards. The stopped, their postures tense.

There was another 'boom."

This time she glanced over, faintly interested.

If the guards were so curious, maybe it was worth taking a look.

Another boom, and the ground of the courtyard shook slightly. Beside her, Lev stiffened.

"What—" he whispered.

The courtyard shook again, and the guards on top of the wall staggered. A few chunks of broken prefab blocks tumbled to the ground.

This was actually quite interesting. More interesting than watching the guards come to kill them.

On top of the wall, the warden was shouting frantically. Guards ran towards the wall cannons, shoving frantically in an attempt to turn them to face something outside the walls.

Another explosion shook the grounds, and one of the guards toppled off the outside of the wall.

And then a shape rose above the prison walls. For half a second she stared at it blankly. And then, for the first time since she'd woken up in her prison cell after the beating, her mind snapped back into laser focus.

"Tae!" she screamed, ignoring pain in her jaw. "You bastard! What the hell are you doing with my ship!"

"Jez!" Lev grunted as she tried to push herself upright and almost toppled over.

"He's got my ship! He's controlling my damn ship! Tae! You dirty bastard! Let go of my ship!"

Tae glanced up at her and gave a tight grin. "Give me a minute, Jez," he called. "I'm in the middle of saving your life right now."

"Forget about my damn life, worry about my ship!"

The guards were frozen, staring around them.

"Go!" Lev hissed to Radic.

"Come on!" Radic shouted over his shoulder, and the other prisoners started forward after him, just a handful at first, then a trickle, then a flood. The guards turned to run, but it was far too late.

Ysbel grabbed the nearest guard by the collar, brought him close, and dropped him with a head-butt to the bridge of his nose. Tanya grabbed another, and did something quick and graceful that Jez's eyes couldn't quite follow, and the guard she was holding dropped bonelessly to the ground. Jez raised an eyebrow. Maybe she needed to get to know this Tanya woman a little more. Masha, too, seemed to be using her fists in a way that was just as frighteningly competent as everything else about her.

"Lev," she muttered. "Let go of me."

"You're going to fall over," he said through his teeth.

"Might not."

"You are going to stay out of this." He dragged her over to a nearby wall, lowered her gently into a sitting position, and propped her up against it. "Stay there."

On the one hand, she'd never liked doing what she was told. On the other, she probably couldn't disobey if she wanted to.

He turned and snatched a shock-stick one of the guards had dropped, tested its weight, then swung it hard into the head of a guard who was running towards them. The man dropped, and Lev shuddered in distaste. She could almost picture the look on his face.

Outside the walls, her beautiful ship was firing at the walls, hovering above the ground. The sight of it still sent a jolt through her.

Damn that Tae.

Still, wasn't much she could do about it, since he seemed determined to ignore her. And, he hadn't crashed it yet, which was quite frankly more than she'd expected.

The all-out brawl in the courtyard was going in the direction of the prisoners by this point. And—

Another explosion, louder than the others. The force field above them seemed to shimmer and falter slightly, although that could have been either her swollen eyes, or Masha's pill.

She glanced down at a sound on the courtyard in front of her.

It was Zhurov. But for once, he wasn't looking at her. He seemed to have dropped his gun, but he'd managed to grab a chunk of pre-fab block, and was running at Lev. Lev hadn't noticed him yet, still turned to face the guards in front of them.

"Lev!" She tried to shout, but her words came out as a garbled mess. Lev didn't even look up.

Damn.

Damn, damn, damn.

Thank the Lady and all the saints for Masha and her pills, because she was pretty certain she was going to regret this. She shoved herself against the wall, and managed a few garbled swear words, even through her swollen lips.

Damn. Her head was spinning, and the whole world seemed to sway under her, but she was on her feet.

She was going to pass out. She was one hundred percent certain she was going to pass out.

"Lev," she called again, and this time he heard her and started to turn.

Zhurov had almost reached him. But he hadn't noticed Jez.

He'd broken her arm. She was pretty certain she remembered that, and probably wouldn't forget it any time soon. But he hadn't broken her leg.

She took a shallow breath, braced herself against the wall with her good arm, and swung her knee up, just as he passed her.

She felt it connect solidly with the portion of the guard's anatomy she'd been aiming for.

His shout rose by three octaves, and he folded in on himself, clutching at his groin.

"Bastard," she muttered, collapsing back against the wall. Her head was still spinning, blackness encroaching on her vision. But she could see well enough to see the look in Lev's face as he turned and saw the guard.

"Right kind of crotch," she whispered. "Told you."

Lev smiled, ever so slightly, then turned to Zhurov.

She felt very, very glad for a moment that she was not in Zhurov's shoes.

Lev raised his shock stick.

"You, my friend," he said, his voice low and almost friendly, "deserve something much, much worse than this. And believe me, you'll get it. But right now, I'm busy."

He swung the stick. Jez winced, but when she looked back, Lev was standing over the fallen guard, calmly handcuffing him.

She noticed, absently, that Lev was cuffing him at the elbows, instead of at the wrists.

She'd had that done before. Hurt. A lot.

Lev didn't look at all sorry. His face showed nothing but a sort of interested calculation.

She raised an eyebrow at him.

Maybe not such a soft boy after all.

Then there was another boom, this one loud enough that it was impossible to ignore. She looked up.

The force field was gone, and in place of the nearest wall cannon, there was a thick cloud of fine dust, glittering in the morning sunlight.

30

Tae, Day 12

Tae barely glanced up at the noise of the explosion. He didn't have to.

He'd done it.

The relief that flooded over him was so strong his hands were trembling.

He clenched his teeth and took a steadying breath. He couldn't afford to mess up. Even one of the wall cannons would cause unimaginable casualties among the prisoners, and if he scratched Jez's ship, she would probably kill him, bring him back to life, and then kill him again.

He didn't watch the ship—he couldn't afford the distraction. Instead, he stared at the blip on his screen that showed him where it was.

There. Fire.

Behind him, another section of the wall vaporized.

Whatever you said about Ysbel, the woman knew how to make good weapons.

"Tae!"

He didn't look up. He didn't have the time or the energy to spare.

There were five more cannons on this wall, and they were already pointing towards the ship.

Jez was going to kill him. If he managed to keep her alive, she was definitely going to kill him.

He'd been working on controlling the wall cannons for two weeks. Two plaguing weeks.

And it wasn't until the wall cannons moved that he realized two things: first, he'd never have been able to hook into the wall cannons because they were manual. He should have figured that out a long time ago, and he'd probably be cursing his own stupidity for at least a month over it. But, second, in an attempt to get into the wall cannons—he'd hacked into the *Ungovernable*. One of the few ships he knew of with the firepower to take out a prison-level shield and wall cannons.

And now their fears about the prison going into lockdown over it had become completely irrelevant.

"Tae!"

The voice, he realized, belonged to Masha. And she sounded afraid.

He frowned and glanced up.

The courtyard had devolved into a mass free-for-all of fighting, struggling prisoners and guards, and the top of the wall was pandemonium, as guards ran and shouted and bumped into each other, trying to point the wall cannons and at the same time stay out of the way of the Ungovernable's guns.

But the area where he was crouched was almost empty of people, except for one—a guard. A guard with his heat-gun drawn, and a grim, deadly look on his face.

For half a second, Tae's instincts screamed at him to run.

But if he ran, he'd lose his control, and he'd lose the guns, and his friends would die. He turned back to his com, grim-faced. Three more cannons. That was all.

If he worked fast enough, he'd make it.

He pressed the controls to fire, and another wall cannon evaporated.

The guard was getting closer, almost in range.

Another cannon vaporized, and he pointed the *Ungovernable* at the final cannon.

The guard in front of him raised the pistol so it was pointed directly at his head.

He didn't look up. He didn't have the time. He let loose a final blast from the ship, then, hands trembling, set the controls to hover the *Ungovernable*, keeping her in the air, so when he got shot, the ship wouldn't crash. He couldn't do that to Jez.

Even though she wouldn't be able to kill him now.

He felt surprisingly calm as he lowered his controls and looked up into the barrel of the heat gun.

He'd assumed he was going to die, from the moment they'd set foot inside the prison. But this time, he'd actually won. He'd saved them—at least, he'd given them a chance.

He thought, somehow, that Caz and Peti, back on Prasvishoni, would have been proud of him.

"Step away from him."

Ysbel's voice was hard and cold and flat. He glanced over in sudden, desperate hope.

She was too far away to get to him in time, but she was holding the dummy weapon, and it was pointed directly at the guard.

The guard looked at her, and gave a grim smile.

"I was the one who confiscated the weapons," he said, voice hard. "I know that's not a real gun."

Tae blew out a breath, hope fading back into that strange calm.

He almost smiled. It was honestly amazing they'd gotten as far as they had on this bluff.

The guard turned back, steadying his gun.

Then the air around him shimmered with heat, and the guard's eyes went wide. The smell of singed flesh and hair thickened the air. Slowly, the gun fell from the guard's nerveless fingers, and slowly, face still frozen in an expression of shock, he tumbled forward to land on the dust of the courtyard.

Tae stared at the man lying on the ground in front of him. Then he turned and stared at Ysbel.

She looked down at her gun with a satisfied air.

"What—" Lev began, in a shocked voice.

"He did confiscate the weapons," Ysbel said. "But, he didn't confiscate the one that was left in the guards' room."

"You were carrying that since we left the guards' room?" Tae asked, voice weak with stupefaction. "And you didn't use it?"

She shrugged. "I didn't need to until now."

Tae looked back at the guard, lying face-down two metres away from him.

He realized, suddenly, that he needed to lean against the wall or his legs were going to give out on him.

Around him, people shouted and cheered, but the noise sounded somehow distant.

On the walls, the prison guards were still scrambling about in confusion, but the warden stepped forward.

Slowly, deliberately, she raised her weapon over her head so they could all see it, then lowered it to the ground in front of her and stepped back.

Masha nodded in satisfaction, and the cheers grew deafening. Tae stared around him bemusedly. Then someone put a hand on his shoulder. He glanced up. Ivan stood there, smiling broadly.

"Well, Tae," he said quietly. "It appears you've done what you said you'd do."

Tae tried to smile back, and found for the strangest reason there were tears in his eyes instead, and a thick knot of happiness in his chest that almost made it hard to breathe.

31

Lev, Day 12

Lev stared around him. The guards on the wall were following the example of the warden, lowering their weapons.

"We'll talk," shouted the warden from the top of the wall. Masha nodded, and the woman made her way down into the courtyard.

Lev tapped his com on a private channel. "Ysbel. Can you watch Jez? I'm going with Masha, to make sure she doesn't agree to anything crazy."

"Of course," said Ysbel. "Is she still conscious?"

He glanced back at Jez and clenched his teeth. She was leaning up against the wall, but her face had gone very pale, and she looked like she might throw up.

"Yes," he said shortly. He tapped off his com and crossed over to her. "Hey. Jez," he said softly. Her eyes were closed, but she forced them open with an obvious effort.

"'S?"

"I have to go take care of something. Ysbel's going to be here until I get back, OK? And then we'll get you somewhere where you can lie down."

"Mm."

He studied her for a moment, chest tight.

"Go on," said Ysbel, from behind him. "I'll take care of her. I promise."

He nodded tightly, then turned and strode off to join Masha. He caught Radic's eye on the way over and gestured him to follow. The man disentangled himself from a crowd of celebrating prisoners and hurried over.

"Get Ivan and come over," said Lev in a low voice. "I'd like you all to be part of whatever Masha's negotiating."

Radic nodded his understanding and slipped away.

With the three of them present with Masha, the negotiations were short and simple. The warden noted the prisoners would die if they left, and that she couldn't override the chips without an authorization key from Prasvishoni, even if she'd wanted to. Masha suggested that, since that was the case, the woman should have no concerns about letting herself and the other guards be locked safely in the cells, as it would certainly be no more than temporary. The warden countered that she'd prefer her people not be killed by angry prisoners as retribution. Masha was not overly sympathetic, but seemed to imagine that as long as the guards went quietly, it wouldn't be much of a problem.

With the exception of one particular guard, Lev put in.

With the exception of one particular guard, Masha amended.

In the end, the warden didn't have much of a choice, and she knew it. Lev watched in grim satisfaction as Radic and Ivan directed prisoners to lead the guards into cells and lock them in, after first removing the key chips from their coms.

"How long until help comes," Lev asked the warden bluntly.

"I don't—"

He stepped closer. "Listen to me. I'm not in a very good mood right now, and I'd appreciate if you didn't play games. How long?"

She took one look at his face and gave a sigh of resignation. "About six standard hours."

"Thank you." He glanced at his com. "I hope you're telling the truth. Because I'm gong to ask my friend to set explosives at the door to each of your cells. She'll disable them in five and a half standard hours. And if anyone should try to get through the prison walls prior to that, they'll go off."

The warden paled. "I—That is, my understanding is that—"

He leaned closer, a slight smile on his face. "Your understanding had better be correct, then, warden."

"I—you'd risk killing us all if my calculations are off?"

He smiled a little wider, but there was no humour in it. "Well. You were willing to kill two children, horribly, because you didn't want them to be a bother. And you were willing to let one of your guards beat my friend almost to death because you thought the guard was useful." He paused a moment. "Do you know how it feels to be beaten almost to death? If you're interested, I'm certain I could arrange something."

She shook her head rapidly.

"I thought perhaps you wouldn't. So—" he shrugged. "Yes. I'm comfortable taking that risk."

As a small group of prisoners led the much-subdued and slightly pale warden off towards a cell, hc noticed her talking very quickly on her com.

Whether she'd been telling the truth about the timeline before or not, he was now relatively certain that no one would show up at the prison gates prior to six standard hours from now.

Masha was watching him, one eyebrow raised. He glared at her.

"What?"

"Nothing," she said with a faint smile. "I was only thinking that you have more capacity for intimidation than I would have imagined."

"Trust me, Masha" he said through his teeth, "that was not intimidation. That was explaining the damn future."

"I see." She was still smiling slightly. "And now, shall we call Tae? It appears that we have about two thousand people we need to break out of prison."

Tae brought the *Ungovernable* down gently into the courtyard. Jez, who was now almost incoherent from pain or painkillers or both, still managed to curse Tae fluently until the ship had come to a rest. Then she slumped back against the wall, whimpering quietly.

Lev glanced over his shoulder at her, gritting his teeth.

"Masha. Can you fly her?" he asked quickly.

"Yes. Despite what Jez may think, I am a fairly experienced pilot."

"Alright. Tae, how many do we need to get over the wall at once to short it out?"

Tae frowned. "Anything over a hundred should do it, I think," he said at last. "I would say a group of two hundred to be safe. We'll have to pack people in. The ship's force field will level out the effect of the shock-chip, so variances in height of the prisoners won't make a difference."

"Good. We don't have a lot of time. Let's start—"

"Lev."

He turned quickly. Ysbel had a concerned look on her face. "I think you'd better come over here," she said.

He drew a breath and crossed quickly over to where she was standing beside Jez.

"She's asking for you," Ysbel said quietly.

"Jez." He hesitated, then put a hand gently on her shoulder. "Jez, what do you need? Are you alright?"

The bruises on her face were swollen and misshapen, and the front of her uniform was streaked with drying blood. She managed to blink her eyes open, and the corner of her mouth twisted up in a gruesome approximation of a grin.

"Hey genius-boy," she whispered.

"Jez. What is it?" he asked.

"You know," she began with an effort, her voice so quiet he had to lean in to hear her. "There's a split in the butt of your pants."

He stared at her for a moment. Then Ysbel gave a badly-concealed snort of laughter.

"There is, you know," she said, when she'd recovered herself. "You must have been very intimidating, since I didn't notice until just now."

He turned and glared at her, tugging his jacket down to cover it. Jez made a noise that was probably supposed to be a laugh. Then she swayed slightly, eyes rolling back into her head, and collapsed.

Lev swore and dropped to the ground beside her.

"Ysbel. Help me. Masha, get a first aid kit, now," he snapped.

Jez's eyes were closed, her body limp. He pressed two fingers frantically against the side of her throat. His hands were shaking, he noticed vaguely.

There was a pulse—weak and rapid, but there. He let out a long breath, shoulders slumping in relief.

At least she was still alive. Although you wouldn't know to look at her.

Ysbel knelt at Jez's other side, and a moment later, Masha appeared with a first aid kit from the ship.

Ysbel carefully straightened Jez's broken arm, then ran the medi-scaner down the back of her head and neck and down the sides of her torso.

"Broken arm, at least four broken ribs," she muttered to herself. "Her neck is fine, I think, but then again, if it hadn't been, we'd have known by now." She ran the scanner along Jez's bruised, swollen face and shook her head. "Her jaw is broken too. I'm not surprised. Actually, I'm surprised she stayed on her feet for as long as she did."

She pushed herself to her feet. "We'll get her on a stretcher and get her into the med bay. I'm no doctor, but I should be able to—"

Lev stood and grabbed one of the prisoners by the arm.

"Get me Ivan. Right now," he said. Something of what he felt must have shown through his voice, because the woman obeyed with remarkable haste. A few moments later, Ivan stood in front of him.

"I need a doctor. And I expect the best damn doctor in this damn prison, and I don't care whether they're a prisoner or a damn guard."

Ivan looked at Lev, then down at Jez, and nodded, just a hint of amusement in his face. A few moments later, he returned with a woman in a prison uniform, with a weary, competent face.

"Here you are," said Ivan. "This is Lucic. She used to be one of the top surgeons in Prasvishoni, until she got thrown in here. The guards still use her if someone gets badly injured."

"Have you practiced recently?" Lev snapped. The woman nodded.

"I did a major surgery three weeks back, and I'm in the med bay here almost daily." She paused, her voice sharpening slightly. "If I understand correctly, my last two weeks of work were largely contributed to by this woman." She glanced down at Jez, and her face softened slightly with concern.

"A beating?" she asked.

"Zhurov," he said shortly. She nodded, face grim, and knelt beside the fallen pilot, performing the same checks that Ysbel had, then stood back and gestured Ysbel forward with the stretcher. Ysbel lowered it beside Jez, and between them, the two women lifted the unconscious Jez onto the stretcher. Jez didn't even stir.

"Has she had anything since the beating?" Lucic asked.

"Yes. Painkillers."

"What kind?"

He glanced at Masha.

"Halprenal," said Masha. The surgeon raised an eyebrow, and so did Lev.

"How many?"

"Two. It was the only way to keep her on her feet."

Lucic shook her head. "Your pilot must have a head like a swamp ox. I'm surprised she could stay on her feet after two halprenal."

"That's because you don't know Jez," Lev muttered. Lucic cracked a slight smile.

"I'm beginning to believe that."

"I'm not saying you should," offered Ysbel, "but if you do get a chance to wire her mouth shut, I'm not going to complain."

Lev glared at her. "Ysbel. As I recall, the only reason she's in this position is because she was trying to save your life."

Ysbel looked at him, eyebrows raised. "I understand that. And I will always be grateful to her. But don't tell me that if we have the chance to wire her mouth shut, you would choose to not wire her mouth shut."

He sighed and turned back to Lucic. "Do what you need to do. But please, do it in the least invasive manner possible. She saved a lot of lives today."

"And believe me, she isn't going to let any of us forget it," Ysbel muttered.

Masha stepped forward, and she and the surgeon lifted the stretcher gently. Lev gritted his teeth as he watched them walk into the ship.

He needed to stay here. He'd been responsible for this, at least partially, and someone needed to make sure everything—

"Lev." He turned. Ivan stood there, watching him in slight amusement. He gestured with his chin to the *Ungovernable*. "Go on. Tae and Radic and I will take care of the rest of it."

He hesitated. "I don't—"

"Go on," Ivan said gently, his smile broadening slightly. "I think you've done more than enough. The rest of us can take a turn now."

Lev glanced around indecisively, then finally he shook his head and sighed.

He wasn't going to be much good to anyone anyways, at this point.

Ysbel, on his other side, smirked at him and leaned over. "I think everyone on this planet knows how you feel about that crazy pilot woman now. Except maybe the crazy pilot woman."

He glared at her. Then he shook his head ruefully, and followed Jez into the ship.

32

After

"Masha."

She glanced over from her seat beside a small table, pushing aside the holoscreen on her com where she'd been studying a long list of document from a chip. Tae stood at the door to the main deck. His face was lined with exhaustion, but he looked happier than she'd seen him in a long time.

She was mildly surprised at the weight of relief the thought brought her. Perhaps two weeks in a cell with the street-boy had done something to her.

The thought was not entirely comfortable.

"Yes Tae?" she said, in a pleasant voice. She knew him well enough by now to see the slight narrowing of his eyes that meant he was re-evaluating how terrifying he found her. She smiled to herself.

"The last of the prisoners are off," he said. "Turns out enough of the prisoners knew tech that if I gave them the basic hack I'd created, they could help with the rest of the ships. They're all short-haul, but—" he shrugged. "It's better than prison."

"They have provisions?"

"Enough for a couple weeks. We scrubbed all the ships, and we're close enough to the outer rim that even when the government comes after them, they'll probably be able to lie low." He shrugged, and gave a faint smile. "Anyways, isn't that what our system was built on anyways? Political prisoners, religious exiles, and some stubborn dirt-eaters?"

"I suppose it was," murmured Masha, almost to herself.

Two thousand prisoners set free. Not a bad haul, really. It would certainly be a black eye to the government back in Prasvishoni.

Something in the back of her mind, though, nagged at her.

That had been the reason she'd agreed to this job, certainly. But it hadn't been the reason she'd finished it.

She pushed the thought back. Time enough to deal with that later.

"And there were enough ships for everyone?" she asked.

"Yes. Barely. We used the guards ships mostly, but there were a couple extra transport ships in storage as well, and some older ones we were able to get in the air."

"You work fast."

"Well, there were a lot of us. And Lev said to be finished in five standard hours, which—" He looked at his com. "We made, barely."

"We never found who it was who sold us out, did we?" she asked. He frowned slightly.

"No. It can't have been Radic or Ivan, I assume, because they almost got themselves killed trying to get everyone out. I talked to them, but they had no idea." He shrugged. "Two thousand prisoners, and most of them we don't know. It could have been anyone."

He was right. Still, she didn't like loose ends.

She sighed and pushed herself to her feet. "Then I suppose we'd best get going ourselves. Is everyone on board?"

"Almost. Ysbel and Tanya are still outside with the children.

They'll be in in a minute." He paused. "How's Jez?"

Masha smiled slightly. "Best ask Lev that, I think. He's still in with her, last time I checked. I'm heading in there now, if you'd like to come."

Tae nodded, and followed her across the small deck, through the mess hall, and into the med bay.

Jez was lying prone on the narrow medical cot, eyes closed, face puffy and bruised and body stiff with bandages. Lev sat beside her, his face drawn, looking down at her with an expression of mixed worry and tenderness that was completely unmistakable. Masha shook her head in mild amusement.

A complication, certainly. Although it had certainly been instructive to watch how a highly-motivated Lev behaved. Tae, too, and even Ysbel.

The position of a certain guard, stripped to his unders and tied onto the top of the wall in the hot sun with a white flag in his mouth containing a full written confession, was evidence of that. If it had been Lev's decision alone, she wasn't entirely certain the guard would have avoided the sedation chamber.

"How's she?" asked Tae quickly, crossing over to Lev. Lev glanced up, and she noted how his expression softened when he saw Tae.

Well. She'd wanted the crew to work together.

She just hadn't been prepared for it to happen quite this fast, or quite this thoroughly. Again, there was something mildly unsettling about the thought.

She'd expected to be controlling it, at least to some extent. But it seemed matters had been taken out of her hands. She wasn't used to matters being out of her hands, and it was not a feeling she enjoyed.

"She's going to be fine," said Lev in a low voice. "Lucic said she'd be sore for a few weeks, but no permanent damage. She was able to set the broken bones with some boneset she had in the prison supplies, so she'll be be back on her feet as soon as her bruises go down enough to let her."

Masha watched the pilot with a slightly icy stare.

Jez was a wild card. She'd always been a wild card. Until she'd met Jez, Masha had thought she was beyond being goaded. But this cocky, restless pilot could get under her skin with remarkable ease. Even unconscious, she had a certain air of cockiness about her.

The pilot had come through in the end, of course. This time. Despite probably almost getting them all killed several times.

But next time? She wasn't sure. And she wasn't sure she could afford to take the chance.

She couldn't deny a twinge of affection for the woman, even as difficult as she was. But affection wasn't something she could afford to base her plans on.

"How is our crazy drunken lunatic?" asked Ysbel from behind her. Masha stepped aside, and Ysbel, Tanya, and two small children filed into the room.

"What's wrong with Aunty Jez?" asked Olya. Lev smiled again, his face softening almost to the point of doting.

"Hello Olya. Why don't you come over here? Jez is going to be alright. The doctor's come, and she bandaged her up."

"That mean guard hit her, didn't he?" She crossed over to Lev, and let him lift her into his lap so she could see better.

"Yes. But I don't think he's going to be doing anything like that to anyone else for a while."

"Why not?"

"Well, because Uncle Tae and I programmed something into that white flag we shoved in his mouth." The way he said the last word made Masha suddenly sure that he'd had other ideas as to where to shove it, and probably been restrained by Tae. "As soon as a government scanner views it, it will upload every single assault he's committed on any prisoner onto every single government communication channel, and jam the programming so that every person across the entire system will be locked out until they hear every last detail." He paused. "There may have been a few personal details that we inadvertently slipped in as well."

"And possibly a very compromising and slightly-exaggerated corruption report," murmured Tae.

"You framed him?" asked Ysbel, in faint amusement. Tae shrugged.

"I wasn't sure if the government would care about assaults on prisoners. So I gave them something they would care about."

"I expect we'll still be having a prisoner transfer to the Vault in a few days," said Lev, in that friendly, mild voice that became something utterly terrifying when combined with his bland, merciless expression.

She'd known Lev had this side to him from reading through his files, but she'd never seen it before now. It was—not something she'd want to be on the wrong side of.

"If they take brush-pigs in the Vault," murmured Tanya.

Tae chuckled softly, and they all turned to look at the figure on the bed.

"So, Masha," said Lev at last, looking up at her. His expression was back to what she was used to seeing, that mild, calculating gaze with the sharp intelligence behind it. "What was on that chip you had me leave in the guards' quarters? I assume that's why it took so long for the warden to get things under control."

She gave a slight smile. "It was her recall to Prasvishoni."

He frowned. "Her—"

"It did take me some time to forge, and some time to get enough information from the guards to make it believable. But when we changed our plans, I thought a distracted warden might be helpful."

"It was," Lev said, giving her that calculating stare of his. "Of course, you could have told us about it."

"I could have. But I prefer not to bring up plans that I am not certain will succeed."

He gave her a piercing glance that was slightly too perceptive for her liking. "I see," he said. "And that's the same reason, I assume, that you didn't use some of the street drugs you gave to Jez to buy our way out, once we'd realized Tanya wouldn't make it because of the chip in her head."

She paused. "Tae thought of a perfectly good solution before I had to," she said in a non-committal voice.

And that, of course, was the thing about this whole situation that made her most uneasy.

Because she should have. She would never have agreed to their ridiculous plan if she hadn't had a backup. So she'd brought one.

And when she should have used it, should have insisted they leave Tanya and the children behind—

She hadn't.

The pilot was rubbing off on her.

Ysbel was looking at her too now, and there was a thoughtful look on her face.

"Well," said Lev, with a slight, knowing smile. "Now that we've rescued Tanya, I assume you have something you'd like us to do for you."

She managed a smile and raised one shoulder in a shrug. "Yes. But first, we'll need supplies, and then there's somewhere I'd like us to go. Deep space, I'll get you coordinates. It's far enough away that we should be untraceable, which I believe would be prudent, considering what we've just done. I'll tell you the rest when we get there."

She studied them.

They were almost ready. Once she figured out how to deal with the pilot, that is.

Jez jerked suddenly, swore, and opened her eyes.

"Tae," she said, her words slightly indistinct, but heavy with urgency. "What happened to my ship?"

"You're on your ship, Jez," said Lev patiently.

She sighed, and relaxed back onto the bed. Then she jerked up again, swore even more loudly, and pushed herself up on her good elbow with slightly more ginger movements.

"Jez. There are children here," said Tanya, her voice gaining a slight edge.

"Hey Olya." She moved, winced, and swore again.

"You're swearing."

"Yep." Jez turned her head gingerly. "Sorry, Olya. You'll have to ask your mamochka what that word means, I don't have time to explain."

"Jez—"

The pilot glanced around the small room in mild panic. "Who's flying my ship? Is Tae flying my ship?"

"No, he—"

"Is Masha flying my ship? Tell me Masha's not flying my damn ship."

"No. Jez. Relax. No one is flying your ship. We just got the prisoners off-planet."

She relaxed back again, wincing at the movement, and Lev leaned forward to tuck a pillow under her back, shaking his head.

"So we won," she said.

"Yes," said Tae. "We won." He couldn't seem to contain his smile.

"And we got everyone out? Even Radic?"

"Everyone."

"Good," she said after a moment, and there was a sincerity in her voice that Masha hadn't expected to hear there. She turned her head. "Hey Tanya! Glad you made it. You know, Ysbel basically hasn't talked about anything except you since I met her. It was getting a little old, to be honest. Even though I'm sure you're a lovely person. I mean, no offence or anything, but it really was a bit much. You'd think she'd have more than one topic of conversation. I hope you don't get too bored with her." She paused, considering. "OK, except for wanting to blow me up. She talks about that a lot too. I think she's probably flirting, but still—" She tried to grin through the white bone-set that had been formed to her jaw. "Although, I mean, if you do get bored of her, I'm available at the moment, so—"

Ysbel was shaking her head. "How did we not wire her mouth shut? We had the chance to wire her mouth shut, and we didn't take it." She turned to Lev, who had a look on his face of amusement mingled with disbelieving exasperation.

"Lucic said the bone-set would work faster, since we had it available," he murmured.

"And you didn't stop her? Had she not met our pilot?"

"Admit it, Ysbel," said Jez. "You wouldn't know what to do with yourself if you didn't have me to talk with."

"Believe me, I would know exactly what to do," said Ysbel. She turned back to Lev. "Are you sure we can't call Lucic back here?"

"Sorry, Ysbel. She's already off-planet."

"I can't believe this," Ysbel muttered. "We had one chance. We can break an entire prison out, but we managed to fumble on this one."

Jez tried to grin again, then glanced around restlessly. "Well, guess I better get up. Ship isn't going to fly itself."

"No, Jez, listen—"

She'd already pushed herself off the bed. She gasped, swore colourfully, and swayed on her feet. Lev leapt up and caught her before she could fall over. She leaned against him, cursing breathlessly for a few moments, and Tanya covered Olya's ears, her mouth pressed into a tight line.

"Jez," said Lev through his teeth, clearly trying to keep his voice patient, "you need to lie down. Masha can—"

"Masha can fly my ship over my cold dead body," Jez grunted, glaring in Masha's direction. "I always sleep in the cockpit anyways. I'll be fine."

Lev cast a long-suffering look at the others, then, shaking his head, he supported the stumbling, swearing Jez out of the med bay.

When they'd gone, the others looked at each other. Ysbel was grinning slightly, and even Tanya wore a reluctant smile.

"So. That's what you have to put up with every day," said Tanya. "I am beginning to believe that maybe you have become a saint."

"Not that much of a saint," said Ysbel. There was a wicked look in her eyes, and she pulled Tanya in for a kiss that was long and slow and not even a little chaste.

"Ysbel!" said Tae. From the look on Olya's face, she fully agreed with him.

Ysbel pulled back slightly and fixed Tae with her flat stare. "Listen to me, Tae. I have waited five and a half years. I killed thirty-five people, and spent five years in jail. I broke into Vitali's compound, stole a ship, broke back into jail, have almost been killed more times than I can count, and helped two thousand prisoners escape a government prison. And right now, I'm going to kiss my wife."

She turned back to Tanya and resumed where she'd left off.

Tae and Olya exchanged glances.

Misko came over to Masha and pulled on her pilot's coat.

Masha found herself smiling despite herself as she bent down. "Yes, Misko? What is it?"

"I'm hungry, Aunty Masha," he whispered, looking up at her with his big, solemn eyes.

"Well. I suppose we could see what's in the mess hall," she said, straightening. "As long as your mamochka doesn't mind."

Tanya, without looking up, waved a hand at them. Tae shook his head.

"Pretty sure they want to be left alone." He sighed. "Coming, Olya?"

The girl glanced at her parents with a faintly disgusted look and nodded. Masha took Misko's hand and followed Tae and Olya out of the room, closing the door firmly behind her.

She glanced down at the boy holding her hand and looking around the ship with curious eyes.

That was the thing that terrified her.

Because what she'd done in that prison hadn't made sense. When they'd realized, a week ago, that they wouldn't be able to get Tanya and the two children out of prison like they'd planned, her job had been simple—convince the others that for Jez's sake, if nothing else, they had to get out. They'd try again later. Then use her street drugs to bribe one of the guards, get them out, and not look back.

She should have done it. She possibly could have, although, watching the four of them together now, she wasn't entirely certain. Her goal was and had been simple—giving the government a black eye by breaking prisoners out of a high-security prison was useful, but certainly not vital. What she needed was her team, healthy and prepared and motivated, and, above all, alive. Nothing else mattered.

But the truth was, she hadn't even tried. She'd looked at this small boy, with his big, solemn eyes, and Olya, with her quick intelligent face, and she hadn't even tried to talk the others out of their mad rescue scheme.

Because she'd felt as sick as the rest of them at leaving this child in a prison like that, to be taken to the Vault.

The thought sent a cold shiver through her.

She couldn't afford this. This was all wrong. Everything she'd done since she was Olya's age herself had been preparing for this. Like she'd told the pilot, she couldn't afford to take risks, and she certainly couldn't afford to let personal feelings get in the way of her plans. And now, with no more impetus than a solemn-eyed six-year-old, she'd risked the entire crew she'd spent years researching and planning for.

Yes, they'd succeeded. But that had been more chance than planning, and she couldn't leave things to chance.

"Aunty Masha?"

She looked down at Misko, and forced a smile. "I'm sorry, Misko. I got distracted. You're right, we should go."

But the sense of unease had wormed its way inside her, and wouldn't let go.

Tae showed the yawning Olya to a small room to one side of Ysbel's.

"You can sleep here. See, there's another bed for your brother. But —" he leaned closer and whispered, "since you got here first, I'll let you pick. I won't tell Misko."

She grinned at him, then scampered into the room to try the cots. He smiled to himself, watching her. She finally settled on one and lay back.

"This is mine." She gave a huge yawn. "I'm not tired," she said, when she could speak again. "But I might just lie here for a few minutes. To make sure it's the one I want."

Tae nodded, not bothering to hide his smile.

She was asleep in moments.

Masha stepped past him a few moments later, carrying a limp Misko in her arms. She brought him over to the empty bed, laid him down, and covered him gently with a blanket.

"He fell asleep while he was eating," she whispered, and Tae nodded.

He wasn't sure he was still entirely comfortable with Masha. But she didn't frighten him quite as much as she had.

"You know," he said quietly, as they stood watching the sleeping children. "I don't know if I ever told you thank you. For—well, I almost got us killed back there, when I couldn't figure out that system. I—thought you'd be angry. You'd have been in your rights to be."

"No," she whispered. "I would not have been." She turned and gave him a calculating look. "You know, Tae, you're quite extraordinary. I knew that when I asked you to be on the team, but I don't know that I fully appreciated it."

He frowned at her. She looked serious.

She gave him a slight smile. "You did well. You did more than any of us could have expected from you." She paused. "The street children back on Prasvishoni—they were lucky to have you. We're lucky to have you as well."

"We will go back for them, right?" he said. "Sometime?" At the thought of Prasvishoni, of Caz and Peti, something had caught in his throat, and was making it hard to talk. Masha looked at him gravely for a long moment.

"Believe me, Tae. I have every intention of honouring my word," she said at last.

That was the best he was going to get from her, and he knew it. Still, it was more than he'd expected.

He was going to go back for Caz and Peti and the others. One way or another, he would. But it would be a lot easier with their crazy, ridiculous pilot, with Lev's calm, calculating intelligence, Ysbel's somewhat disturbing ability to blow things up. And Masha, of course. Somehow, he had a hard time picturing their crew without Masha's calm, competent leadership.

And Ivan, and Radic, and Anya and the others.

Perhaps they weren't as entirely alone in the system as he'd imagined them to be. Perhaps there were other people willing to risk prison or even death, if that's what it took, to help a stranger. Even a street kid, like him.

Masha turned away, and he noticed a slight tension in her posture, a mild unease.

He shook his head and glanced back at the sleeping children.

He was likely misreading her. He'd never been good at guessing what Masha was thinking.

When he looked up again, she was gone.

Ysbel raised up on her elbow and looked down at her wife, lying beside her. Tanya's head lay against Ysbel's shoulder, one arm thrown around her.

"My Ysi," Tanya murmured softly. Ysbel turned to kiss her hair.

"I missed you. More than I can say."

"I missed you too," whispered Tanya.

"I'm so sorry," said Ysbel, at last. Her voice was heavy with tears. "I'm so sorry I wasn't there to help you. I'm sorry the children had to grow up in that place."

Tanya looked up at her, shaking her head. "No, Ysbel. I'm sorry we were not there with you." She paused. "I thought they'd killed you, when I heard about the explosion. I was sure they'd killed you."

"I hoped they would," Ysbel whispered.

"But not anymore."

"No." Ysbel smiled gently. "Not anymore."

"Did you kill them all? Everyone who did this to us?"

"No," said Ysbel. "Not all of them. Most of them, though. But I know there were others. There were the government officials who ordered the job. Three of them. I know their names. And there were two of the operatives who I was not able to get, and the site manager who had suggested they needed my help, whatever way they could get it. There was one more, as well. The person who planned it. I was not able to find their name. But I will, one day."

Tanya smiled that small, wistful smile that Ysbel remembered so well. "But you don't have to, anymore," she said. And Ysbel smiled too. It felt good. It felt like it had been so long since she'd really smiled. Like this woman laying next to her was a piece of her, and she was broken without her.

"No," she said. "I don't. Because my time is much better spent with you and with our babies. Those others are not worth my time." She paused, and turned so she was looking her wife in the eye. Tanya met her gaze. "But," she said softly, "if I meet one of them, if I see them, I swear to you, I will kill them without a second thought."

For just a moment, there was something bleak and hard in Tanya's expression, something that hadn't been there five years before. "That," she said softly, "I will not argue with."

Then she smiled, and the bleakness melted into the background, although, Ysbel thought, it might never go away completely.

The last five years had changed her. It had changed both of them, and they would never be the family they had been before.

Tanya laid her head back on Ysbel's shoulder with a sigh, and Ysbel leaned her cheek against her wife's hair and closed her eyes.

But then, maybe, that was alright.

Because they had each other again. And whatever family she made with this woman, whatever their lives looked like now—if she had Tanya, it would be something she would love with all of her heart.

Jez lay back in the pilot's seat and ran her good hand over the control panel. She smiled to herself as she fired up the ignition.

Her whole body still ached. But sitting here, in the cockpit of the *Ungovernable*—it was better than medicine. It was better than whatever had been in those white pills Masha had given her.

It was better than anything.

"You strapped in, genius-boy?"

"Jez. I've flown with you before. I'm always strapped in."

She grinned, at least, as well as she could with the damn boneset on her jaw, and pulled gently back on the throttle. The *Ungovernable* lifted into the air and pointed its nose towards the sky. She pulled back a little harder, and they shot upwards, and the controls trembled slightly in her hands, and the atmosphere burned around them, and then, finally, the beautiful, perfect blackness of space surrounded them. Behind them, the planet glowed a bright white and brown, and to one side the small sun glowed and burned. Ahead, the tiny brilliant specks of stars burned against the black of space.

"You love it, don't you?" asked Lev softly, staring out ahead of him.

She didn't answer. She didn't have to.

"I think maybe I'm starting to see why," he said, still looking ahead.

She turned her head to watch him. He was wearing a faint, wistful smile, and the light from the sun glowed off his regular, even features.

He was a soft-boy, yes, but maybe that wasn't the worst thing in the world for someone to be.

He seemed to feel her eyes on him, because he turned and caught her gaze, and for a moment she was looking directly into his dark, intelligent eyes.

Her breath caught, ever so slightly, and she felt momentarily lightheaded.

She wasn't certain she wanted to know why.

But it wasn't an entirely unpleasant feeling.

He smiled slightly. "I'm glad you're feeling well enough to fly," he said. "It wouldn't have been the same with Masha in the cockpit." He paused. "I'd be less likely to throw up, for one thing."

"Damn Masha to hell. I'd be dead before she was flying my sweet beautiful angel," she grumbled, forcing herself to look away from him.

"You very nearly were," he said quietly, and there was something in his voice that made her breath catch again. She steadfastly avoided looking at him, even though she could feel his eyes on her.

"Nah. I was fine."

"I was worried about you."

"No need to be." She hoped she sounded jaunty, instead of slightly breathless. Because that would be stupid, and she might be a lot of things, but stupid wasn't one of them.

Usually, anyways. She was pretty sure.

Very possibly she was being very stupid right at this moment.

"So. Where we going?" she said, staring ahead so hard she thought her eyes might start watering.

"Well, Masha suggested we lay low in deep space for a couple weeks," he said. "And to be frank, I don't think it's a bad idea. I think we just made even more people angry with us than we did when we stole this ship, and that's saying something."

She tried to grin, swore, and glanced over, forgetting she wasn't looking at him. He was watching her with faint amusement, and there was an expression in his eyes, tender and—something else.

She closed her eyes for a moment, fighting down the shakiness in her muscles.

This was not something she was prepared to deal with. Not right now.

"Well," she said, "guess at least we got Tanya back. Bet she and Ysbel are pretty happy right now."

"They probably are," he said softly, and there was an unfamiliar tone in his voice, rueful and just a little sad. "You know," he said, "there's something I've been meaning to tell Ysbel." He hesitated, then sighed. "I suppose now is as good a time as any."

She glared at him. "You crazy? I mean, don't answer that. I know you're crazy. But give poor Ysbel some time. Figure she might want a day or two without anyone telling her anything." She managed a slightly lascivious look. "Maybe a couple days with no interruptions, if you know what I mean."

He sighed. "Jez—"

She snickered, and he shook his head.

"I suppose you're right. What do you think then, since you're apparently the expert at this?"

"Damn right I am," she smirked.

"Tomorrow then?"

"Nah. Give them a week. Can't be that urgent, if you've been meaning to tell her for a while."

"I suppose," he said. There was still that odd tone in his voice, and a slightly wry edge to his smile. "A week then. And then I'll tell her."

"She'll probably be glad to hear it," said Jez flippantly.

"She probably will," he said, voice quiet.

For a few minutes, neither of them spoke. At last, Lev said, "Well, Jez, we're going to deep space. I'll plot you a course. But in the meantime, why don't you show me what you love about flying?"

She closed her eyes for a moment. Her body hurt like someone had beaten her with a metal pole, which, she supposed, wasn't entirely wrong, and talking hurt, and one of her eyes was swollen almost all the way shut, and she couldn't even grin properly, and she still had to deal with Masha, somehow.

But she was in the pilot's seat, and there were controls under her hand, and she was out in space. And more than that. Radic was out there, somewhere, and Ivan, and a whole bunch of other prisoners. Even Vlatka.

Somehow, the thought made her happy. Happier than she would have thought, a few weeks ago.

And beside her, in the co-pilot's seat, Lev was sitting, probably smiling that little smile he had. The one she didn't want to think about.

But that she actually kind of liked.

Masha glanced down at the scroll of letters on her com, chewing thoughtfully on the inside of her cheek.

She should probably have been in bed a long time ago. But there was something nagging her about their time in prison. Something Lev had said.

Someone from the outside was looking for Jez.

No one in the system should have been able to look for her. They shouldn't have known she existed, or if they did, they should have assumed she was dead. Masha had been very, very careful.

They certainly should not have been able to track her to the prison planet.

Before they'd left the prison, she'd gone up to the guard rooms and grabbed all the chips she could find. Never a bad idea to have more information. She'd pass them along to Lev as well, and he'd probably think he'd died and gone to paradise.

Still, there was one thing that she needed to check.

And here it was. Buried in the notes in the prison file.

A tag beside Jez's prison number. And on that tag, buried deep, a name no one in the system should have access to anymore.

Jez Solokov.

And under the name, a notation, hidden well enough that you might not notice unless you were looking. "Currently sought. C level credit reward."

C level credit reward. There were few people in the system who merited that sort of reward money. Certainly not a scrappy, irritating ex-smuggler pilot, no matter how good she might be.

And for that price, there would be a lot of people looking. Just as well they were going to deep space to lay low for a while.

And yet—they'd been in the prison for a mere two weeks. And somehow in that time, someone had managed to infiltrate the aliases Tae had set up, find Jez, and tag her.

She glanced through the small porthole window of her cabin.

They'd done a hyperspeed jump a couple hours ago. They'd effectively disappeared. There was nothing for her to be worried about.

Still …

She shook her head grimly.

Apparently it was past time to find out a little more about this pilot of hers.

The End

ENJOYED THE BOOK?

I HOPE YOU'VE ENJOYED Jailbreak, the second book in The Ungovernable series. Thank you for reading!

If you did, I have a small favour to ask you: Would you please leave a review? It may seem like a silly thing, but reviews are very important to authors like me, as they help other people find my book, which in turn helps me to keep writing. Even a line or two would be unbelievably helpful.

If you haven't read it yet, Zero Day Threat is the first book in the series, and it's available on Amazon. The third book, Time Bomb, is coming on July 15th.

In the mean time, if you subscribe to my mailing list, I'd love to send you an exclusive short story prequel featuring Jez Solokov, *Devil's Odds.* I'll also let you know about future launch dates, give-aways, and pre-release specials. And I always love to hear from my readers, so feel free to drop me a note!

If you'd like claim your free short story and subscribe to my newsletter, head over to my website: www.rmolson.com

Also, feel free to connect with me on Facebook: https://www.-facebook.com/rmolsonauthor

or Instagram: https://www.instagram.com/rolson_author/

Printed in Great Britain
by Amazon

49037196R00177